Bronwyn Scott is a commun[...] at Pierce College and the prou[...] wonderful children—one boy and two girls. When she's not teaching or writing she enjoys playing the piano, travelling—especially to Florence, Italy—and studying history and foreign languages. Find her on Bluesky, @bronwynscott.bsky.social. She loves to hear from readers.

Also by Bronwyn Scott

Cinderella at the Duke's Ball
The Viscount's Christmas Bride

Daring Rogues miniseries

Miss Claiborne's Illicit Attraction
His Inherited Duchess

Enterprising Widows miniseries

Liaison with the Champagne Count
Alliance with the Notorious Lord
A Deal with the Rebellious Marquess

Wed Within a Year miniseries

How to Court a Rake
How to Tempt an Earl

Discover more at millsandboon.co.uk.

HOW TO SEDUCE A VISCOUNT

Bronwyn Scott

MILLS & BOON

All rights reserved including the right of reproduction in whole or in part in any form. This edition is published by arrangement with Harlequin Enterprises ULC.

This is a work of fiction. Names, characters, places, locations and incidents are purely fictional and bear no relationship to any real life individuals, living or dead, or to any actual places, business establishments, locations, events or incidents. Any resemblance is entirely coincidental.

Without limiting the author's and publisher's exclusive rights, any unauthorised use of this publication to train generative artificial intelligence (AI) technologies is expressly prohibited. HarperCollins also exercise their rights under Article 4(3) of the Digital Single Market Directive 2019/790 and expressly reserve this publication from the text and data mining exception.

® and TM are trademarks owned and used by the trademark owner and/or its licensee. Trademarks marked with ® are registered with the United Kingdom Patent Office and/or the Office for Harmonisation in the Internal Market and in other countries.

First published in Great Britain 2025
by Mills & Boon, an imprint of HarperCollins*Publishers* Ltd,
1 London Bridge Street, London, SE1 9GF

www.harpercollins.co.uk

HarperCollins*Publishers*, Macken House, 39/40 Mayor Street Upper, Dublin 1, D01 C9W8, Ireland

How to Seduce a Viscount © 2025 Nikki Poppen

ISBN: 978-0-263-34533-9

09/25

This book contains FSC™ certified paper and other controlled sources to ensure responsible forest management.

For more information visit www.harpercollins.co.uk/green.

Printed and Bound in the UK using 100% Renewable Electricity at CPI Group (UK) Ltd, Croydon, CR0 4YY

For my B, who, like our hero, Luce, knows how hard it is to be the youngest and to find your own path. I am excited to see where your path leads.

Chapter One

*Little Albury in the Surrey Hills,
Late January 1827*

Lucien Parkhurst, the ton's newest viscount, was a self-proclaimed chionophile and a consummate lover of all things winter. His recently acquired neighbours in Little Albury would not take issue with that moniker. On any given day, while they were sensibly tucked up in their country homes and cottages, the young viscount could be found striding about the environs of the Surrey Hills in his greatcoat and muffler, head bare, the wind having its way with the dark waves of his hair. When he wasn't striding, he was riding a great black horse named for the Celtic warrior, Vercingetorix who, for the sake of efficiency, answered to Vere.

Tonight, though, the gravity of the chill weather had sent even the redoubtable Vere to his warm stall in the stables and his master indoors along with the rest of Little Albury. The only difference being that while the other residents were scanning the skies with grim worry, Lucien scanned them with growing hope.

He'd been watching the grey clouds all afternoon for signs of that most blessed—and in Surrey most rare—occurrence, snow. If there was to be snow at all in these parts, better known for their chalk downs, it would be here in the hills where elevation gave snow a fighting chance.

Luce stood at the bank of long-arced cathedral windows of Tillingbourne Abbey's library and looked hopefully out into the darkness. The windowpanes were cold in testament to the weather but the fire at his back filled the room with a comfortable heat. There were lamps enough for reading long into a late hibernal evening—the kind of quiet night that was perfect for snow.

There was nothing quite like going to sleep amid a soft snowfall and waking up to the ground covered in pillows of white. Nothing like a morning spent out of doors, strapping on snowshoes and being the first to tramp across acres of pristine whiteness.

Nor was there anything like a snowy evening for reflection. Snow forced one to stay inside with one's own thoughts. These days he had plenty of those.

He'd come to winter at Tillingbourne in large part to sort those very thoughts. To figure out who he might become—a question, that for various reasons, needed answering in the next six months. This might indeed be his last chance to shape his identity. To plot his own course in life, as opposed to the course plotted for him by others.

'Your brandy, my lord.' A footman entered and set a tumbler beside the armchair at the fire—Rowley, Luce thought his name was. He'd been learning all the staff's names since he'd come back from his brother's Christmastide wedding in Wales.

'Thank you, Rowley.' Luce smiled his appreciation from across the room. 'I won't be needing anything else tonight.'

Everything in those two sentences felt foreign to him. The words, the giving of an order, responding to the title 'my lord' as if he'd been born to it, which he hadn't. The title was his by mere happenstance, plucked at random by the King from the pile of gifts that were the monarch's to give. Now, he had a title, an estate and the expectation that, if he wanted to keep these things in perpetuity, he would marry before the year was out.

That year had begun in July when the title had been bestowed on him. He had six months left. His other two brothers had already married and satisfied the monarch's terms. Their titles were safe now, as long as they produced a son to inherit.

Luce rubbed at his eyes. He was feeling the pressure. He didn't want to disappoint his grandfather who'd had a hand in arranging the titles. He didn't want to disappoint the local community. If he chose to be the viscount in truth, he needed to marry. It hardly made sense, nor did it seem fair to the local community, to invest himself in the role of Viscount Waring only to have his legacy erased upon his death. And yet, if not for those considerations, he'd not be seeking a wife on his own accord. He'd not planned to marry for himself, not for a long while.

Although now that he was considering marriage, the conditions were not conducive. Winter was not ideal wife-hunting season. London was depleted of company and people in the countryside were separated by miles of road and bad weather. A man was limited to the prospects in his immediate vicinity.

In Little Albury, those prospects bordered on dismal. It wasn't for the lack of Little Albury's interest. There were women aplenty who had made it clear they wouldn't mind helping his matrimonial cause to the altar. It was for a lack of *his* interest.

He simply couldn't see himself with any of them. Not with the quiet, doe-eyed Clara Benton, granddaughter of an earl, nor the squire's daughter, Arabella Malmsby, who was vivacious to a fault. Nor any of the daughters of the local gentry who aspired to the ranks of the peerage.

Vivacious or quiet, they were all the same once one got past the outer trimmings. They would all make a steady wife who would exist competently and unobtrusively in the background of his life—well maybe not Arabella, but the rest certainly would.

All of them were unobjectionable choices. He wanted more. His brothers had both made love matches. Why shouldn't he aspire to the same? This was one way in which he did not wish to differentiate himself from the family.

He may have to wait until spring and a journey to London. It would be cutting it fine on the deadline. He'd only have a few weeks to find a bride and convince her to marry before July, which might be harder to do in reality than in theory. Tillingbourne Abbey was very much a work in progress in terms of being ready to bring a bride home. All except the library. He'd restored that first.

Luce glanced towards the long library table where he spent hours researching and writing about various subjects. His latest botanical treatise had been published last spring. His current work was a memoir for his grandfather. It was meant to be a gift for his eighty-ninth birthday in April. When Luce wasn't writing he was decoding ciphers for that grandfather who, even at his advanced age, kept a very active hand in the darker edges of the diplomatic world.

Luce supposed he could apply those same research skills to his bridal hunt. He could spend the winter poring through Debrett's and sending letters of enquiry in advance of the Season to fathers of eligible daughters. He could engage his mother for suggestions. He could compile a heavily curated list. But all that seemed rather counterintuitive to the point of making a love match or something close to it. The Parkhursts were famous for such matches and his brothers' recent marriages had solidified the generational trend.

The recent duress he felt to follow suit was just another example of the self-imposed pressure he struggled with to balance his own sense of independence with his devout loyalty to the family, to his brothers.

His whole life had been a battle between the fervent yearning to belong, as his brothers belonged, and his own desire to step outside the family circle. For him to be recognised for himself as a scholar in his own right. Something that was deuced hard to do when one was a member of the Four Horsemen and the youngest of four brothers, three of whom had already carved out dashing reputations before he'd even reached puberty. Much of his road in life so far had been strongly pre-determined.

Luce made his way to the waiting brandy and his chair, set at an angle to take in both the warmth of the fire and the view of the outdoors. He sank into the chair with a pleasant sigh, reminding himself that even within those pre-ordained parameters, he had carved something of his own niche as a scholar. A lover of languages and of women—he'd upheld the family reputation on that last one admirably and if it hadn't been for the current situation, he might have continued in that vein.

He'd been in no matrimonial hurry before the title. There'd been no succession to secure and no inheritance to protect. In fact, being unmarried was a benefit in his and his brothers' line of work as the Four Horsemen—Britain's covert answer to diplomatic situations gone awry. He lived an uncertain and dangerous life. Six months ago, all that had changed. It still felt as if it were a dream—a bad one.

The Horsemen had been sent to apprehend a saboteur at the Wapping Docks who was intent on blowing up a ship loaded with privately sponsored money and arms bound for the Greek war of independence. They'd been successful in their mission at the price of losing their brother, Stepan. His body had never been recovered from the water. Either he was missing, or he was…dead.

Luce took a long swallow of brandy, letting it burn his throat, his thoughts. It was still too hard to think that word, let alone say it out loud. But what else was there to think? It had been six months with no word, no body. The reality of that jarred him anew when he woke every day. Another day without Stepan. Another day of coping with the knowledge that Stepan was gone for today. For tomorrow. For ever. For the rest of the mornings of Luce's life. Of which, God willing, there'd be many but one never knew. Stepan was proof of that. A Horseman's life was uncertain and complicated.

Luce raised his glass to the flames in a toast. 'To you, brother, wherever you are.'

Stepan had no idea of what he'd set in motion the night he'd disappeared under the waters or of the consequences—public, private and personal.

To the public eye, the king had awarded the three brothers titles in gratitude for their bravery and service to their country while subtly thrusting them onto the marriage mart without their consent.

Privately, however, the brothers knew those titles for what they were—a sop for the loss of a brother. As if titles and estates could ever replace what Stepan had been to each of them personally—a brother, a friend and a peacekeeper when tempers flared.

To Luce, especially, Stepan had been the bridge that spanned the gap between a young boy and his older brothers who outpaced him by up to six years.

The difference in ages didn't matter so much now except to tease Caine, the eldest, that he was about to turn forty. But when a boy is six and his idol of an older brother is twelve the difference in years seem more like a chasm than a gap. Stepan had always seen to it that he was never left out and never left behind. Stepan had even delayed going away to school by a year so that Luce could come with him. That had been the great compromise. Luce went to school a year early and Stepan a year later so that they could go together.

Now, Stepan was…gone. And Luce was Viscount Waring, in possession of Tillingbourne Abbey, an esteemed but somewhat derelict estate that had survived the Tudors but been conquered by time. Luce was reclaiming it room by room. This place would bear his stamp, be uniquely his alone.

Luce glanced towards the bank of long windows. Was that a speck? The firelight made it hard to see through the outer darkness. He set aside his brandy and crossed the room. Yes, it was a speck. Then there was another and another. He felt himself smile.

It was snowing. For a moment all was right with the world. He stood for a while watching it come down, the plump flakes growing thicker and denser, before he returned to his chair content to spend his evening with a book, a brandy and the blessed snow.

The cursed snow! Wren slipped, her boot soles sliding on a dark patch of slick ground. Snow turned everything to ice and wet. She blinked the thickening flakes off her lashes and pulled her muffler up a little higher to ward off the chill. Snow was nothing but a nuisance at best, dangerous at worst, and that was what it was tonight—dangerous—at least to her. It was slowing her progress to Tillingbourne Abbey and thus it was slowing the delivery of an urgent message to Lucien Parkhurst, one of the Four Horsemen.

She patted the secret slit in her coat in reassurance that the paper was still there. The Earl of Sandmore, Lucien's grandfather, had entrusted it to her and no other. It was that important the note make it through. It was not merely a note, but a code, that if broken could offer an advantage to the Greek independence fighters supported by private British citizens if and until the British government officially aided them.

If anyone could crack the code, it would be Luce, the Horsemen's scholar and resident polyglot.

Delivery of this message was the first stage of a two-part mission. The second stage was to quietly follow a lead that had come to the earl regarding his missing grandson. Someone who matched Stepan Parkhurst's description and the timeline of his disappearance had turned up in a village by the sea.

Of her mission to find Stepan, she was to say nothing to Luce, do nothing that would get his hopes up or inspire reckless action. She would deliver the message and go. Both stages of the task required discretion, stealth, blending in without being detected. Who better to undertake the task than Falcon, the earl's most reliable emissary for over twelve years?

She'd argued hard for the assignment. She'd wanted to go for both professional and private reasons. It was to be her last. After that, she was to slip into anonymity, retired. Because of an error on the road and the risk that someone now might associate her with her *nom de guerre*—Falcon. She'd made one mistake in all the years she'd been Falcon and that mistake had cost her.

Most never got to leave the game by choice—not that it had been much of an option in the end. Retiring her was the earl's decision more than it was hers. Now that the earl had handed the reins of the network over to Caine Parkhurst, he wanted to see her settled and safe. It had been bound to happen, she knew, but she also knew that her slip had expedited it.

As for her, she'd wanted a chance to see Luce Parkhurst up close before she went. She'd followed Luce's career, idolised him from afar for years. She'd envied him the charmed life of the Parkhursts, his doting grandfather—the earl—and the large, loving family that surrounded him. She'd mourned silently with him when he'd lost Stepan. If there was a chance to restore his brother, to heal the pain Lucien carried over the loss, she wanted to be part of that. It would give her an opportunity to make a return on all that the Parkhurst family had given her over the years, even though they knew her not at all.

Wren blew into her gloved hands to generate warmth. She flexed her fingers attempting to ward off stiffness. She needed to be able to hold a knife if the three men behind her on the road were who she thought they were. She'd acquired them after the last village where she'd stopped briefly to warm herself at a crowded pub.

That stop was turning out to be another mistake, understandable as it was on a cold night. Heat and warmth would always be a practical luxury to her after a childhood of having gone without. Her hands were dreadfully chilled. Without them functioning, she'd be no use to anyone tonight. Without her hands, her life might very well be forfeit over the code she carried.

She did not think the men behind her intended to be noticed, which meant they weren't out for a casual evening journey between villages. The weather was not conducive for such an outing and men in groups liked to sing as they walked—riotous tavern songs with bawdy lyrics to pass the time. These men were quiet, silent. She'd only picked them up because of the moon, which hung full and white and damnably bright in the snow-filled sky.

Snow always made the evenings lighter. That was yet another reason to detest it. True, if there was enough of it, snow could muffle sound, but it also stole the chance for stealth. There was nowhere to hide. If she could see them the men could see her. That was not what she was hoping for.

Wren squinted against the snow. There were lights in the distance. The Abbey. She was nearly there. A mile or less to go, across open ground and a gradual incline.

She loosened the knife at her waist. A slim, sharp Italian wrought stiletto. The men were letting her get awfully close to her destination. That concerned her and made her re-think what they were after. The message certainly. But they could have tried to waylay her far sooner than this. Three to one on a lonely road were much better odds for them if they'd only come for the message. She was starting to suspect they'd come for more than that.

Cold knowing spread through her. They were after the message *and* a Horseman. They'd waited this long on purpose. They were following her to get to Luce Parkhurst in retribution for the Horsemen's dismantling of Cabot Roan's arms empire in the autumn.

Stepan was already lost. The remaining three Horsemen were vulnerable. She would merely be collateral damage to these men when she was done leading them to Luce's very front door. This was how wolves hunted. They stalked, chased, ambushed. She swallowed. At least now she knew when they'd strike.

She doubted if she could lose them in this light. But she could possibly outrun them if the snow didn't play her false. She was fast and fleet under normal conditions and she had those conditions tonight if one did not count the snow. She wore trousers and a coat. No unnecessary frills and full skirts to get in the way. If she could beat them to the Abbey, she'd have the advantage of a few precious minutes in which to warn Luce. Her heart pounded irrationally at the prospect of seeing him when it ought to be pounding with fear, with the anticipation of the fight to come.

This was not how she'd thought she'd meet him—*Good evening, I'm from your grandfather and there are three men coming to kill you.*

Instead, she'd had images of being invited in. Of being offered a tea tray beside the fire in the library his grandfather mentioned he'd been restoring. They would talk about books they'd read, of Horsemen business, the message she'd brought. Perhaps he might even ask her to help with the cipher.

To work with the brilliant Lucien Parkhurst would be a divine experience. It might still happen, she consoled herself. *If* they both lived through the night. If she wasn't smart, this might be her last mission in a different sense than it had been intended.

She felt, more than she saw, a movement on her left flank. The wolves were closing ranks. If she didn't bolt now, there'd be no distance to spare between them. Wren gathered herself and began to run, aware that somewhere behind her, the men had begun to run, too.

The end game was in motion. She was flying, light and nimble over snowy ground, her body fuelled by the thrill of the chase, of leading them on. She'd never been caught. They were falling behind, the gap between them widening. She let out an exultant crow as she turned down the drive to Tillingbourne Abbey, the final leg. She was in an all-out sprint now, her concealing cap long gone, her hair streaming out behind her bright in the moonlight, life itself coursing in her veins. In these moments, she was alive! This was what she was made to do. To court danger and then outrun it.

She reached the door, pounding hard with her fists in her urgency before she turned and drew her blade. She heard the men panting before she saw them, spilling from the drive, heavy and winded. They were not as far behind as she'd hoped, but she'd tired them and she could use that to her advantage.

Blades flashed in their hands as they approached. 'We want the message. Hand it over and no one gets hurt.' The thickset man in front opened negotiations, his chest heaving with his exertion.

'I don't do business with liars.'

She knew they couldn't let her live. What if she'd seen the message? Even if it meant nothing to her, she could still relay it to others perhaps. They couldn't take that chance. They were here for containment.

She flourished her knife and smiled when it stopped their advance. They weren't close enough to strike. Yet.

'If you wanted the message you would have tried for it long before this. Why walk all this way?'

She hoped someone would open the door soon. She was practical about her odds here. She'd take one of them, maybe hurt a second one badly, but she'd not take all three. They were too big. Their sheer size would overwhelm her if they rushed her all at once—a wolves' ambush.

'Kill, maim or live, which one do you think it will be for you? And you?' she bantered, brandishing her blade one more time, letting them know she'd read their thoughts and they matched her own.

Each knew she'd likely kill one of them and gut another. Each were weighing the odds they'd be the one to walk away unscathed. They had to act soon. The longer they waited, the more likely it became that it wouldn't just be her they would have to face on the doorstep.

The thickset one snarled. It was all the warning she had before they came. The outcome of this doorstep skirmish would be decided in a matter of seconds now.

The thickset one reached her first. She thrust hard, feeling the sharp blade stab past layers of muscle and fat. The force of it vibrated up her arm but she held on, withdrawing the blade and whirling to face another as he fell. She wielded the knife up high in fencing fashion to parry a thrust, but she'd left herself open. She wasn't quick enough. She felt a blade slice her side. Felt the warmth of blood and the sting of pain.

Ignore it her mind cried. She had to protect the message, had to protect Lucien Parkhurst.

One of the men grabbed for her and she kicked out at him. He stumbled, losing his grip on his knife in the process and she staggered forward, her blade dealing damage with the last of her strength. The man gave a groan, his eyes wide with shock at his misjudgement. She pushed him away and he slumped in the snow.

One more to go and she hadn't the strength. He lunged for her, grappling for her knife, his hand encircling her wrist trying to shake the blade free. She'd be no match without it. She kicked and fought, feeling her power ebb. Her shirt was wet. It must be soaked through now. She was dizzy and the world was starting to spin.

The front door opened at last, light spilling out like a benediction. A blessing, a farewell…and a form with it. *Lucien.* She'd know those dark waves and dark eyes anywhere. Ferocious and feral, his features were fierce as he charged the third attacker and pulled the man from her. She felt his weight leave her, felt her own weight leave her, and then it seemed that life its very self followed.

At least she'd made it. Lucien would find the message. He would search her coat. She'd not failed the earl or the Horsemen. But oh how ironic, she thought, to have come this far, gotten so close, only to die on the doorstep of her desire at the very last.

Chapter Two

Whoever she was, she was *not* going to die, this waif of a girl dressed in trousers. He wouldn't allow it. Luce knelt beside her, pushing back her coat, ripping at her shirt to get at the wound. Dear lord, there was so much blood. It was everywhere, drenching her coat, soaking her shirt. *And* she'd been stabbed on his doorstep. Who stabbed waifs on viscounts' doorsteps in the middle of snowfall at midnight? No one. But people *did* stab messengers that sought the Horsemen. Good God. The message must be important. If so, why had Grandfather sent her? She was delicate and pale with silvery hair like an angel's. And yet she'd managed to skewer two before he'd made it downstairs.

Luce stripped off his cravat and pressed the hasty wadding to the wound, his mind rapidly prioritising his actions. The bleeding had to be stopped. Immediately. She would need stitches. Her care came before his questions.

Luce lifted her in his arms. How had someone this light managed two brute-sized men? He angled her through the door, juggling her in his arms. She moaned in protest. That moan was proof of life. Thank God.

'You're safe. I'm taking you inside. We'll see to your wound,' he assured her.

One never told a fallen comrade how bad an injury was. The rule was to be positive, to minimise the severity of the situation so that the injured didn't panic. Luce hoped the slice wasn't as severe as it looked. Sometimes a wound just bled.

Luce's servants had been woken by the commotion and had come to see what had happened. Luce issued orders to them as he climbed the stairs with the waif in his arms.

'Rowley, take the footmen and tie up any of the men outside who are still alive. Put them in the wine cellar. Mrs Hartley, I need hot water and medicinal supplies. Send a maid up, one with a strong stomach.'

He set his household in motion, thankful the girl in his arms was feather-light. He'd not realised how many steps comprised his staircase, or how long the corridor was. Perhaps that was his haste talking. There was little time to lose.

'In here, my lord.' A maid scurried past him, holding open the door to a guest room. 'This chamber has been aired.' The maid hurried about the room lighting lamps and laying a fire. Luce would have to remember to thank her later for her efficiency in a time of crisis.

Luce laid the silver-haired waif on the bed and pushed aside the tatters of her clothing, getting his first good look at the injury. He sucked in his breath. That wasn't a slice. It was a *gash*. Behind him in the room, he could hear the arrival of hot water and supplies.

'Another pad please.'

The layers of his wadded cravat were soaked through. Someone was beside him, pushing a clean cloth into his hand. He folded it and pressed it to the wound.

'Shall I send for the doctor?' the efficient maid—he remembered her name was Rose—asked.

'Yes, at once.'

Although he held out little hope there would be much help from that quarter. The doctor would be an hour at least in coming, perhaps more with the weather. That assumed the doctor was even at home and not already out braving the elements to deliver a baby or attending to some other medical need.

By the time the doctor arrived, Luce thought grimly, it might not matter. The injury may resolve itself by then. Either he'd get the situation under control or not. He didn't want to think of the 'or not'. This slip of a girl had fought three men on his doorstep. She could not die. Not until he knew who she was and why she'd come.

'More hot water,' he barked, his voice rough with his own desperation. 'Let's get her cleaned up. Mrs Hartley, prepare a needle for stitching. Rose, be ready with the brandy. And both of you, wash your hands before you touch anything.'

Thank goodness Grandfather had made sure his grandsons knew a few doctoring skills, enough to see them through more than one scrape.

'A lamp please, Mrs Hartley, when you're done with that needle. I need more light.' He bent to the task of cleansing the gash and prepared to apply stitches. The waif had beautiful skin, so pale and clear, which made the gash all the more vivid. A wave of anger surged. How dare someone think to mar the perfection of her with their blade?

'Keep her still, Rose,' he snapped gruffly when the waif's body flinched.

To his patient, he murmured a litany of reassurances as he worked. 'You're very brave, my dear. You fended off three men, you can do this.' He hated the idea he was causing her pain even as he was trying to save her life.

Luce tied off the last stitch and sat back, letting Mrs Hartley wrap yards of bandages about the girl's midsection. Luce stretched, the muscles of his back and neck taut from the precision of his efforts. But his discomfort was nothing compared to his patient's.

His patient. The waif. *Her*. There was more to her than those nondescript labels. Luce looked down into her sleeping—or was it unconscious—features, his mind a riot of questions. *She* had a name, this girl with the silvery hair and pearly skin. What was it? What had brought her to his doorstep tonight of all nights? Who were the men who had followed her? Who'd tried to kill her? Now that the initial crisis had passed, he could put his mind to those questions at last. He washed his hands and stepped out of the room while Mrs Hartley and Rose put her into one of his nightshirts.

Rowley was waiting with a report. 'There was only the one man alive. He's in the cellar as you asked, my lord. We've posted a guard for when he wakes up.'

'Excellent.' Wherever Grandfather had found the

staff, he'd done well. 'I'll question him in the morning. And the other two?'

'They're in the icehouse. Shall I send for the magistrate?'

Those bodies were going to be a problem. The ground was frozen. Digging graves would be hard work, impossible work, for a few days.

'We'll need two coffins and the discretion of the undertaker. Perhaps you could pay him without making it seem like a bribe.' The fewer questions the better. Luce didn't want to explain to Little Albury why the new viscount had two dead bodies to dispose of. 'By the way, which two didn't make it?'

'The thickset one and the one with the thin face.'

Luce raised a brow in surprise. Those had both been hers. The man he'd dealt with was the one in the cellar. That slip of a girl had taken out two grown men. His admiration for her rose. 'Was her weapon recovered?'

'Yes. I brought it up.' Rowley withdrew the knife and handed it over.

Luce held it up to the light. A stiletto. It had been cleaned and the blade shone with deadly intent. She'd taken out two men with this? It was a wicked, sharp blade, to be sure, but it *was* a civilian's weapon, not an assassin's. He hefted it, feeling the perfection of its weight. Still, it was exquisitely made and well-balanced. Stilettos were traditionally offensive weapons for stabbing, hard and swift. It was impressive that she had the strength for it and the tenacity for it. Knife work was not for the faint hearted. It was violent, bloody, up close and personal.

He handed the blade back to Rowley. 'Thank you. Let everyone know that they've done well. I am pleased with our efforts tonight.' He needed to get back to his patient although there was nothing more to do for her but wait, watch and hope that his skill had been enough to bring her through. Even so, it was likely to get worse before it got better.

Inside the room, he pulled up a chair next to the bed and settled in for his vigil. He'd take the first watch. Mrs Hartley had volunteered for the second. The door shut quietly behind him as Rose and Mrs Hartley exited, leaving him alone with this exquisite mystery.

And she *was* exquisite, now that there was time to appreciate the details of her. At the moment, she looked peaceful in her repose, like a fairy tale princess, with the long waves and curls of her hair fanned across the pillow.

He'd never seen hair—natural hair at any rate—quite that shade. He could see now that he'd been wrong to call it silver. The word did not do it justice.

It was not silver, nor was it blonde, but something beyond. White-gold perhaps, like Bolivian platinum or the shimmering ice-crystal-white of a snowflake. It gave her an otherworldly appearance tempered by dark lashes sweeping the pale pearlescence of her cheeks. Even though she'd lost blood, her skin was naturally pale. He reached out to stroke her cheek. He told himself it was to check for fever, to see that her skin remained cool, but in truth he simply couldn't resist. He knew before his hand reached her that touching her skin would be akin to touching silk. Warm silk, unfortunately. He'd keep a close eye on that. Fever was nothing to take lightly.

'Who are you?' he whispered. There was no answer. No fluttering of lashes. She was entirely lost to sleep, to exhaustion.

Luce sifted through the events of the evening and made his own deductions. She'd travelled on foot. How far? There'd been no horse with her. She'd arrived only to stand and fight. That she was one of Grandfather's many messengers seemed plain. That she carried urgent information worth killing for seemed plain too.

Whoever she was, he knew three things about her—she was beautiful, brave *and*, despite appearances to the contrary, she was deadly. Perhaps that was what Grandfather saw in her. She was someone people would underestimate, to their detriment.

Luce let out a calming breath. He would solve the mystery of her when she awoke. Until then, he could turn his attention to what she carried. What had been worth almost dying for? Had it been on her person or had she carried the message in her mind? If it was the latter, it made her survival all the more urgent. If she died, the message would die with her. Certainly, Grandfather could send it again, but valuable time would be lost and with Grandfather time was always of the essence.

Luce glanced around the room, searching for her clothes. He spied them draped over a spindled chair by the fire. He rose and retrieved them, starting with the coat first. That seemed the most likely place. He patted the pockets, rifled through them, finding nothing. Definitely one of Grandfather's messengers then. They never carried anything extra on their person. Nothing that would give away who they were or who they worked for. They were to be anonymous.

He glanced at the bed where she slept. It would be hard to be anonymous with snowflake hued hair. Beauty was meant to be noticed. It had its purpose, too. Beauty enticed. Men would tell a beautiful woman anything. Likewise, a woman would tell a handsome man her own husband's secrets if asked in the right way. Over the years, Luce had learned the power of a touch here, a smile there, a lingering gaze, a hand to the small of a woman's back as they strolled through a crowded ballroom. Quiet attentions were the most potent, the ones that made a woman feel seen and appreciated. It was a sad commentary on husbands that there were so many lonely women willing to talk in exchange for so little.

Luce turned the coat inside out to better see the lining. Was the message sewn inside? Was there something he'd overlooked? Ah, there! A narrow slit beneath the arm not easily noticed even with the coat turned inside out. The opening was only large enough for two fingers. He rooted around carefully, the tips of his fingers brushing against a slip of paper, slim and flat. Not rolled or folded. Nothing that would bulge. He retrieved it, marvelling at how small it was. A quarter sheet of note paper, no more, on which the fate of something as large as a nation might hang in the balance, proving to Luce yet again that the pen was so much mightier than the sword.

He brought the slip back to his chair for further study. It was as he anticipated: a code. Something that must be written down in order to be cracked. With coded messages, nuances like spacing mattered. Everything was part of the pattern. It could not be memorised for oral delivery without potentially losing a vital component.

Graphical shapes met his stare instead of letters drawn with straight lines. The code was likely written in Arabic. He looked closer. No, not Arabic. That didn't seem quite right to a more closely trained eye. There were more dots than Arabic usually employed. Perso-Arabic then. He'd have to get his books out tomorrow. He set the code aside and glanced at the bed. What else could she tell him about the coded message? He reached for her hand, taking it in his own, lacing the delicate elegance of her slim fingers through his own. 'Please, wake up, lovely one. I am going to need you.' Then, out of reflex, he raised her hand to his lips and kissed it.

She *had* to wake up. There was a message to deliver. There were men to fight. Luce would need her protection. The earl could not afford to lose another of his Horsemen, another of his beloved grandsons. The Greek cause was counting on her. So many were counting on her if she could just wake up.

Some vital part of her pushed its way forward into consciousness but it was difficult. Her limbs were heavy, there was an ache and pain and she was so very hot. Better to stay asleep her body counselled her mind. In sleep there was healing, there was peace. To wake up would mean hurt and illness. Those would be the price of consciousness. Did she really want to chase that?

This wasn't about want. This was about need and she *needed* to wake. To sleep was dangerous. What might escape her lips if she slept? What secrets might she give up in the throes of fever? For surely that was the source of her heat.

From a distance, she heard a voice, pleading, wishing, for her to wake up. A hand enfolded hers, its grip firm and healthy, lending her strength as it drew her forward to wakefulness. Lips brushed her knuckles with an unlooked-for gentleness. She was closer now. She could hear words. *Wake for me, I need you.* Yes. Yes, she thought. She would wake up for this. For him.

She forced her eyes open to meet his gaze, dark and warm like melted chocolate before milk was poured in. A smile of relief and joy took his face in gradual increments. His expression gave away much. He'd been worried for her. He was still worried. Her injury must be severe, then. It certainly felt severe. Between the ache in her side and the fever, she would not last long in the waking world. She would need sleep, but before she slipped back, she had to tell him. 'My coat…' She could barely make the words. They stuck in her throat.

He had a glass of water to her lips. 'I have the code,' he offered softly. 'You're not to worry. The message has been delivered. Your attackers are dealt with. You got two of them. I will question the other and learn who sent them.'

Wren swallowed, grateful for the cool water and for his news, delivered as it was in gentle tones and concise words as if he knew she didn't have long. That every waking second counted. 'Is it bad?' Her voice sounded stronger but that strength was an illusion. Already her eyelids were heavy.

'I've stitched you up. The doctor has been sent for.' He was holding her hand again. She liked the feel of it, the sense of connection it wrought. She wasn't fighting alone. 'There will be fever but we will get you through this.'

She wanted so desperately to give a nod. She could not make her head move. She thought she managed a small smile instead as her eyes closed. She could rest now. The business of the message had been dealt with.

'Wait.' Luce's voice was sharp. 'What's your name?'

She made a desperate effort to whisper, 'Wren. Wren Audley.' That's when she knew just how worried he was and just how badly she was hurt. He wanted her name in case he needed it for a tombstone. But she couldn't die. Not yet. There was a code to crack and Stepan to find. There was work to do and she couldn't do it dead.

Chapter Three

She didn't die, although there were times over the next three days when she thought she might, especially if one counted dying of embarrassment. For someone who detested being dependent on others for even the merest of assistance, Wren had been reliant on the immensely kind Mrs Hartley and the stoically practical Rose for everything, large or small. And Luce, too. Whenever she'd been awake, he'd been there at her bedside. She'd rather have starved than let him feed her beef broth from a spoon as if she were an infant, but Luce wouldn't hear of such foolishness.

Wren did understand though that she was lucky the sting to her pride was greater than the sting of her injury. A mid-grade fever had subsided, leaving her grouchy and restless in a bed she was truly too weak to leave. That didn't mean she hadn't tried. Day two, she had attempted to get out of bed and managed to stand up by herself for all of twenty seconds before taking a tentative step and falling over. Her folly had brought Luce running to pick her up off the floor and a visit from the doctor to check her stitches.

Such bravado had added two more days of bedrest to the doctor's orders. Unfortunately, Wren couldn't argue with the suggestion. She was kitten-weak in ways that went beyond the gash in her side. Bedrest would ease her wound, but only time would restore the blood she'd lost. That last contributed prominently to her grouchiness. She could hardly track down word of Stepan stuck in a bed, wearing one of Luce's nightshirts. But she decided, after her two days of extra bedrest were up, it wouldn't stop her from helping with the first part of her mission. Her brain was in perfect working order even though her strength was not. She could still contribute on that front.

Fuelled with determination, Wren carefully got out of bed and stood slowly, this time making sure to hold tight to the poster as she inched towards the dressing robe draped over the chair. Luce's chair. Where he sat when he came to visit, which wasn't as often as she'd like but she understood. He had a message to decode and time was of the essence. He was working. He didn't have time to read aloud to her or play cards. Although, Mrs Hartley had mentioned he'd not left her side that first night when she'd been in the most danger. It was only when the danger had passed that he'd vacated his chair, seeing her for a few minutes for a bedside supper. He spent those minutes giving her an update on her health and offering assurances that she was healing well. But they had not discussed the message after that first night. Nor had he asked any further personal questions.

Wren reached for Luce's robe, a black silk garment that smelt faintly of winter woods and spice. She breathed it in and laughed at her silliness. Of course it would happen this way: that she'd manage to capture Luce Parkhurst's attentions only while she was asleep. That was how her luck was. She often got what she wished for but in ways she'd not intended. Wren gingerly slid her arms through the sleeves, her movements stiff and slow. A person never quite realised how connected one's muscles all were until some of those muscles were out of operation. Any motion of her arm pulled at her side. It would be a while before she could even think about using her stiletto. Just the thought of trying to stab with it in her present condition made her wince.

Now for the door. Just five steps. She rested triumphantly when she reached it without mishap. She opened the door and stepped into the hall to make the journey to the library. The length of the corridor looked daunting. She would take it one door at a time, she told herself. There was no rush. Thank goodness this was not like her usual jobs for the earl where stealth was required. There'd be nothing stealthy about her progress today and she certainly didn't have the strength to hide. If any of the servants came upon her in the hall, she'd have to persuade them to help her along instead of sending her back to bed.

It was indeed a journey by the time she reached the library but well worth it for those windows. She leaned quietly against the door frame, gathering herself from that final effort, and took it all in. The enormous bank of cathedral windows that let in copious amounts of daylight even in winter, the pleasant warmth of the room she could feel even from where she stood and the man who sat, enthralled in his work at the long table with hair mussed, jacket off, shirtsleeves rolled up and glasses perched on his fine, long nose. Not even the windows could compete with the sight of that.

'Beautiful view,' Wren commented, dragging her reluctant gaze back to the windows. 'I see the snow has lasted.' The limbs of the sycamores lining the drive glistened in the sunlight beyond the windows, majestic and magical in their snow-kissed glory.

'Wren! What are you doing out of bed? Did you walk all the way on your own?' Luce pushed back from the table and raced to her side.

'All the way down the hall,' she offered wryly. 'It must be a whole hundred yards. *Quite* the journey,' she glibly mitigated the accomplishment. 'You needn't fuss.' But silently she was grateful for his arm about her and the support he offered as he settled her in a chair beside the fire. Her efforts had cost her more than she'd anticipated.

Luce gave her a stern obsidian stare. 'You could have fallen. For someone so eager to be up and about you seem very willing to risk bedrest again.' He reached for a soft velvety throw the shade of deep mahogany and draped it over her lap.

'I'm not in my dotage,' she scolded even as her fingers luxuriated in the plushness of the blanket and her mind basked in the indulgence of being cared for in spite of her protests to the contrary.

'No, but you *are* barefoot in a nightshirt in a house undergoing renovations in the middle of January.' Luce took the seat across from her, his gaze making her keenly aware of her rather unsatisfactory dishabille. She must look a fright, drowning in his nightshirt and robe, her hair a-tangle from lying abed. The words 'waif' and 'orphan' came to mind. Hardly words for how she'd like Luce Parkhurst to remember her.

Luce tapped his fingers on the arm of the chair, a smile curling on his mouth as he offered a friendly scolding of his own. '*You* are stubborn. You don't like others taking care of you, even when you need it.'

'I don't like *owing* others. It makes a person weak.' She didn't allow people to fuss over her in part because she knew no one would. Who *was* there to fuss over her? There were no parents, no siblings, no beloved friend. If she were to disappear, only the earl would note her absence. When he died, there'd be no one. It was best not to get used to such pleasures when she knew she'd lose them. 'Relying on others can be dangerous in my line of work.'

'Which would be what, exactly?' Luce queried with a hard stare that made her wonder if he'd believe a half truth or at least accept it if he couldn't believe it.

'You already know. I work for your grandfather. I run messages for him.' All true. There wasn't a single lie among those words, except that they weren't complete. She did more than run messages. But did it matter? The words wouldn't be true much longer. Soon, she'd be retired. Wren pushed the thought away. She didn't want to think about that yet. Who would she be if she wasn't Falcon?

Luce gave a considering nod. 'What else do you do for him?'

'Why do you think there's anything else?' She knit her brow in an attempt at subterfuge, hoping to throw him off the scent, minimal as that hope might be.

Luce gave a chuckle. 'Because, Miss Wren Audley, you left me two dead men on my doorstep to discreetly dispose of courtesy of your blade. It's a most wicked weapon for a messenger to carry. Which brings me back to my previous question. What else do you do for my grandfather?'

'A girl alone in the world can't be too careful. I like to cover all my bases, Mr Parkhurst, or do you prefer Lord Waring these days?' She offered the question with a smile made to distract. If subterfuge didn't work, perhaps redirection would. She'd far rather talk about his new title than talk about herself.

But he wasn't fooled by her enquiry or her smile. 'Luce is fine. And a girl alone indeed. It's an odd choice for my grandfather and a rather fraught one. He must be very sure of your abilities to put you in such situations.'

'He is, and you should be, too. I'm only sorry I

didn't get the third man.' Perhaps distracting him by discussing business would be more successful.

Luce gave another enigmatic nod. Was that a nod of approval? Or a nod of concession acknowledging he'd get nothing more out of her at the moment? She hoped for the latter. 'It would have been better for the third man if you had killed him. Then his identity could have died with him.' As would have anything the man knew. It was always a shame to lose information but sometimes that was the cost of doing business.

Wren leaned forward, impatient to hear the rest. 'Well? What did you learn? Was he hired by one of Roan's old minions set on revenge? Or was he from the Ottomans, sent to "retrieve" the message before it can be decoded?'

Luce laughed, his mouth curling up into a smile, appreciation twinkling in his eyes. Good. He liked her boldness. It didn't intimidate him like it did other men. 'If you already know, why do you ask? It is both, by the way.' He paused and the glance he gave her this time was definitely a considering one. 'Are you sure Roan's minions are after us? It doesn't seem the most logical of choices.'

She had to be careful or she'd give too much away even in a short sentence. 'We must consider all possibilities.'

'What about *probabilities*? I am surprised Roan's minions would have the time to bother. I would have thought they had enough to worry about cleaning up their own losses after Roan's demise. Does Grandfather think it is likely anyone will cross the Channel in winter simply for revenge?'

'Revenge is seldom logical.' What she did not share was that the earl did, in fact, think it a probability of sorts once the weather cleared. They would come not only for revenge. Some of Roan's minions were personally connected to the Ottoman forces and to the man Stepan had killed in the water. They'd cross the Channel for revenge *and* to retrieve the code. The earl was indeed worried enough to send her to track down a man who *might* be Stepan so that he wasn't taken unawares should the probability become a reality. But she was not to let on about that to Luce.

She met Luce's gaze with unwavering directness. 'I think the earl has lost a grandson and is concerned about losing others. He is riddled with guilt and grief over what happened. He blames himself. He feels as if he made a mistake. It has, perhaps, made him overly cautious when it comes to the Horsemen.' And when it came to her. It was that same grief that had the earl urging her towards retirement. The echoes of that conversation were ever-present in her mind. *I want you safe before the time comes when I am not here to protect you*. Because she owed the old man everything, she could not deny him this one last thing.

Mistakes? His grandfather did not make mistakes. For a long moment, all Luce could do was stare. Her audacity astounded him as much as her insinuations. This angel-haired ragamuffin with the quicksilver eyes deigned to tell *him* about *his* grandfather? To offer insights into the great man that was the Earl of Sandmore? To suggest the man had weaknesses? Who was she to dare such a thing?

Luce rose and walked to the console holding an array of decanters, in part to collect himself and in part because a drink was certainly in order despite the early hour. He poured two brandies and offered her one. She accepted the glass matter-of-factly, which was telling in its own way.

Luce re-took his seat. 'I find it intriguing that you believe you know my grandfather so well as to understand his mind on such personal matters.' And yet there were signs she might be right. When Caine had married in August, Grandfather had turned the day-to-day running of the Horsemen and the Sandmore network over to Caine. At Kieran's wedding in December, Grandfather had settled a considerable sum on Kieran and his new bride for the upkeep of their estate.

'I have been with the earl for a long time,' she offered, and took a sip of the brandy with a manner that suggested she drank it often. He admired her confidence even dressed in borrowed night attire. She might be sipping brandies dressed in a ball gown for all her elan at the moment. It was hard to remember she'd been stabbed and writhing with fever five days ago. In fact, it was hard to remember much at all with her sitting there in his dressing gown. He couldn't recall his nightwear ever looking so good and that tangle of platinum hair was positively seductive.

'How long *have* you been with Grandfather?' Luce gathered himself. It was ridiculous to be so affected by her. He'd had plenty of conversations with plenty of beautiful women and never once had trouble keeping his thoughts in order. It couldn't be terribly long. He was thirty-two and he'd been with Grandfather since he was twenty. Twelve years. He'd cut his teeth on Napoleon's war. She was what, twenty? Twenty-two? Although she could pass for younger. Sitting there, swamped in his night clothes, one might mistake her for sixteen on a casual glance. A closer glance would reveal the error, though. She was no waif. That was an illusion and perhaps a convenient, oft used disguise. He'd had hours to truly discern the truth of her while she'd lain unconscious with fever.

'Fifteen years,' she replied over the rim of her glass, her eyes intent on him because the minx *knew* her answer would shock him. Beyond the shock though was disbelief.

'Do you expect me to believe that?' He grinned into his glass. Her subterfuge was falling apart. 'It's not possible. You would have been a child.' The look on her face stalled the glass at his lips. '*Were* you a child?'

He'd not considered that and if he was being honest this conversation had elevated his curiosity, which had been on a barely contained simmer since he'd carried her bleeding body upstairs and patched her up. She was a woman full of contradictions. An angel who wielded a blade with the devil's own deadly precision. 'Perhaps you wouldn't mind telling me how you became acquainted with my grandfather? Did you find him, or did he find you?'

She shifted in the big chair and adjusted the blanket, her robe slipping open to reveal the soft curve of a breast beneath the nightshirt. 'He found me picking pockets where I shouldn't have been when I was eight.' She gave a smug smile and made no effort to readjust the robe. The minx enjoyed shocking him in all ways. Luce schooled his features, pretending to take each revelation in stride.

'I was living on the London streets, running with a gang of pickpockets, sleeping on straw in a damp cellar in St Giles, eating whatever I could cadge or cajole. One day, I picked the wrong pocket, or perhaps the right one. Your grandfather caught me and offered me a choice. Either he could turn me in or I could work for him.' She gave a delicate lift of her shoulder on her good side. 'I could tell from the look of him that he was a man with power. If he turned me in it would be straight to the prison. The choice was easy. But some days I regretted it and I am sure your grandfather did, too. It was hard work, harder than I thought it would be, and I was stubborn.'

Luce's brow arched in sardonic precision. 'I wouldn't have guessed it.'

'You see, I couldn't just go straight to work for him, I had to be cleaned up in all ways. I needed schooling, I needed manners. By the time your grandfather was done with me, I could speak, read and write three languages. I knew how to address all ranks of people, how to dress for any occasion, how to dance, how to shoot, how to use a knife, how to ride, how to fight and a hundred other things I had no idea I would need to know,' she finished proudly.

Luce studied her afresh. Grandfather had done

well. Any hint of the street had been entirely erased from her voice, her movements. He would not have guessed her beginnings had been so meagre, so bright was the polish on her now. But perhaps her story explained her tenacity on his doorstep, the will to fight, to win at all costs, without hesitation. Perhaps the scrapper in her had not been bred out. 'I assume this means you have no parents? No brothers or sisters?' Grandfather would not have taken a child with a family.

She nodded and the pride with which she'd ended her tale faded. 'There's no one. I don't remember my parents.' Her fingers were worrying the blanket now. He'd hit on a difficult subject for her. She might not remember them, but she remembered something.

A gentleman would let it be and Luce was usually a gentleman. But not always, not when there was information to be had. She'd finished her brandy and he swapped her glass for his, pressing the fuller glass into her hands. 'Not a single memory? Surely you did not spring into the world as an eight-year-old pickpocket.'

The quicksilver eyes dimmed to grey. 'I'd lived in the rookeries with the other children since I was three. It was all I knew. I don't think children have any earlier memories before they're three.' She glanced at him, perhaps waiting for him to challenge her before she went on. 'There was an older girl, Maggie, who looked after the little ones at night. She would tell us stories. Sometimes she shared her bread with me if she had extra. The best stories she told were the ones about each of us. She even gave each of us a birthday. It was usually the day we were brought to the cellar, but we didn't know differently. We barely knew our names. She told me I was brought in October by a man who said my name was Wren. I had a blanket with me and the clothes I wore.'

'Where does Audley come from, then?' Luce enquired, genuinely curious even as he was morbidly enrapt in her horrific tale. His heart went out to the little girl who'd had the tenacity to take her circumstances in stride and survive.

'Your grandfather found me on Audley Street. It was the beginning of a new life for me so it seemed appropriate to have a new name of sorts.' She flashed a brief smile trying to make light of a maudlin tale. 'That is the sum total memory of my origins. Needless to say, the blanket and I have long parted ways and I am much better off for having met your grandfather.'

What an awful story. There were gaps but they were easily filled in and some things were best left unspoken because they were too hurtful to say aloud—that her family had sold her to the pickpocket gang. It did happen. A family with too many mouths to feed would often trade their children in exchange for coin.

Luce's stomach twisted at the thought of abandoning, or worse—selling one's own child.

She would not want his pity. She had barely tolerated his help when she needed it. Pity would be met with scorn. He understood the reasons, though. She'd been forced to be self-reliant, forced to distrust. She'd lived a life devoid of love and connection. She'd not let it destroy her. Instead, she'd forged her strength from it. Impressive. And sad.

He wasn't sure his reaction was entirely one of pity. He wanted to protect her. To show her what life could be like when people were surrounded by family. By the caring of others.

'After all of that schooling, what do you do for Grandfather?' He asked his question again. If she was a messenger, she was certainly a high-end one with an education equal to that of he and his brothers.

'I pass messages for your grandfather and I collect bits of information here and there. I go where the Horsemen cannot, just like any of his many agents and messengers.' She stifled a yawn with her hand.

She was being vague again and she was tiring,

perhaps thanks to the brandy or perhaps due to being out of bed for the first time in nearly a week. Luce reached over to take her brandy glass and set it aside. 'I've worn you out. I'll help you back to bed.'

'No, please. I've had enough of bed for a while. We haven't talked about the code yet.' She yawned again.

'We can talk about the code later,' Luce insisted.

'You'll send me back to bed and forget about me like you have all week. You disappeared once I was out of danger.'

'Because I had work to do. The code must be solved.' And because staying beside her had proven to be too distracting. He had originally brought his work to her bedside but he'd spent more time wondering about her than he had trying to create a cipher. He'd been entranced by her hair and by the ethereal expression on her face. He'd made up stories in his head about who she was. All proof perhaps that he'd been too long without a woman beside him or that his brothers' married states were taking a toll on him. So, he'd put himself beyond distraction and removed himself to the library where he staunchly remained except for the few minutes each day he allowed himself to check on her at dinner and assure himself that her recovery was well under way.

'A compromise then,' she negotiated with a smile.

'I'll rest here on the sofa and when I wake up refreshed you can share what you've discovered about the code with me.'

Which wasn't going to be much. He'd made little headway on it. 'Fine, we have an accord. But let me help you to the sofa for my peace of mind.' Perhaps the best way to assist her would be to make her feel as if she were helping him instead.

'I feel silly taking a nap at eleven in the morning,' she murmured as he settled her on the sofa. 'It's not even time for luncheon.' But she was visibly losing the fight. Already, her eyes were shut.

Luce tucked the blanket about her. 'You have two hours until lunch, plenty of time to nap. You forget you left half your blood on my doorstep along with the bodies.' It would be a long while before he would be able to erase the memories of that night, watching her blood seep out of her as fast as he could staunch it. He studied her face. She did seem pale. 'Grandfather would never forgive me if something happened to his pickpocket princess.' She didn't hear his jest. She was already fast asleep.

Chapter Four

It turned out he lied. He did not wake her. Luce let her sleep through lunch for both their benefit, although if anyone had asked he would have argued it had been primarily for her sake. She was the one recovering from a serious wound, after all. The adventure to the library had taxed her nascent return of strength. The other part of that reality, though, was that he was recovering too from the force of her revelations, which had both intended and unintended consequences. One of which was that they made it impossible for him to get back to work on Grandfather's memoir.

She looked like an angel when she slept. He knew. Empirically. This wasn't the first time he'd watched her sleeping. He'd spent a hellish two days at her bedside watching her do the same thing. Even in the midst of fever and pain, she'd slept with a serene quality. And now, she was at peace again while his own personal world and tenets he'd once believed unequivocally true, were, if not in turmoil, teetering on the brink of it.

His grandfather—a man he'd grown up admiring as the grandest, smartest, most powerful and yet kindest man in the world; a man who was busy but always made time for his grandsons; who saw to the welfare of every family member even if they weren't in the line of succession, had recruited an eight-year-old orphan with the intention of grooming them for the network. For life as an agent, private spy or courier. For entrance into a game one could never leave.

To Luce, whose own relationship with the Horsemen was fraught with the tension between uniformity and individuality, making that decision for another, especially a child, seemed ethically and morally wrong.

He and his brothers had a saying 'once a Horseman, always a Horseman'. The expression was meant in many ways. A motto of solidarity. A reminder that your brother always had your back, even when he disagreed with you. But it was also a reminder of the permanence of membership. One could not quit the game, one simply survived it. After Stepan had gone missing Luce had tried to leave, tried to retire to his newly gained estate and forget about the game. For various reasons, he'd been unsuccessful. He could not leave his brothers out there alone without him. He might be willing to give up his loyalty to the Horsemen and the network, but he'd never give up his loyalty to his brothers, and so the contradiction bound him. Now, a new contradiction was testing his loyalties to the grandfather he loved.

At its core, Grandfather's decision to recruit Wren made sense, too much sense. Where there was one, were there others? Was the network full of orphans deliberately recruited as agents, spies and couriers for one of the most powerful private citizens in the country?

An orphan was the perfect candidate, Luce mused. An orphan had no family who might be used against them. The younger the better, too. If recruited young enough, there would be no fraternal or sororal bonds of the street, no friendships or loves to compete for their loyalty. All their loyalty and gratitude could be saved for Grandfather and the network.

That had certainly been the case for Wren. Luce watched Wren make a small adjustment in her sleep, a long length of her exquisite hair falling over the edge of the sofa. It was hard to imagine this angelic beauty as a street urchin. But that was testimony to Grandfather's efforts. It was no small thing he offered the orphan—shelter, food, clothing, education and a career. Where else would the street rat have such an opportunity?

That was the rub, Luce thought. The answer was nowhere else. Grandfather had to know that what he offered could not be duplicated. That for the child looking to break away from the streets, there was no choice but to accept. There was no choice but to be bound to him and the network. It was a deal even a canny street child could not truly fathom. A Faustian deal indeed, as Grandfather was no doubt aware. *That* was what made Luce uncomfortable. There was a remarkable lack of consent in the arrangement when all was stripped away. The child was trading a street boss for another boss who would exact his payment just as the street boss did, only in subtler terms and under a different guise. Which begged the question—was that what Grandfather had also done with him and his brothers?

Luce rose and went to the long windows, looking out over the clean, white snow. He didn't want to let his thoughts run in that direction but how could they not? He and his brothers were not much different than the parentless orphan whom no one was counting on. He and his brothers were the sons of his grandfather's third son. The spare to the spare, in a male rich family tree where the prospects of inheriting were less than nil. In terms of the succession, no one was counting on them. Luce's uncle, the heir, had multiple sons of his own. All of whom would be married within the year given the developments of this past Season.

Grandfather would have seen the succession dynamics early on when his sons started having children. Had Grandfather decided then to recruit him and his brothers? No one was counting on their branch of the Parkhurst family, no one except Grandfather and the network. It was to Grandfather and the network that they owed their purpose, their lives and now their estates and titles.

To be untrue to that would be to be ungrateful for the things that had come their way and to be ungrateful to the man who'd made all that possible. Luce looked out onto the snow-covered grounds of Tillingbourne, a place he was coming to love as his own. He knew sons of third sons had a difficult go in life, that Society felt they weren't truly gentlemen because they had to work for their living.

He and his brothers had been allowed to rise above that. Which made his own lack of abject appreciation harder to grasp. What would his brothers think if he raised such speculation with them? Caine was devoted to Grandfather and the purpose of the network.

If Caine had to choose between his brother and

the things that had shaped so much of his life, which would he choose? The old dilemma whispered. Belonging to the Horsemen meant acceptance within the family, equal footing with his revered brothers. Would that acceptance still be there if he stepped outside of it? And did he truly need to step outside of it to find what he was missing?

'You didn't wake me.'

Luce turned at the sound of Wren's sleepy accusation. 'You needed the sleep and luncheon could wait.' He gestured to the tray on the long table, untouched, as proof.

She gave an impish smile. 'Good, I'm tired of beef broth and I'm starving.' She tossed off the blanket and Luce crossed the room to assist her to the table.

'I could have made you a plate and brought it over,' he scolded, getting his arm about her to steady her. Wren was an apt name. She was petite in stature, delicately boned and yet hardy and strong. She wasn't brown like a wren though, that's where the analogy stopped. She was the color of winter. Her hair and her skin, shades of white.

'I can make my own plate.' She gave a resigned sigh. Resigned over being helped? Over her invalid state at present? Or something else? Luce wisely said nothing. He simply pulled out a chair for her at the long table and allowed her to assemble her own plate, as long as she sat down to do it. He was coming to understand that negotiating with Wren Audley was likely going to be a series of compromises on his part.

Dealing with Luce Parkhurst was likely going to require a firm hand and direct speaking. He wasn't an unreasonable man, but he was a protective one. He'd have her wrapped in cotton wool if she allowed it. Wren made a modest sandwich from the bread and meat. As delicious as the food looked, she knew better than to rush her stomach after a strictly beef broth diet.

Luce nodded approvingly as she took a small bite. 'That's right, take it slowly.' She wanted to snap back that she knew how to take care of herself, that she'd been wounded before, that she knew what to do. But that would give too much away. She held her tongue and focused on chewing instead. He was just trying to help.

'I read your paper on the impact of alkaline soil on the flora of southeast England.' When in doubt it was best to focus conversation away from oneself. 'What are you working on now?' Wren nodded towards the papers strewn on the table.

'A memoir of sorts for Grandfather. I want to finish it by spring.' Luce paused as if he were in conflict with himself. 'When did you see him last?'

Luce Parkhurst was a protector indeed. There was concern in those dark eyes of his for a man who likely did not need protecting any more than she did. Sandmore was one of the most powerful men she knew. 'Right before I left to come here.'

'How is he? Is he well? At Christmas, I worried the journey to Wales was too much for him even with all of my father's careful planning not to tax him.'

A moment of connection rippled through her at the realisation Luce felt it too, that same fear she harboured down deep when she took time to reflect. That someday, sooner than later, Sandmore, the one person in the whole world who cared for her, who knew who she was, would die. Her life would change that day. She could not let herself hide from that truth with little lies and explanations to compensate for the reality that the earl was showing his age. She wouldn't let Luce hide either.

'The earl has been sleeping a lot during the day since he came home and he mostly stays in his study so he doesn't have to leave the fire.'

She could see that the remark bothered him and she felt compelled to mitigate its impact. 'But he still handles copious amounts of paperwork with his usual dexterity and clarity of thought.'

Wren paused before adding softly, 'Even great men age. It's difficult to grapple with. He's been such an enormous part of my life that I wonder who I will be without him once he's gone.'

She'd find out soon enough when this final assignment was complete and she slipped into the world as someone else. It would be hard. Sandmore had treated her like a cherished granddaughter and he'd become her family. She'd let herself care for the old man and now she'd pay for that caring in the losing of him, proof that she was right to avoid long-term ties.

Nothing lasted for ever. Not the family she'd once had, nor the family she'd made. Love was a fool's ideal. It was ephemeral, existing in moments. The foolishness was in knowing it was doomed from the start and reaching out for the futility of it anyway. Love was not sustainable, not for her. And yet, part of her would still run towards it, the part that wanted a family of her own. Retirement would make that possible. It was not something she'd allowed herself to think about for a long while, but now circumstances had changed, allowing the impossible to creep back in despite knowing better.

Luce was frowning. What had she said to upset

him? 'I feel like I should apologise for that. For Grandfather being such a large part of your life. He catapulted you into a world you had no choice about belonging to. It's a very dark world and a dangerous one. Not a world most would choose to join.'

'Is that what you think?' His remark had taken her entirely by surprise. 'It's no more dangerous than life on the streets. In truth, I've never thought of my situation in terms of choice, but opportunity.'

'Perhaps you should.' Spoken like a man who had the luxury of consent, a gentleman for whom the world was indeed a different place. Street rats had no such privilege.

'Why? I've always been very grateful for what I have.' She had an education. She'd been able to travel, to see Europe. She had control. She made decisions for herself. It was far more than a three-year-old left in the stews could hope for.

'Maybe you shouldn't be.' Luce reached to make another sandwich. He'd devoured his in three bites while she digested the bitterness behind the comment. 'Are there others?' he asked. 'Other orphans in the network?'

She shook her head. 'I wouldn't know. We don't know each other. Anonymity keeps us all safe in case anyone is ever questioned. I don't believe there are others. If there were, they weren't raised at Sandmore.'

'But you were. It's a marvel we didn't see you. *Did* we meet you at some point? Did you live at Sandmore?' Luce wondered aloud, taking them off on a slight tangent.

She nodded. 'In the beginning, when I was young. I needed a lot of schooling simply to be ready for more schooling. The earl felt I would learn better if I could combine education, etiquette and...' She was looking for a word and Luce knew what it was.

'Espionage. I think that's the word you want. Grandfather's three Es,' Luce supplied.

She laughed. 'Yes, espionage. As I grew, the earl often sent me with others for training and later I was able to attend a finishing school. The older I got, the less often I was at Sandmore. And you were not there often in those days. You had your schooling to finish and Napoleon to fight. It is no wonder the path of a grown man didn't cross with a young girl's.' And yet, there'd been that one time she'd spied him through a keyhole talking with the earl.

She'd not heard what they said, but she'd seen him—the tousled waves, the broad shoulders. Not so different from his brothers in that regard, but then he'd tossed back his head and laughed—a wondrous, warm sound. In that moment, the mythical Horseman she'd heard so much about became human, tangible and real. It was the moment she'd fallen for him. Not the legend but the *man*, and she'd promised herself that one day she'd meet him, face to face. That was all she could promise herself. Just a meeting. A man like him wasn't meant for a street rat like her.

She'd give too much away on her face if she let her thoughts linger on that memory. Wren furrowed her brow, letting her mind find its way back to the original conversation. 'Do *you* think the network is made up of orphans?' Why had she never thought of it? She'd spent her life thinking she was the only one. 'Does it matter if it is?'

Luce's dark eyes turned thunderous. 'It damn well does if my grandfather is deliberately and regularly recruiting young children from the street and thrusting them into a life of espionage under the threat of taking them to the magistrate if they refuse. It's no choice at all. No child is going to pick Newgate over hot meals, shelter and clothes.'

She took a slow bite of her sandwich, seeing the source of his bitterness more clearly now. 'Is that what happened to you? Were *you* forced to be a Horseman?' Why had that not also occurred to her growing up? In Sandmore's household, she'd been raised on stories of the gallant four who rode forth dealing death and destruction in order to protect England. She'd not considered their consent in that role any more than she'd considered hers. Survival was the lens through which she viewed everything.

'It was different for me than it was for my brothers,' Luce said. 'I was the youngest of four boys. Many decisions were already made by the time I was old enough to participate. Caine and Kieran had been working for Grandfather for a few years already. Everyone, even myself, assumed I'd follow in their footsteps, and Stepan's. It seemed unconscionable to not support my brothers and, at the time, it was something I'd spent my life yearning for.' He gave a chuckle. 'I thought being a Horseman would solve all my problems. That I would be one of them, not the little brother always lagging behind, trying to catch up, trying to prove myself.'

'Did being a Horseman help?' she prompted, intrigued by this glimpse into a very private side of Luce Parkhurst.

'In some ways. It gave me an identity and it gave me membership into a group. It met some of my belonging needs. Now the die is cast, *has* been cast for some years. There is only going forward. Once a Horseman, always a Horseman. My brothers and I are bound to it by birth and bonds. Together for ever, which is a very long time even with brothers one loves.'

'At the price of your individuality,' she divined. How illuminating. He had not said as much, but she heard the message beneath his words. Loyalty did not come without its own price. In that regard, he and she were not so different, each of them thirsting to belong and yet searching for their individuality, both of them struggling to understand who they could be outside the bonds of the groups they belonged to.

Despite his struggle, Luce had chosen his family over himself. How very admirable of him. Luce Parkhurst was loyal, brave and protective even at a personal cost to himself.

She was collecting impressive attributes in regard to him. All of them things a Horseman should be and yet she sensed they were both the source of unhappiness and happiness for him. She'd never questioned her identity, not until now when she faced losing it, but it seemed Luce had questioned his.

She tipped her head to one side, taking him in. The long elegance of his nose, the wire-rimmed spectacles, the loose wavy dark hair and rolled up shirtsleeves. He looked very much the part of the wild academic. It was undeniably a sexy look, mostly because it was uncultivated and, she suspected, it came quite naturally to him. One did not curate such a look in the mirror. Sitting in the library, she felt as if she were seeing Lucien Parkhurst, individual man, in his native habitat without the trappings of the Horsemen, without his brothers.

It occurred to her that this was where he preferred to be—among his books, his mysteries. It was no wonder his expertise for the Horsemen was in code breaking—a puzzle to be solved. Solving required thought and research. In that way, the two halves of his life—his life as a scholar and his life as a Horseman, intertwined. It made her wonder what he would choose if he could. She posited the bold question, 'Would you leave the Horsemen if you could?'

His gaze turned stern and shuttered. 'It is a futile question and you well know it. There is no leaving the game. Perhaps that's why I object to you having had the lack of choice in joining. One cannot simply choose to get out.' His answer told her all she needed to know. He *would* leave if he could, just as she'd stay if she could.

'Speaking of the game,' she moved on smoothly, filing that bit of information away, 'how is the code coming? Have you cracked it yet? You promised to tell me.'

'No, but I feel I am close to having a cipher.' He passed her the paper. 'It's written in Perso-Arabic, at least that's what the letters are.' He reached for a book and opened it to a marked page. 'The Perso-Arabic alphabet is here. You can see the symbols match. This is really nothing more than just verification I have the language right.'

He presented her with another sheet of paper. 'Here, I have written out each translated word so that we can read the message in English. It took a while. I am not as conversant in Arabic as I am in other languages.'

In *six* other languages to be exact. Luce Parkhurst was a polyglot. He had mastered French, German, Spanish, Portuguese, Latin and Greek before he was twenty, while having a more than passing ability in Russian, the Nordic languages and Arabic. He was far too humble about his talents.

Wren took a moment to read the message. 'It doesn't sound cryptic to me. Two men meeting, sharing a meal.' Her specialty was unravelling people and obtaining information, not interpreting it.

'You're right. It's not cryptic. One could read it and assume it was just a message, one with no high-level information in it. However, the fact that someone intercepted it, coupled with the fact that you were followed and stabbed in an attempt to retrieve it, affirms that there is hidden value to this. It is unusual for the Ottomans to use codes at all. The

Greek resistance uses them often, but not the Turks. The codes in the region are commonly designed around the structure of a *krifó scholió* or a 'hidden school'. The Ottomans might have used one as well, especially if they were in enemy territory and worried the message would be intercepted.'

She was having trouble concentrating on the details. Her mind was far more interested in the man who was speaking. He was breath-takingly intoxicating like this, entirely in his element. Intelligence was damnably attractive to her and he had looks and intelligence to spare. 'Show me.'

Luce searched for a clean sheet of paper, printing out a sentence as he spoke and a ripple of want shivered through her. 'For instance, maybe I use religious references and on the surface, my letter appears to be about a church service and the vicar's sermon. But someone who knows the cipher would know that any reference to the vicar is actually a reference to a certain general and the church service is actually a reference to his troop placement.' He pushed the paper towards her, 'Now, read this with that in mind.'

'"Attendance at church was sparse today. Many folks are down with an ague given the dampness of the season. There were perhaps only twenty in attendance for the vicar's sermon and for that reason, I believe he cut it short.'" She looked up from the paper with a grin. "'Our general did not follow through on an attack given his lack of troops due to illness in camp.'"

'Very good. They're not always that simple or straight forward but now you see what I mean by a hidden school. The trick is to figure out what the 'school' or context is. Is it religious? Is it historical? Is it mathematical? What is important and well-known enough in that region? Once we understand the context, we can decode the references. This is very much a cipher that has to be built in layers.' He gestured towards the pile of books on the table. 'Hence, the research.'

She laughed. 'Hence? I like that. It's a word we don't use nearly enough.' But it *was* a word Luce Parkhurst would use. An old word, a scholar's word, and it was awfully sensual.

He leaned back in his chair and pushed a hand through his hair, smiling. 'Well, that depends if we're using it as a verb or a noun. As a noun, it's still active, less so as a verb.' He was in his element. Anyone could see it. Surrounded by books, playing with words, solving puzzles. This was what brought him joy.

Wren stood, stiff from sitting too long. She needed to work her muscles if she was to regain her strength.

She made a slow walk to the window. It was late afternoon but already the long shadows of night were gathering. 'It gets dark so soon in the winter.' She wrapped her arms about herself as if the cold could reach her through the windows. 'Still, it's an extraordinary view. You can see all the way down to the village.'

Luce was beside her, draping the throw about her shoulders. 'I don't mind the dark. Winter is my favourite season.'

'It's not mine.' She tugged the blanket tight around her. 'I remember freezing in the winter. The cold would go on without end until I thought I'd simply die of it. Many did. Some of the children in the cellar would go to sleep and not wake up. My blanket, my singular possession, very likely saved my life until your grandfather came. Then he saved me in truth.' She slid him a smile to soften her words, knowing now that Luce carried a deep-seated love-hate relationship with the role he played within his grandfather's network.

She'd learned a lot about Lucien Parkhurst today. He was not all he seemed. He was in fact, quite a sexy, intellectual bit more, which only served to increase her intrigue with him. If she had any sense, she'd take that as a warning and leave as soon as possible. She floated the idea casually. 'I should be able to travel within two or three days.'

'I doubt it,' Luce answered with equal nonchalance as if this discussion was of no great import. 'You are in no condition to sit in a jouncing carriage or on a bouncing horse. Even if you were, Mother Nature has other ideas.' He nodded towards the outside where night and snow had conspired to fall together. White flakes lit the darkness. 'We'll have six inches on the ground by morning and another six by the end of the day tomorrow. Supposing you were fit to travel, which you are not, the roads won't be any good to you for a while, even after the snow melts. I think you are here for the duration.' He gave her a friendly smile. 'I can think of worse places to wait out a snowstorm. You can help me crack the code.'

That was the problem, the very *big* problem. She could think of worse people to wait it out with, too. She'd wished for exactly this—time to work alongside the legendary Luce Parkhurst. But one ought to be careful what one wished for because wishes came with strings. Now that she'd gotten what she wanted it was so much more than she'd expected.

Chapter Five

Wren Audley was much more than expected, although Luce supposed that wouldn't take much given that he'd expected no one at all and she was definitely not 'no one'. Not if his sleep patterns were proof. Thoughts of her had been keeping him up at night although the reasons for those thoughts had changed as her stay lengthened and her proximity increased. He could no longer confine her to her bedroom and pretend she didn't exist when her presence got to be too much. He was intrigued by her and everything he learned about her fed that intrigue instead of sating it.

Luce slid a look over the rims of his glasses to where Wren sat across from him at the long library table. The snow had kept her here as predicted and the past week of rest and good food had worked wonders. Her strength had returned to a degree that she could spend her days with him in the library and perambulate under her own power about the corridors, peeking beneath Holland covers with him in unfinished rooms as he discussed his renovation plans. Health pulsed beneath her naturally pale skin, bringing a soft pink tinge with it to override the deathly white that had characterised her early days with him. Today, she was dressed in a blue gown of merino wool loose enough to not disturb her stitches, courtesy of Mrs Hartley's efforts, and her hair was plaited in a thick braid that hung over one shoulder.

If one didn't know better, one would never guess a little over a week ago she'd lain unconscious and fever ridden, fighting for her life. But Luce did know better. She might appear to be all right, but it would be a while before she was entirely restored to health. She'd proven to be resilient but one could not hurry the body in replenishing lost blood. She'd still need to stay a while longer. Surprisingly, the thought did not sit poorly with him, despite his original intent of hibernating alone. It was clear that her company was more welcome to him than his company was to her. She'd made it plain that she wanted to be gone as soon as possible, which prompted the question of why? Was there some place she had to be?

She looked up and caught him staring. 'What is it?'

Luce gave a slow smile, unbothered by being caught out. 'You look like winter, all blue and white.'

She laughed and tossed her braid. '*You* look like you're not concentrating on the code.'

Luce tipped his chair back on two legs and pushed a hand through his hair. 'I wasn't getting anywhere with it even when I was concentrating. I know I'll crack it. Eventually. But at the moment I am entirely blank.' Now that they had the message literally translated, their efforts had focused on trying to deduce what the 'school' might be. So far, all they'd done was eliminate options.

'It's because you're restless. When you aren't looking at me, you're looking out the window. You want to be out there, in your precious snow.' She waved a hand towards the windows. 'You've been cooped up inside too long on my account. It's not your nature to be indoors all day.'

'What do you know of my nature?' Luce chuckled but he couldn't disagree. He *was* restless and he did some of his best thinking outdoors. He'd foregone his usual rambles in order to work on the code and to stay near in case she needed him. A good host didn't set out after breakfast and leave his guest alone until supper. Grandfather would expect better of him.

She didn't answer but gave him a smug smile that

suggested heavily she felt she was in possession of a great secret. 'Up with you.' She rose slowly from her chair, a reminder that she was still recovering despite her looks to the contrary. 'Let's go for a walk. The fresh air will do us both good.'

Luce *did* feel much better outdoors even if they did stay on the grounds. Mrs Hartley had found Wren a shawl and the gardeners had shovelled the paths earlier so that they were able to stroll in the cold late-afternoon with relative ease, although Luce kept a tight grip on Wren's arm lest she fall. He gestured to the barren snow-covered beds. 'I found the original plans for the gardens in the library, from back when this place was a fully operating monastery. I added a few flourishes and a little modernisation so the gardeners will be able to re-establish them in the spring. This garden here will be dedicated to herbs, both for the kitchen and for medicinal use. Through here,' he led her beneath an arch way that opened into another garden, 'will be a scientist's garden. It was once used for growing and collecting species of plants from all over the world. I want to recreate that. Perhaps in time it might again become a place of interest for botanists in the region and they will want to visit for study.'

He noticed she suppressed a shiver despite the shawl. Perhaps he'd kept her out too long. Her blood was thin at the moment. 'The orangery is over there. It's a work in progress like the rest of the house. Let's go in. There isn't much to see yet, but it's warm and we are using it to keep some cuttings and trees alive through the winter.'

The orangery was indeed warmer and he could see that Wren relaxed immediately as he guided her around the space pointing out special cuttings. 'I hope I haven't bored you?' Luce brought his tour to a halt beside what once had been the orangery's pride: a fountain basin done in Talavera tile from Spain.

'Not at all,' she said. Perhaps she was just being polite, although he didn't think she was in the habit of saying things she didn't mean. 'This house suits you. It's full of history.'

There she went again, telling him about himself. Luce sat on the wide rim of the basin. 'Sometimes I feel as if you know far more about me than you should on short acquaintance.' He gave her a speculative look. 'Have we met before?' he asked, not for the first time. He would have remembered her, he was sure of it.

She shook her head and sat carefully beside him, smoothing her skirts. 'The earl talks of you, all of you, at least to me. So, yes, after fifteen years as one of his agents I do feel like I know you.' She gave a coy duck of her head that Luce found charmingly irresistible. 'We've not met, not technically, but I did see you once through a keyhole.'

'That's rather alarming.' Luce chuckled. 'Keyholes imply a certain level of decadence. Was I dressed?' He could only imagine what he might have been up to and who he might have been up to it with. There'd been a steady parade of lovers over the years, although no one staying for long, which was how he preferred it.

She shook her head and laughed. 'You were wearing a long coat and talking with your grandfather. Something he said made you laugh. It was at Sandmore and it was all very decent, I assure you.'

It was at Sandmore. She spoke of the place like one would a home. It had been more to her than just a place to live between trainings and school terms. It was a reminder that she shared fifteen *close* years with his grandfather. She'd also used the term agent this time, not messenger, and Luce was fairly certain his grandfather didn't tell just anyone about his family. Once more, her references spoke of the immense trust his grandfather had in this particular agent and of the type of relationship his grandfather shared with her, which seemed to border on the paternal.

'I am almost jealous of you,' Luce confessed. 'Visiting Grandfather's home in the summers was a treat nonpareil for me and my brothers. We coveted our time there.' Talking to her was like talking to a stranger who wasn't a stranger. There was so much more about her that he wanted to know—who she was, how she fit in to the Sandmore network—and yet they also had memories of a shared space, memories of a shared beloved person. They'd walked in each other's footsteps without realising it. 'When did you go on your first mission?'

Wren gave a laugh and blushed with humility. 'I don't know if I would call it a mission. I was twelve and I didn't have to leave Sandmore for it. It was a little nothing thing. The earl had some gentlemen and their wives to supper. He'd told me that two of the men were working secretly for France and that they were planning on using the supper as a chance to pass messages. It was my job to pick their pockets and ensure those messages never the left the house.'

Luce shook his head in amazement and disbelief. 'I don't know whether to laugh or be offended that Grandfather used a twelve-year-old for such an important task. Were you successful?'

'Of course I was.' Her eyes danced and she leaned forward confidentially, a casual hand resting on his thigh that sent his blood racing. Usually it was the other way around. When was the last time a woman's touch had roused him so thoroughly? So immediately? Had she done it on purpose or did such gestures come naturally to her? Had she even noticed she'd done it? Luce certainly noticed.

'It turned out it was vital information, too. It was good practice for me and it proved to the earl that I could be trusted for other missions. Although, they were all at home for a while.' *At home*. Luce did not miss her reference again to Sandmore as home. Grandfather must have cared about her very much.

'I didn't go abroad until I was old enough to be out in society. I went to Paris for the earl when I was sixteen.'

'Sixteen is not old enough to be out in society let alone travelling to the Continent,' Luce corrected.

'I wasn't alone. The earl had arranged chaperones. I stayed with the Comtesse de Varigny. It was all very above board.' She shrugged off the concern.

'I *know* the Comtesse de Varigny. She's quite, um, progressive, to say the least. Hardly a proper chaperone for a young girl.'

'Well, I didn't *look* like a young girl. With cosmetics and the right clothes, I *can* pass for older.' And for a lovely courtesan, the kind of young woman the Comtesse would take under her wing. Luce could imagine how that visit went.

'You could also pass for younger,' Luce said pointedly. 'I thought you were a waif when you collapsed on my doorstep.' All of his protective instincts were awake and wanting to work on her behalf even though she clearly didn't need them.

She shrugged and replied, 'People see what they're told to see, what they expect to see.'

'Or what you *allow* them to see.' Today, she'd allowed him to see quite a lot. She'd been given to share her own history with him. And why shouldn't she be? He was a safe place for the sharing and that was undoubtedly rare for her. Where else or who else could she share her story with if not a Horseman, the grandson of her benefactor? And Luce was lapping it up like a cat with cream, each piece of information a gift that helped him unwrap the mystery of her while simultaneously deepening that mystery.

She was not daunted by the implied scolding in his words. 'You do it, too. You're careful with what people get to see. The people of Little Albury look at you and see the new Viscount Waring. I doubt you do little to dissuade them to see otherwise. Your brothers see you as the fourth Horseman. I do not think they see your dilemma and dissatisfaction with that role. Do they? Do they know you'd put it all behind you if you could?'

He shot her a sharp look. She was too perceptive by far. 'I'd not realised I'd given myself away.'

'This *house* gives you away.' She smiled kindly.

How many men had she smiled at in the same way? How many of them had disgorged their secrets to her as a result?

'You love it here with your plans to reconstruct the gardens in line with their heritage. Your efforts in rebuilding the library and your designs for the rest of the house. You *want* to be the viscount. You want to make a life here,' she surmised, all too accurately for Luce's taste. She cocked her head and Luce felt the full force of her gaze. 'Does that mean you'll marry before July?'

'Oh no, you don't.' Luce laughed and made a warding gesture with his hands. 'Discussing matrimony with a woman is always a dangerous conversation.'

Especially when she had her hand on his thigh and he'd not even discussed the topic with his brothers when they were together at Christmas, or his father with whom he was very close. It had seemed too personal, too private. But not with her. She was far too easy to talk with.

'Not when the woman is me. You have nothing to fear, cross my heart. I am not likely to marry.' It was one more item they had in common, one more way they'd walked the same path without knowing it, and yet to hear her say such a thing pained him. The way she spoke of his grandfather, of her time at Sandmore, made it clear to him that she craved belonging. That she craved a family to make up for the one she'd lost. The network had taken that choice from her.

'I did not think to marry this soon if at all, but things changed. Now I find I *must* marry if I want to make a legacy of this estate. I don't want it to fall into ruin again. It would mean all my efforts were for naught. However, that poses the question of whether I can simply marry perfunctorily to satisfy the requirements? I'd prefer my marriage to be something more than that. I want it to be something meaningful. I am not sure I have the time to find that, though.'

'You would settle?' It was asked quietly, without judgement, and it suddenly felt right to be sitting in the half-done orangery discussing this intensely private topic with her—someone he'd not met ten days ago. No wonder Grandfather valued her as part of the network. She could pry secrets from the most hardened and guarded of hearts, and perhaps she had. He found he didn't like thinking about that—about other men sitting in orangeries with her, talking about the things that haunted the depths of their souls.

'A title and estate are hardly "settling".' Luce made the argument out loud that he'd made so often in his head over the past months. 'It's an enormous move up in the world for the fourth son of a third son. Many would say only a fool would toss away such opportunity. Grandfather included.'

'You cannot bear to disappoint him.' She gave a gentle laugh, her delicate hand offering a commiserating squeeze of his leg. 'The earl does inspire deep loyalty.' She paused and studied him, giving him the full attention of her eyes. 'Loyalty means a great deal to you, doesn't it? You are loyal to your brothers, to your grandfather, to some extent at the expense of your own personal preferences. Now, you are faced with that same dilemma here at Tillingbourne. You are loyal to your tenants, to your village, even though that loyalty will require you marry a woman for whom you have little affection. Shouldn't there also be room for loyalty to yourself amid all of this sacrifice?'

'I think the word for that is selfishness.' He gave her an appreciative grin. She would never know how much her insights pleased him, warmed him. To be understood by someone was an enormous gift and she'd given him that at a time when his personal world often seemed bleak.

'I appreciate the thought but no, I don't think there's room for selfishness. I do, however, think there is room for compromise and Tillingbourne is it,' he explained. 'To be the viscount allows me to put my stamp on this place and to pursue my ideas for my studies, for this home, for this village. It does grant me some of the individuality I am seeking, some of the chance to step out from my brothers' shadows. In exchange, I must marry and perhaps it will not be a love match.'

It very likely wouldn't be.

'Perhaps it is the price that must be paid for the chance to be on my own in some small way. To not marry is to doom both of my dreams—to doom the estate and this village as well as to doom my own quest to be more than a Horseman, more than one of four brothers. I think the greater good, and my own good, is served through marriage, love withstanding.'

'It's your version of utilitarianism,' she commented softly.

'Yes, it allows me to be loyal to the most people and at least partly loyal to myself.'

It sounded rational when explained that way and yet Luce couldn't help but feel that deep down he would trade all that logic for the right woman, a woman who inspired him to greatness and to grand passion. This was why one could not be ruled by selfishness. It was an uncomfortable thought.

Luce sighed heavily. 'Speaking of loyalty, I am

failing Grandfather at present, unable to unlock that code. My lack of familiarity with the Turkish region is working against me.' He rose and walked a few paces.

The shadows had stretched while they'd talked. The afternoon was fully behind them now and no good could come of being in the orangery after dark with a woman whose hand rested too comfortably on one's thigh. Especially when that woman had been keeping him up at night with images of her in his black robe, her hair tangled and loose falling over her shoulder while she matched him in authority on foreign policy—a most wicked and rare combination.

'We should get you back to the house. Mrs Hartley will have supper ready and it's getting cold even in here. She'll not forgive me if you catch a chill.'

Luce took her arm and tucked it close to his side. 'You're a very good listener. Thank you for that. I appreciated being able to talk about my gardens.' And his life, his dilemmas and his desires. This conversation had been about far more than gardens.

She flashed him another charming smile. 'It's easy to listen when the subject is interesting.' Flatterer, Luce thought not unkindly. He knew flattery when he heard it, but the compliment warmed him anyway.

***

The walk and time outdoors had restored Luce's energy and his spirits. He was far more optimistic when he walked into the library. He inhaled deeply, savouring the aroma of hearty cooking. Mrs Hartley had set up supper in the library for them as had become their practice and because the dining room was not ready for use. Generous slices of cottage pie were set on plates and red wine sparkled in the goblets.

'It doesn't get any more English than this.' Wren's eyes lit up at the sight of the food.

Luce held her chair out for her before moving to his own. 'The Irish might disagree. They like to claim cottage pie as their own.'

'But it was Sir Walter Raleigh who introduced the potato to Ireland and he was most definitely English,' Wren argued easily and impressively. Grandfather had done his due diligence with her academics.

Luce took his seat and raised his wine glass. 'To Walter Raleigh and cottage pie on cold nights.'

Wren laughed at his toast and he took a ridiculous amount of pleasure in having made her smile. Making women smile came naturally to him, so why it should matter so greatly that he could make this one specifically smile bore thinking on. Perhaps it was because she'd nearly died in his care. Perhaps he felt responsible for her. Or perhaps it was simply because he liked her. She was easy *to* like. She was pretty and intelligent, they shared certain key similarities and she had no intention of ensnaring him in marriage. In short, she was perfect for him.

She took a forkful of the thick pie and closed her eyes as she chewed. 'This is delicious,' she said after she swallowed. 'Something I've appreciated in my travels throughout the Continent for the earl is a chance to eat many regional cuisines. Bouillabaisse in Marseilles, ratatouille in Provence, pasta in Florence. Food marks a region. It defines a culture.'

She might have said more. Luce was too busy staring at her, the pieces that had eluded him all week finally tumbling into place. 'That is exactly it,' he said excitedly. 'The food in the message. That's the hidden school. It's all about the menu for the meal they discuss. The dates, the grapes, the kebabs…they all stand for something. We just have to figure out what it is.' He rose from the table, cottage pie forgotten, his mind racing. 'I've got a book of foods from the region here somewhere that details their histories and import to the culture. We can start with that.'

She laughed. 'We are going to finish our food while it is hot. Bring the message and your book to the table. We can work a little while we eat. But we're definitely not letting this food go to waste.'

Ah, a compromise, Luce chuckled to himself as he retrieved the book. He'd known from the start this woman would demand them of him and he'd not been wrong.

Chapter Six

Luce was right. Wren stared at the map spread on the library table anchored with paperweights, its surface dotted with various figurines they'd collected from the around the room to act as ships and troops. The hidden school was indeed the food and the meal itself. The mantel clock chimed a sonorous reminder that it was past midnight. They'd left their cottage pie and red wine hours ago.

Wren stifled a yawn, exhausted. This was her longest day by far since her injury but it would take more than sleepiness to drag her from Luce's side. If he could keep working, so could she, although she was starting to think he was indefatigable. His brilliant mind showed no signs of slowing down. The library table bore testament to his mental agility. Books lay open, key pages marked. She'd appointed herself the official note taker so that he could pace and think out loud.

To watch Luce Parkhurst in action as he worked through a puzzle, methodical and sure, was yet another revelation of his depths. His reputation in certain circles was by no means overstated. She took a small measure of pride in knowing she'd contributed a little.

'Wren, read back the notes on the figs.' Luce leaned against the table, palms braced on the tabletop, shirtsleeves rolled up, his coat long since discarded as he studied the map. He looked a wonderful, wild mess, his glasses sliding down his nose, his waves askew. His rather glorious backside on display in those tight breeches made her mouth go dry. How was a girl—even a well-seasoned girl such as herself to whom the male body was not a mystery—supposed to think with all that masculine geometry on display—the broad shoulders, the lean waist and those long, muscled legs?

She cleared her throat and read back the information. Luce moved one of the objects on the map and stood back. 'There, that makes more sense.' He turned to her, a smile taking his face, a spark in his eye as if he'd done battle with a foe and conquered it. 'I think we've got it. Check my math, as it were.'

She left her notes and came to stand beside him as he began. 'The Ottomans no longer control the Ruemli.'

He traced a circle on the map with one long finger. How had she not noticed the elegance of his hands before? A little thrill ran through her at the thought of those hands on her, touching her with the same reverence he touched his books.

'They still hold Athens though and a Greek state cannot be complete without it. They have the advantage there.'

He tapped the paperweight representing the Ottomans in Athens.

'The Greeks will have to take the city. It's no secret that's where the next battle will come *if* the Greeks can get that far.'

Reaching for a dog figurine positioned in the water, he continued. 'That's where the note comes in. The Ottomans are going to blockade the Saronic Gulf, here. In order to stop supplies to Eleusis, or Eleusina if you prefer the modern name, there.'

Luce tapped another spot of land at the north end of the gulf and drew a circle around Eleusina and the surrounding hills. 'The Ottomans are tired of General Karaiskakis harrying them on the ground and winning. He's taken territory and disrupted their own supply chain.'

Wren nodded, processing what that meant. 'Eleusina is a vital part of the supply line for Greek forces.'

She knew just how vital it was. As Falcon, she had been there in the spring, supped with the Greek guerillas while she gathered intelligence for the Sandmore network.

'Instead of fighting Karaiskakis on the ground and risk losing as they have been, they'll strangle him and prevent him from fighting at all. No supplies mean no army.'

Anger flooded her. 'Karaiskakis has fought all autumn, making victories out of nothing, winning back ground lost this past spring. There is no money for salaries for his soldiers. The men who fight with him do so out of their love for independence or out of their love of him. To be thwarted now...' She let the thought trail off in frustration and impotence. She made a fist. 'When will England officially join the fight? It's been six years! The British navy would be quite helpful in protecting the gulf just now.'

Luce folded his arms across his chest, his mouth set in a grim line. 'We *have* sent funds and arms. Six hundred thousand pounds in gold, in fact.' Luce's jaw was tight as he issued the reminder and she recognised too late that in her own passion she'd stepped out of line. His brother had sacrificed himself for the cause.

'All the more reason to see the effort succeed.' She placed a conciliatory hand on his arm, her tone soft. 'People, your own brother, have given much individually. It would be a shame to falter at the last.'

She had travelled the breadth of the Continent in aid of the cause and at no small risk to herself. The Ottomans were in earnest. She did not want her efforts to be in vain.

'Grandfather is doing his best to assist with private support while rallying more overt troops and aid in Parliament.' Luce made his usual gesture, a hand raking through the thick depths of his dark waves. 'We have done our jobs, Wren. You deliver information, I decode it. *We* don't make policy. That is for others.' He drew a deep breath and they stood silently for a long while, staring at the table, at the map, frustrations ebbing away in the wake of accomplishment. At some point, they'd moved together, perhaps it was she who'd taken the small step, or perhaps it had been him so that now they stood side by side, arms wrapped about one another's waists in silent communion.

'Do you realise what we've done tonight?' Luce's voice was low, private. 'We've saved lives, Wren. Possibly thousands of them. Grandfather can use this information to rally support. General Karaiskakis can use it to stockpile supplies, evacuate civilians if need be and better position his troops to great effect. Perhaps he will be able to prevent or offset the blockade.' His grin widened, the spark back in his dark eyes. 'We might have created a turning point in the war. The last push needed to see victory.'

'You did. You solved the code. You were the one who figured out the food represented different ships and the courses the geographic placement. I was merely a dogsbody taking notes and fetching books,' Wren corrected.

'You gave me the idea when I couldn't see past my own thoughts.' Luce gave her an appreciative squeeze. 'We make a good team.' He nodded towards the map. 'You are quite knowledgeable about the geography of the war. Have you been that far south?'

'Yes. I was there last spring until Missolonghi fell.' Up until now, he'd not asked about any of her missions particularly and she'd been grateful for that. It meant she hadn't had to outright lie to him.

Luce furrowed his brow. 'I thought only Falcon went that far south. It's behind enemy lines and Grandfather isn't keen to risk too many agents.'

'It's a large territory.' She said as she shrugged, brushing off the reference. She'd said too much. 'One person could not possibly cover it all.' Although she had. She was unaware of any other network agents being down there.

He was looking at her intently, admiration in his gaze. Warmth unfurled in her belly at his regard.

'I suppose we have you to thank too, then, for those reports. They were critical in being able to raise the arms and funds that were sent in July.'

She'd impressed him. She seldom got the chance to impress anyone. The problem with being a covert operative was that no one was supposed to know what you did. If people knew—well, then that meant you'd messed up and you were probably dead. Unlike Luce. He didn't have that particular level of anonymity. In their circles, he was a known entity.

He turned to her, his gaze lingering on her face, his eyes gentle in their contemplation. 'I might have solved the code, but it wouldn't have happened without you. Not just because you said something at supper that helped generate a key idea. *You* risked your life to bring the code to me. The movement is in your debt.' He skimmed the curve of her jaw with the back of his hand. A warm thrill moved through her as she intuitively felt the conversation changing, the atmosphere around them shifting. This was no longer about Greek independence. This was about them and the attraction that had been brewing. 'You're an incredible woman, Wren Audley.'

There was an invitation in his words and echoed in his touch. An invitation brought on perhaps by the excitement of breaking the code and the lateness of the hour. An invitation that she ought not accept.

He was a well-known rake. This would not be a mere kiss, at least not for her. And yet this kiss, and the potential affair that waited beyond it, would be over before they'd begun. It would be short-lived and it would end when she left in the very near future. Later, when he learned her secret, he would regret it.

They were both experienced masters in the art of affairs. One small step backwards would signal a quiet decline of the invitation and nothing ever needed to be said about it. It was what ought to be done. But she did not step back. She stepped instead into his touch. Her cheek nuzzled his hand where his palm cupped it.

'And you are an extraordinary man.'

'Think what we could be together.'

He murmured the potent seduction. His mouth had hers, then, in a tender capture of lips that caressed and cajoled and she complied fully, opening her mouth to him with a contented sigh. How wondrous to be kissed by a man who turned the meeting of mouths into a slow, sensual journey as if he had all the time in the world, as if the kiss was an end within itself and not a mere formality in preface of things to come. She tasted the tannins of dinner's wine on his tongue, tangled her own with his in a languorous exploration.

It was a pleasant discovery to find that Luce Parkhurst was a full-bodied kisser. A man who kissed with his mouth, his hands, the whole length of him. And what a delightful length it was. He was warm and hard against her. She could not pretend indifference. Her own body thrilled at being surrounded by his strength, by the confident proof of the desire he seemed more than willing to satisfy with a kiss for now and a promise of more for later. She breathed against his mouth, a sigh of pleasure escaping her even as her own hunger ratcheted. Perhaps it would be she who escalated the kiss and perhaps that was what he intended. A woman would be safe with him, as a man, as a lover, and the pleasure would be divine if she committed. Commitment seemed inevitable but it was not going to be decided tonight in the glorious heat of the moment.

'It's late. We should both get some sleep,' he murmured at her neck and stepped back, letting his gaze linger, dark with want, on her face as if to assure her stepping away had been difficult. 'I need to draft a letter to Grandfather before I retire. The mail coach will still be able to run in this weather, even if a single messenger on horseback cannot, and the coach leaves tomorrow from the village. I will go into

Little Albury in the morning to see it sent. If you feel up to a trip you are welcome to come. If not, if there's anything you need, make me a list and I'll get it.'

'I'll go with you.' She smiled, answering his gaze with her own unspoken message of a promise for later. Apparently, her body and mind had already decided. She took his hand in a small squeeze. 'Goodnight, Luce.'

'Goodnight, Wren.' It was all so civilised one would never guess what had been decided in the space of a glance. Somewhere between cottage pie and maps of Greece, they'd become a team in more ways than one tonight.

For better or worse, Wren thought as she prepared for bed. An affair with Luce Parkhurst—even a short one—as theirs would be, came with more strings attached than usual and at a time when she couldn't afford *any* strings let alone several. She couldn't even tell him about the rest of her mission. She pulled on her borrowed nightshirt, breathing in the smell of him, her body still echoing with the feel of his touch, of his mouth. It was hard to vanish if one had strings. Strings made knots. Strings pulled one back to their past. Strings could lead people to her. In short, strings were dangerous. Not just to her, but also to those tied to her. He was not the only one who struggled with loyalty dilemmas. The longer she stayed here, the harder it was to choose the earl over Luce. Another sign it was time to go.

Wren slipped beneath the covers and turned down the light. But sleep didn't come immediately. Normally, her mind was busy with thoughts of a mission, of the information she'd gathered and there'd been plenty of that she could mull over from tonight. But at present, her traitorous mind was too busy reliving personal moments instead. That kiss, his mouth on hers. Imagining him in the warmth of the library, sitting at the table, his glasses sliding down his nose and reaching up every so often to push his hair back as he penned a letter to the earl. Would it be hard for him to write? Was he distracted, too? Would he be thinking of her? Or was he urbane enough, rake that he was, to set aside the episode and get back to work as if that kiss had not been of any particular moment?

Once, she would have been able to do just that. But not with him. Not with that kiss. She'd felt it to her toes and it would not soon be forgotten even if she chose not to repeat it. But heaven help her, it seemed likely she would.

Good God. He'd kissed Wren Audley, his grandfather's agent. That was not a mere mixing of business and pleasure, it was an absolute *integration* of them. He'd kissed women for business before. Seduction, after all, was a powerful tool in retrieving information. Never had he kissed a woman for business and pleasure all at once. He'd learned from Kieran's mistake—a mistake that had nearly cost his brother his life. Kieran bore a scar near his liver as a reminder. When on the job, kisses were for business only.

But Wren Audley was not merely business. It had been personal with her since she'd landed on his doorstep. She'd been a life to save. He supposed battling for her life, stitching the very fabric of her life back together had escalated his sense of connection to her. Perhaps her beauty had played a part in that as well. It certainly had invoked pathos on his part. Beautiful things were rare in this world and ought to be preserved. But they were beyond beauty now. She was more than her delicate good looks. She'd been a partner to him tonight, and indeed, every night since she'd been out of bed. Sitting with him in the library, drinking brandies, reading books, talking, strolling the unfinished corridors of the house and listening to him go on about his plans.

Luce poured himself a drink. Perhaps he'd simply been alone too long and was desperate for company. He would have bought that argument except for tonight. She'd not merely been a patient listener, but a partner in truth, working alongside him. Her expertise had been invaluable. While he'd not readily admit it to anyone, especially not his brothers who would get a good laugh out of it, he'd gotten a little aroused listening to her discuss supply lines and the Greek cause. She'd been there, she'd seen it all firsthand.

That one thought chased itself around in his head as he returned to the table and outlined his findings for Grandfather. The image of her with her stiletto—dressed in trousers, sitting around a campfire with the guerrillas, her hair in a long braid like it had been today—was a strong one. What a woman she was. There was no woman in London her equal. For all the delicacy of her looks, Wren was strong, hardy, resilient and determined.

Luce dipped his pen, re-reading the presentation of his findings. He'd been sure to highlight Wren's part in assisting. He wanted Grandfather to know how valuable she'd been and to assure him that his agent was recovering. Ideally, he would usually send such findings by private courier but with the weather that was not an option, not when weather wasn't a concern in Greece. The Egyptian navy—allies to the Ottomans—could be moving into place at any time, unfettered by weather. Better to risk the mails than to wait. Lives and democracy depended on it.

Satisfied with the account, Luce paused, debating how to broach the next subject. He wanted to ask Grandfather about Wren. What had she been doing that far south? What had she been sent to find in Greece that the redoubtable Falcon could not? And yet, he wanted to ask for the right reasons. For the sake of business, he did not need to know. It was only to sate the hunger of his curiosity. Wren Audley had shown herself to be a revolutionary spirit tonight and a passionate one. He could still see her quicksilver eyes turning the color of dark slate with her desire, the pulse note at the base of her throat beating a rapid tattoo at his touch. And oh sweet heavens, the way she'd returned his kiss, running her tongue over his lip, letting it linger boldly with his so that he did not mistake her interest. She'd been his partner in that, too, not a timid debutante who shrank from her passion and his.

He did like a woman who knew her own mind and Wren Audley was certainly that. The best lovers were those who were equal partners in the pleasure, who asked for what they wanted, who took what they needed and understood he would do the same. Needless to say, Wren Audley with her unflinching gaze, her light touches at his arm and on his leg, would be such a woman. She would be more than that.

Luce sanded the letter and sealed it without asking his questions. He wished he could seal his thoughts as easily. It suddenly seemed superficial to classify her in a category that was purely about the physical. He knew intuitively that to be with her would require care and consideration. It would be meaningful and life-affirming if not changing. She'd risked her life and he had saved it. Together, they'd gone on to save other lives and possibly alter the course of the war. These were the invisible threads that bound them together.

He knew already she would be a woman he would not easily forget. And yet he wanted more. But to what end and for how long? This *would* end. She *would* leave. He gave a bittersweet smile, reconciling reality with the echoes of his desire. Better to have paradise for a short while than to not have it at all. He would make the most of the time he had with her, starting tomorrow with a venture into the village full of hiemal delights sure to please even Wren Audley, despiser of all things wintry.

Luce chuckled to himself. For tomorrow, Wren would need to be warm. That much had been abundantly clear from their conversations. The greatcoat she'd worn on arrival had not survived the altercation on the doorstep and a shawl would not be enough for the village. A trip to the attics *tonight* would be required if *tomorrow* was to be a success.

Chapter Seven

Luce had the cloak waiting for her at breakfast, draped over her chair. He watched surreptitiously over the edge of his newspaper as she entered, wearing the blue wool dress she'd worn for the past several days. He saw the moment she spied the cloak, the slight widening of her quicksilver eyes, the way her hand moved to caress the heavy burgundy wool and the swans-down lining with something akin to reverence or perhaps relief.

'It's for you, to keep you warm today on our outing.' Luce set his paper aside. 'We'll do something about your wardrobe, too. There's a good dressmaker in the village.'

'That's not necessary.' She could not take her eyes or hands from the cloak and it warmed him to see her so pleased. Life on the road for his grandfather could require austere measures at times. Living among the Greek guerillas certainly would have.

But she'd also been to Paris and there would have been silks and satins there. She smiled. 'I am used to doing with very little when I work.'

'Are you working now?' Luce poured a hot cup of morning coffee. 'I'd say you were on a repairing lease recovering from an injury and that deserves a few dresses.' He poured in a splash of cream, just how she liked it, and let his eyes meet hers with a silent message—*I am observant. I see you.*

For a woman whose livelihood depended on being unseen, or at least unknown, to be seen would be a novelty. A luxury. As the youngest of four brothers, he knew something about that. It was a constant war to claim his own individuality, especially when all four of them looked alike to a stranger. She'd given him that gift yesterday in the orangery. Today, he'd like to repay it.

She took the cup and flashed him an appreciative smile before sipping. 'You remembered the cream.'

He remembered more than cream. He remembered everything about her. Every like and dislike. Every nuance. Every gesture. Surely every man she met would feel the same. It was difficult to see how she cultivated any stealth at all when his body was still humming from their kiss last night.

'As for working—' she reached for a slice of toast '—aren't we always working? Do we ever get to lay down the mantle of the network?' Rhetorical questions only. She was right of course. The network never slept.

'I declare today a holiday,' Luce countered. 'We were up late last night with work. We can be allowed a day off. I will post my letter. We'll see the village and take care of your dress situation.'

One could never leave the network, that much was true, but here in Little Albury, tucked into the Surrey Hills, one *could* step away from the network on occasion. Little Albury might be regionally important to the smaller villages in the environs, but Londoners didn't seek it out. A Horseman was as safe as he could possibly be.

The thought gave him pause as he reached for his coffee cup. Wrexham, where Kieran lived, was also safe, located in a valley just over the border, a good four-day journey from almost anywhere. The same could be said for Barrow, outside Newmarket, where Caine had taken up his estate. Perhaps the three titles bestowed by the monarch hadn't been so arbitrary, after all. He saw his grandfather's hand in it. They couldn't leave the network but his grandfather had seen to it that they were as safe as he could make them. Just as he was making Wren.

'Are you ready?' Luce rose and held her cloak for her, settling it about her shoulders while she fastened it at the neck.

She took an experimental turn, letting the cloak swirl about her. He wondered how long it had been since someone had given her a gift. Or surprised her with a kindness. Beyond his grandfather, she was alone in the world. He had his brothers. Whether he was on a mission with them or not, he was seldom alone. Even here in Little Albury, his brothers were only a letter away.

'This is divine. I shall be warm today.' Her eyes danced when she looked at him. 'Wherever did you find it?'

Luce shrugged, making light of the effort of tramping through the dark searching for it after midnight. His stubbed toe was still sore this morning.

'In the attic. There's a trunk full of clothes from a former viscountess. I'm afraid nothing else is of much use, as it's all quite dated. But cloaks never really go out of style.' He reached into his coat pocket. 'There were gloves, too. Hopefully they will work well enough for today. We'll see about a pair of your own.' He offered her his arm and a playful smile. 'Now that you are fully kitted out, come this way with me. Your chariot for the day awaits.'

It was *not* a chariot, or even a carriage that waited for her in the stable yard. It was far better. A second surprise in the span of minutes. 'It's a sleigh,' she exclaimed. A beautiful one that might have been straight out of a painting and it was pulled by a glossy-coated Cleveland Bay in bells and harness.

'A two-seated cutter, to be exact.' Luce helped her in and settled luxurious sable lap robes about her. 'There is absolutely no chance of you getting cold today.' He laughed and jumped in beside her, looking the quintessential Englishman in his greatcoat and muffler, dark waves hatless beneath a crisp blue winter sky.

She was definitely *not* worried about being cold, not with Luce Parkhurst's thigh pressed against hers. He was a large man and the two-seater was a small space. It was impossible not to touch. Even through the layers of lap robes she could feel the heat of him. Or perhaps it was her own heat she felt. A heat that likely had little to do with staying warm and everything to do with her reaction to the man seated beside her.

It had been an entire night and she was still feeling the effects of their kiss. The gift of the cloak had only made the butterflies in her stomach flutter faster. Did he guess how rare gifts were in her life? She hoped not. Happiness, joy and presents made her feel vulnerable and that was something she could not allow for more than the span of a few moments at a time. Vulnerability made a person reckless, and recklessness got a person killed. Other things got a person killed, too—caring and love. The ties that bound eventually choked, especially when secrets were involved. There could be no ties here.

The moment Luce set the horse in motion, Wren fell in love with sleighing. The gliding, the sharp wind in her face, pushing at the deep hood of her cloak. The cutter seemed to skim over the ground. In a carriage, one rumbled and bowled. There was nothing smooth about carriages. But in a sleigh, it felt as if she were flying and she adored it. Perhaps because she was warm. Warmth certainly made it easier to appreciate the cold.

'You like this,' Luce accused with a smile. 'See, winter isn't all bad.'

She laughed her joy into the wind, free in the moment. 'It's wonderful!'

The man she was with was wonderful, too. Last night, he'd been passionate. This morning, he'd been proactive in seeing to her comfort and he'd showered her with an embarrassment of riches whether he realised it or not.

Perhaps he was right—today could be a holiday for them both. The code was solved, her wound was healing and her strength was returning. Today could be a few hours away from the network. A few hours to enjoy the company of a thoughtful man, a handsome man, both highly seductive aspects. As long as she didn't get carried away. It would be too easy to let this get out of control. She slid him a sideways glance. It was obvious why he was one of London's favourite rakes. And no wonder, if the rumours were true, the king was so intent on seeing him settle down. He was a danger to all womankind with that dazzling smile and dark gaze, both of which made a woman feel she had the full sum of his attention.

'It is only my first time sleighing, but I *do* think I like it,' she confessed with a mischievous grin. 'I also have come to the conclusion that winter is a wealthy person's season. It's easier to enjoy the cold when you're warm and you need money for that. Warmth can be expensive.'

'A very astute observation.' He slanted her a look and there it was—that gaze that said she had the whole of him in that moment, all the attention he possessed, and he *knew* he had the whole of her. It was a gaze that went straight to her soul and knew her inside out. Foolish as it was, she hungered to believe that, hungered to believe she was truly known by someone. But that was the stuff of fantasies. She came from nowhere. She barely knew herself. No one *could* know her. Not even a redoubtable Horseman. Her whole life had been lived under an alias. Her safety and success relied on being and remaining unknown. That was what the earl was trying to protect by sending her away. Still, the fleeting illusion of being known was a grand feeling, full of its own special warmth even as it was full of impossibility. She couldn't help but smile. For now she wasn't alone in the world. That might be the best gift he'd given her.

Little Albury was another welcome surprise, another unintended gift. The village was a fairy tale come to life. Snow sparkled on the spire of the village church that graced the end of the high street, shopkeepers industriously shovelled the walkways in front of their stores and shop windows gleamed cleanly, showing off displays of tempting goods. The smell of fresh-baked bread and biscuits emanated from the bakery as they drove past.

'We're stopping there first.' Wren inhaled with delight and Luce laughed. Everywhere she looked, there was prosperity and peace. Children ran down the street pelting each other with snowballs, celebrating the rare treat of snow.

What would it be like to belong to such a world? A world where she wasn't always looking ahead or looking behind for danger, wondering who she could trust and where the next peril would come from. She'd never allowed herself to give it much thought. There'd been no point. Families, love and small towns without danger were all dreams that were out of reach. Diplomatic couriers didn't live in bucolic villages, didn't fall in love, didn't have families because the risk of the past re-surfacing would always be there, waiting to steal happiness in an unguarded moment. It was no great loss, she'd told herself over the years. Such a life would be boring. She would tire of it in a short time. But now that she'd *could* contemplate such a thing the wondering returned. Would there be a new place for her in a village somewhere in the new world that waited for her?

'Do you see it?' she asked Luce softly. 'This is what you and I fight for. Sunlight on a snow-covered village with a church spire and streets where children play.' She'd kept England safe so that children could live like this. So that children did not grow up as she had.

Beneath the lap robes she felt Luce's gloved hand squeeze hers. His voice was low at her ear. 'Yes, I see it. And today you and I shall be part of it.' Part of it. Belonging to it. Not just a guardian watching from the outside, but a participant.

At the livery, Luce made arrangements for the horse. 'Keep him warm,' Luce instructed the ostler. 'We'll be a while.' Then he grinned at her and it seemed the sun had come out in full force. 'We're going to make a day of it. Starting with the bakery, then the inn to drop off my letter for the mail and then we have shopping to do.'

'Again, I must protest.' She wouldn't be here long enough to make the effort of new dresses worthwhile. She appreciated the thought, though not the collateral images it conjured of Luce walking down the high street not with her but with the wife that would follow. These considerations, these kindnesses, were how Luce would care for his wife. He would see to her needs, anticipate them before she could even ask. There would be no secrets between them. His wife would want for nothing. What a luxury that would be. To not have to be self-sufficient every second of every day and to know that someone had her back.

Wren reminded herself that luxury was expensive. It came at the price of her freedom, something she was long used to having. She was entirely autonomous. She consulted no one. She did as she pleased when she pleased. She was not interested in being any man's wife. But this was not any man. This was Luce Parkhurst who could make a woman swoon with a smile and who made her feel like a partner, not a possession.

Luce tucked her arm through his. 'Don't argue. You have one dress, borrowed from the housekeeper's sister. Be reasonable. Tillingbourne is a work in progress and very much a bachelor residence at present. I am woefully unprepared to host a female guest. You'll need some things of your own while you're here. Combs, brushes, tooth powder, hair pins, stockings. I have a younger sister, I know these things,' Luce laughed away her protest.

But to her it was no laughing matter. 'Exactly how long do you think I'll be here? When the snow melts, I'll be gone. The roads should be passable within a week.' She'd be off to find his brother.

'The roads may be but not you. Your timetable is not the weather but your own health. The doctor says it will be at least three more weeks until you have recovered from the loss of blood.'

'Three weeks? Impossible. That will make it nearly the end of February.' She could not stay that long, not with the possibility of finding Stepan still weighing in the balance and the enemy on the move. Her mission was only half done. If Stepan was truly out there, he would be in danger.

'Do you have somewhere else to be?' Luce joked. 'I am sure Grandfather can do without you for a while. He knows you're recovering. I sent a note out that first night to let him know you'd arrived and that you'd been hurt. He'll not expect you for a bit and he knows you're in good hands.'

Hands that were too good. That worried her. It would be easy to put off departing, easy to make the excuse that she stayed to heal, when in reality she simply didn't want to leave. Luce Parkhurst was addicting that way with his gaze and his gifts, his quick wit and intelligence. The longer she stayed, the harder it would be to leave. Among other things. The longer she stayed, the greater the risk she'd give up her secrets.

Luce held open the door of the small bakery and she was saved from answering his question by the scents of cinnamon and sugar.

'Lord Waring.'

The baker, a heavy-set fellow with thick forearms wearing a wide apron, greeted Luce jovially from behind the counter.

'Good day, Lepley,' Luce returned the greeting.

Wren was impressed that Luce knew the baker's name. Perhaps she shouldn't be. Luce was good with information. It stood to reason he'd know everyone in his milieu. Knowing names was a valuable commodity, a security measure among other things. It was a way to protect one's personal perimeter and note when a stranger entered it.

'And who is this? A guest of yours, Lord Waring?' The baker's gaze went to her and Wren was glad for the protection of the cloak's deep hood. She was used to being part of a crowd. Here in the bakery or walking the streets with Luce, the recognisable and popular viscount, she'd stand out by association.

'This is Miss Audley, a friend of my grandfather's,' Luce made the introductions. 'She was visiting when the snow fell and delayed her travel plans.'

Oh, he was smooth. It was all true although it certainly created a far different understanding of her visit—one with fewer knives and dead bodies in it.

'Welcome to Little Albury, Miss.' The baker wiped his hands on a towel. 'You're not the only one, stranded. The inn is full of travellers caught between coaches. Only the mail coach is running for a bit. Vicar Paterson even put two gentlemen up at the vicarage. Can't complain though, the extra traffic has been good for business.' He gave a wink. 'Now, what can I get for you today, milord?'

Luce waved off the formality. 'Waring is fine. But no milord. Until six months ago, I was a normal fellow.'

That made Wren want to laugh. Title aside, Luce was not normal. 'We'll take two of your wife's delectable, iced cinnamon buns. Miss Audley could smell them from the street and insisted we stop here first.' Luce made small talk with the baker as he wrapped their buns and she noted how at ease he put the man. One would not guess their status differences from the conversation. Hmmm. How useful that might be. The baker was an informant although she doubted the baker knew it.

Outside, Luce passed her a bun and she gave him a knowing look. 'Shame on you,' she scolded with a laugh. 'You're pumping that poor man for information and he doesn't even know it.'

Luce chuckled and took a bite of his own bun. 'Maybe I am or maybe it's just habit.' He gave a sly look. 'Like protesting new dresses because you're used to travelling light or not letting anyone assist you because you're used to being alone,' he added pointedly.

She couldn't argue with that, so she finished her iced bun in silence. The bun was still deliciously warm and the icing left her hands sticky by the time they'd dropped off Luce's letter and reached the dressmaker's. She surreptitiously reached beneath her cloak to discreetly wipe them on her skirts.

'You can use my handkerchief,' Luce said quietly, reaching into the deep pocket of his greatcoat for a pristine white square. He arched a playful brow that made her laugh before he handed it over. 'On one condition. You must promise not to tell Cook we stopped for buns. She's been trying to duplicate the recipe ever since I arrived and has been, shall we say, unsuccessful? I think there's a secret ingredient only the baker's wife knows.'

'It sounds like you have a new code to crack.' She gratefully took the handkerchief and wiped her fingers. 'Your turn, you've bit of icing, just there.' She pointed to the corner of her own mouth to illustrate.

'Could you get it for me?' It was said sincerely, but she'd have bet her last pound there was mischief in his eyes. He was teasing her, daring her. The arrogant man likely knew there was no chance she could objectively look at his mouth after last night. The moment she *had* looked, she'd wanted nothing more than to lick the icing from his lips, to taste its sweetness on his tongue. Well, she had a little mischief in her as well.

'I certainly could get it for you. Step aside with me for a moment.' Wren tugged him into a short alley between shops and pushed him up against the brick wall while she had him off balance. She reached up on tiptoes and pressed her mouth to his, her tongue dispensing of the icing in a wicked flick.

His hands were at her waist and laughter, low and masculine, rumbled in his chest. 'I did not see that coming.'

She laughed up at him, her arms about his neck. 'Maybe you should have. It was exactly what you asked for.'

'You make me want to forget about the dressmaker's.' His eyes were dark, as they had been last night. Full of want and desire. His mouth quirked in his devastating smile. 'But I am on to you, Minx. That's probably what you want. Your seductive wiles are no good on me,' he joked. They both knew that wasn't true. Even now, she could feel his arousal press against her. 'Off to the dressmaker's with you. We are *not* leaving here without a gown or two.'

She turned serious. 'Truly, Luce, I appreciate the offer, but I'd rather not be fitted for gowns, not with my stitches and scar,' she confessed quietly. 'It will be noticed. There will be questions and that can lead to talk.'

He nodded and she felt herself breathe easier. 'Perhaps a compromise then. Ready-made? Will you tolerate that, Wren?'

'Yes, readymade. Shall we seal the accord with a kiss?' She gave a throaty laugh and he indulged her most delightfully. They were extraordinarily wicked together, kissing in an alley in broad daylight, but oh how fun it was.

They made short work of the dressmaker's with two gowns packed in a box beneath Luce's arm. They stopped to admire the window at the milliner's who was also enterprising enough to sell gloves and other winter accessories. 'Those shearling lined gloves would be good for sleigh riding,' Luce noted.

'They would be.' Wren cocked her head to take him in. 'Which brings me to something I've been wondering about all day. How is it that you have a sleigh? And don't tell me it was just sitting in storage at the estate. This is not usually snow country.'

'I brought it back from Sweden on my grand tour,' Luce answered easily.

She wrinkled her brow in question. 'Is *that* where you went? It's an odd choice. Gentlemen usually go to France and Italy for the tour.'

'War on the Continent made leisure travel difficult for several years. But Sweden was getting interesting and we had no eyes up there. Napoleon's one-time marshal, Bernadotte, was king of Sweden, at Napoleon's pleasure of course, until Bernadotte broke with him and joined the anti-Napoleon Alliance two years prior to my visit. Grandfather felt it would be in our interest to cultivate a relationship with Bernadotte for the immediate future and beyond.' He slid her a look. 'Grandfather believes foreign policy interests will shift northward in the coming years and we need to have strong relationships in place with our northern allies.'

'So you went as a scholar and as an ambassador.' She was doing the math in her head. Luce would have been nineteen, nearly twenty, in 1814. Fresh out of university and ready to join the Horsemen. 'Your first mission was Sweden, although it looked to be something else entirely.'

He'd been up north working against Napoleon while his brothers, Kieran and Caine, had been on the Continent, working behind the scenes in the eye of the conflict. Everyone in such covert circles knew the latter. But Luce had been making vital alliances in Sweden—no one knew that. Just as no one really understood his contributions to code cracking and the many lives his efforts had saved over the years. Much like her own work. Unsung. They were alike that way.

Inside the shop, she settled on the shearling lined gloves but declined a winter bonnet on the grounds she had the hood of her cloak, much to Luce's disapproval. But pretty bonnets were conspicuous.

'I doubt you are this stubborn with my grandfather. He would not tolerate it,' Luce scolded, moving her to the inside away from the curb as they made their way back to the livery. He was always protecting, even in small ways. Did he even realise he did it?

'That's different. He's responsible for me.'

'And I am his grandson, an extension of him. When he is not able to look after you, then it falls to me to act on his behalf.' Luce adjusted the packages beneath his arm. If only all men were raised with these ingrained manners.

'Do I need "looking after"? I knifed two men on your doorstep. I'm hardly in need of protection and gentlemanly manners.' Nor was she terribly used to either. It was frightening new territory.

'You are entitled to both, regardless,' he replied tersely. He might have said more but at the moment three men came around the corner. Luce apparently recognised the bluff man in the middle immediately. 'Vicar Paterson. These gentlemen must be the guests Lepley was telling me about.'

Wren froze, grateful for the anonymity afforded by her hood. Her grip on Luce's arm tightened in warning. These men weren't guests. They'd been in the pub with the others who'd followed her when she'd stopped to warm herself the night she came to Tillingbourne. She regretted that decision. As a result, she'd been followed and stabbed. Now the consequences of her mission continued to follow her here into this bucolic winter paradise, where just a few hours ago she'd foolishly felt safe. It was a sharp reminder that her work wasn't done, she hadn't retired yet and the holiday was over.

Chapter Eight

The tightening of her grip told Luce two things: there was danger nearby, perhaps right in front of them, *and* she feared it. While it seemed implausible that the loquacious Vicar Paterson posed a threat to anyone other than the risk of being talked to death, Luce had made a habit early in his career as a Horseman to assume all was not always as it seemed. He made a small gesture of covering Wren's gloved hand with his to assure her the message was received and she was indeed safe as long as he stood at her side. Not that she needed protection. But he'd rather not have her flash her stiletto at Vicar Paterson. In that case, it would be hard to persuade anyone she was just a guest at the Abbey.

Luce smiled politely but did not offer his hand to the men. He would not shake hands with men who were a source of Wren's sudden unrest. 'How are you finding our corner of the world?'

The taller one met Luce's gaze coolly. 'We are enjoying it fine. The vicar is a most generous host.'

'Yes, indeed!' the vicar broke in excitedly. 'We've discovered we have ever so much in common.' He gave an expansive chuckle as he made the introductions. 'This is Mr Calvin Paterson and his cousin, Mr George Wilkes, down from Yorkshire.'

Luce did not like the look of them. On closer examination he noted what Wren had likely seen already. They were respectably dressed, as if they were gentry, but beneath their clothes they sported burly builds not found among gentlemen and there was a shiftiness about the eyes of the taller one when he'd glanced in Wren's direction. It made Luce want to step in front of her as a shield. She seemed to melt into the depths of the cloak, becoming invisible. Why? To escape recognition? What did she fear from these men? Luce itched to get her alone and ask his questions.

'You will not believe this,' the vicar went on, oblivious to the rising tension. 'You may have noticed the similarity in the name. I'll allow that it's not an uncommon surname but you may recall, Lord Waring, that I am originally from Yorkshire. We spent the first night they were here discovering a distant family connection.' The vicar gave another happy chortle as if he couldn't believe his good luck in stumbling upon an unknown relation. 'We've had the most wonderful discussions reminiscing about Yorkshire and my wife has been in alt having guests to entertain.'

The vicar was right, Luce *didn't* believe it. The coincidences were too damn convenient. His mind was racing over scenarios. The snow was, unfortunately, a reasonable explanation for their presence and for them being unable to leave until their mission was accomplished. The weather made it plausible for strangers to be in a town that saw very few outsiders, except those passing through on the coaches. To the ordinary onlooker, like Vicar Paterson, the weather explained away what might have otherwise been a suspicious prolonged presence.

But the ordinary onlooker didn't know Wren had been chased by three men to Tillingbourne Abbey at midnight. That two men had died and a third had been sent to Sandmore before the second bout of road-closing snow had set in. Those who *did* know though, *might* come looking for answers and for their comrades who'd failed to return. That was the scenario that made the most sense to Luce. If he was right, they'd come looking for Wren at a time when her wings were clipped by her health and by the weather. Even if she could run, there was nowhere she could run to. Damn, Luce wished she'd told him there might be others in pursuit. He could have been better prepared.

'I've had a splendid idea, just now,' Vicar Paterson enthused. 'We should have you to supper, Lord Waring. Now that you're fully in residence and returned from the holidays, my wife and I need to welcome you properly. We can make it a little party for our snowbound guests.' Luce found the idea less delightful than the vicar did.

'I'm sure it would be lovely,' Wren interrupted, all sweet sincerity from the carefully cultivated anonymity of her cloak, 'but I haven't any gowns ready. My luggage didn't fare as well as I did in this current adventure.' Luce felt the pressure of her grip and he picked up his part.

'I appreciate the offer, Vicar. We shall have to consider our situation before we accept. May I send you a note?' Luce shook the Vicar's hand, eager to get Wren away. 'We must be off. I've promised to show Miss Audley some of the sights.' It was a handy excuse. There'd be no more sightseeing. They were going straight home. They had business to settle.

The drive home was accomplished in silence, offering Luce time to align his thoughts. Without warning, the tenor of the day had turned from a light-hearted shopping spree, which picked up where their kiss had left off last night, to something darker—full of danger and quite possibly deceit. Luce was less concerned about the danger. The men posing as the Vicar's guests were merely an external threat. Luce was used to those. They were all part of every job the Horsemen did. It was the potential for deceit, the threat from within, that prodded the deep places of him. He'd not realised how much of his trust he'd given to Wren without being asked to give it. He'd merely volunteered it, something he never did with others. He'd made assumptions because they were on the same side and because he felt he'd held all the power. After all, he had rescued her. He'd stitched her up, overseen her healing.

The most damaging assumption he'd made was that she'd told him everything he needed to know because they were a team. He'd been wrong about that and as a result, he'd been caught by surprise today because he'd been taken in by a pretty face, by *her*. All of her. Her looks, her touches, her intelligence, her kisses… The list was quite extensive because so much about her was appealing to him. That kiss in the alley…good heavens it had rocked him from head to toe. And all the while she'd been hiding the information that the three men on his doorstep had friends.

Yes, he was angry. But to her credit, she had

seemed genuinely surprised and not a little afraid. He'd have to keep his own temper under control if he wanted answers from her. The last thing he wanted was for her to shut down or to bolt. One did not win the trust of someone who was frightened by heaping more fright upon them with threats and rants. His mother had always believed one caught more flies with honey than vinegar and his mother was usually right.

Luce followed that advice, wisely holding his tongue until they were ensconced before the fire in the library. He placed a calming cup of tea dosed with a little brandy in Wren's hands, making it clear that her comfort was his priority in the moment. He poured a dollop in his cup as well and took the seat across from her before he began. 'All right, would you like to tell me who those men were? I take it they're not the vicar's long lost Yorkshire relations?' He'd get the information first and save the castigation for later.

'They were in the pub I stopped at the night I came to Tillingbourne.' She made a frown. 'Stopping was a mistake. I should not have gone inside to warm myself. It exposed me. I might have gone right past all of them and they would never have known. But I was cold and I was concerned my hands were too numb to be effective if I needed them.' She shook her head. 'The irony is that I wouldn't have needed my hands if I hadn't stopped. It was just so bloody cold.' Especially for the orphaned girl who'd spent years shivering on London streets, Luce thought. Her one weakness had been her undoing.

'No doubt they've come looking for news of their comrades, news of the code…perhaps they've even come for me.' Wren gave a resigned sigh. Luce nodded. Most likely they had come for her. Such men were quite keen on revenge.

'Do you think they recognised you?' It would be best if they hadn't. And yet, it would only buy them a little time. If the snow had prevented people from leaving the village, it would have prevented her from leaving as well. Those men would know that. They could be certain the woman they sought was still here.

'I don't think they recognised me. I let the hood hide me and I doubt I looked much like the waif who'd come into the pub.' Luce could agree with that. Without the trousers and coat, she didn't look boyish in the least.

'But your hair?' Luce prompted. A man would not forget hair like that on a boy or a woman.

She touched a hand to her head. 'I had it under a cap that night, at least while I was at the pub.' She paused a moment. 'Luce, we need to consider that they could be here for you, too. If they knew I carried the code, they also knew who it was going to. Fortunately, the vicar introduced you as Lord Waring. The names Waring and Miss Audley will mean nothing to them.'

'Unless they ask the vicar what my surname is.' The subterfuge of names provided minimal protection. A veil easily pierced. These men were no fools. They knew a Horseman was in the village. It wouldn't take them long to put the pieces together given there were no other nobles in the immediate area and given the vicar's penchant for gossip and talk.

Her quicksilver eyes fixed on him with earnestness and it was all he could do not to reach out and take her hand in reassurance. 'I am sorry, Luce. It was such a lovely day. All the delightful surprises. The storybook village with its happy children. The bakery with its iced sticky buns. And now I've ruined it.'

She was irresistible like this, all sincerity and gratitude. The combination made a man feel powerful, made him want to do things for her—like forgive her and overlook her omissions. Luce fought the urge to do just that. To set aside his anger and his right to castigate her for what had happened. But she'd withheld information and that had consequences.

'I've come to learn that people like us have to live *in* the moments and *for* the moments because that's all we get. We don't know what comes next. In the next hour or around the next corner.' He snapped his fingers. 'In an instant, things can turn and moments can end just as they did today.'

She smiled and he sensed she wanted him to smile back. Not yet. He would not relent, not with a smile or with his words. He would not let her off that easily. 'You did not ruin the outing. We had a few precious hours enjoying each other's company. But you did jeopardise my trust.' He let his gaze linger on her, stern and strong. '*You* should have told me from the beginning those men who followed you here had friends.' He did not hide the accusation in his tone. 'I thought we were a team and you took advantage of that.'

'Your assumptions are not my fault,' she replied coolly. Under other circumstances, he'd admire her aplomb. Right now, though, he'd appreciate some penitence.

'Are we *not* a team?' Luce pressed. 'Are we not on the same side?'

'We *are* a team.' She was all calm assurance, her eyes wide with more of that earnestness she did so well. 'Luce, I did not say anything because I wasn't sure of them. I didn't want to unnecessarily borrow trouble. There were a lot of people in the pub that night. They could have been two regular men.'

She leaned forward.

'Honestly, what use would it have been for me to tell you? There were twenty people in the pub that night. Thirteen of which were men. Four with dark hair, seven with blonde and two with grey. That would have meant nothing to you. There is nothing out of the ordinary in that. And quite frankly, we had more important things to take care of between my recovery and cracking the code, than worrying over who else might have been in the pub with nefarious intentions.'

She put a hand on his leg.

'Luce, I would not withhold information from you that could put you in danger. That makes no sense.'

Luce did not miss the qualifier. It wasn't that she *wouldn't* withhold information. She'd only share if she personally deemed it useful for him to know.

'Many things in our particular world make no sense. Men sell arms to both sides of a war,' he said in response.

'For money. That makes sense even if it does not seem ethical.'

Wren squeezed his leg. He probably shouldn't let her do that. He was quite susceptible to the intimacy of that squeeze, the intimacy of her nearness, the openness in her gaze and, by extension, he was susceptible to the logic in her appeal.

'Luce,' she whispered. 'If you fall, I fall. My safety depends on yours. I gain nothing by keeping you blind. You know that.'

He did know that. There was nothing to be gained for her in having him at a disadvantage. He drew a cleansing breath and set aside his anger. Some distance might help as well. He would think better if her hand wasn't on his leg, her touch reminding him of other aspects of their relationship.

Luce took up a position before the windows. The last of the afternoon sun was sparkling its farewell on the snow. The snow wouldn't last much longer, a day or two, and then the roads would begin to be passable.

Wren came to stand beside him. 'I have a confession,' she said, lacing her fingers through his. 'Sun on snow is beautiful. It looks like the ground is covered in diamonds.' She leaned her head against his arm, not tall enough to reach his shoulder. 'Winter wasn't awful today.'

'That's because the sun was out. It was actually mild today. There's a word for the warmth of sun on snow— apricity.'

'You are full of archaic words, Luce Parkhurst.' She gave a soft laugh.

He liked the sound of her, the feel of her, the ease with which their bodies communed. He wanted to forget that he had doubted her, that he should be applying the same standards to her as he did to everyone else when it came to trust and belief. One had to earn those things from him. But when he was with her, all he could think of was how she made him feel—seen, heard and appreciated as himself, not just as one of four. Not just as a Horseman.

'The snow will be gone soon, Luce. After today, I think I should be, too. At least I can lead the men away from you.'

'Absolutely not,' Luce snapped, more upset with himself than he was with her. He'd made her feel as if she couldn't stay; that she had to leave before she was fully healed. 'No, those men being here are exactly why you *should* stay. We should face them together instead of letting their presence separate us. That only makes us easier to conquer. You are not strong enough to be travelling alone and exposed. Don't let them flush you out like dogs on a hare. Grandfather would never forgive me.' Nor would he ever forgive himself if she ended up hurt or worse because she'd left too soon.

'We need a plan,' Luce forged on ahead as if it had been decided she would stay. 'I'd prefer to take the fight to those men instead of waiting for them to come to us. Go on the offensive, as it were. We have the advantage currently since they don't know yet who we really are. Why not take a leaf from Grandfather's book?' Luce slid her a glance. 'We'll borrow Vicar Paterson's idea and invite them to dinner here. You can resurrect your pickpocket role again. See what they've got in their pockets. We'll have the kitchen staff slip something into their food and ship them off to Sandmore.'

'Have them to dinner here? In your unfinished dining room?'

'It wouldn't take much to polish the table and set out the silver. In the candlelight you can't tell how old the wallpaper is. At any rate, I am not looking to impress them.' He was looking to get them as far away from Wren as he could so that she could heal in peace.

She slanted him a saucy look. 'Well, it might be quite the adventure to feast with our enemies right beneath their noses, after all.'

'Wouldn't be the first time for either of us.' Luce gave a low chuckle as they made their way back to their chairs, a sense of accord restored. Mostly. He'd learned his lesson: he could not let personal feelings override the need for caution when it came to assumptions. Perhaps she had learned her lesson as well: teams did not withhold information. But something about her reaction in the village still niggled.

This time, Luce forewent the tea and poured brandy alone into the teacups. Wren tucked her feet beneath her and took the cup. She had made that chair her own. It would be difficult to look at it and not see her in it when she did leave. 'In the spirit of full disclosure, I want to enquire about something in the village. When you squeezed my arm, you were not just alerting me, you were afraid. Why was that?' He'd noticed because the fear seemed out of character for her, this woman who wielded her knife with deadly precision.

She offered a small smile over the rim of her teacup. He would have to learn to guard against that smile better so as not to be distracted from her answers.

'You are very intuitive. I *was* afraid, but not of them. I've met my enemy face to face before. As you say, this is not my first time.' Her quicksilver eyes were steady on him as his body considered the double entendre of her words. Recalling the boldness with which she'd pulled him into an alley and kissed him, stirring last night's sparks to life. Wren Audley was nothing if not intrepid.

'I was afraid of what those men represented. I hated knowing that my mistake had brought them into this peaceful place. I was afraid for the innocent people who might unintentionally be drawn into their web. People like the very gullible Vicar Paterson. I regret also, bringing them into your sanctuary. This is where you come to get away from the world and, despite your best efforts, the world has come to you.'

Dear lord, she'd read him like a book. She'd not seen through him, but *into* him and she'd made the perfect response. How long had it been since anyone had thought of his needs? Or seen what it was that he uniquely craved? His own space, his own life. Sometimes family, even a beloved family, could be formidable. Sometimes the Horsemen were overwhelming.

'You take too much on yourself. It was not a mistake to ensure you didn't freeze.' He could give her absolution on that point. 'Anyone with common sense would have chosen the same.'

'You are kind to say it.' She could not quite meet his eyes in her humility.

'I am *truthful* to say it.' Luce sat back in his chair. 'I would like you to be truthful as well. May I ask you something?'

She laughed. 'That's hardly a fair question. You know I have to say yes, or where will all our talk of teams and truth be?' Then she sobered. 'Yes, you may ask me anything.'

He wanted to believe that was true. But experience had taught him otherwise. Where there was one secret, there was often another. If she'd not told him about the other men at the pub, what else might she conveniently be withholding?

He let his eyes hold hers for a long moment to indicate the gravity of the request. 'I will only ask this once, so be sure of your answer. While we are clearing the air, is there anything else you are keeping from me?'

Chapter Nine

He could have asked her anything but that. Just moments into their fragile truce, she was going to break faith with him again. And yet, to keep peace with Luce meant betraying the earl to whom she owed everything. The earl had explicitly asked that she say nothing about the lead regarding Stepan until they were sure, fearing that false hope might lead to reckless action. She was protecting Luce by not telling him, although she doubted he'd see it that way if he knew.

'You know better than to ask that,' she chided him with a smile meant to distract him as much as he was trying to distract her. Good lord, but they were both shameful flirts, using each other's tactics against each other. The lingering glances, the little touches and the long kisses. Seducing each other to protect their own secrets. But maybe there was one secret she could share with him that might be offered in appeasement.

'There is something. I've kept it to myself because it did not seem relevant to our situation. This is to be my last mission for the earl before I retire.' She let out a shaky breath. It was the first time she'd said the words out loud. It was a far different thing to speak them out loud than it was to think them. That had been hard enough. Saying the words to another made them real.

'Retire? At twenty-three?' Luce didn't quite believe her.

She gave a small nod. 'Your grandfather wants it.' She did not elaborate on the reasons why, which were both personal and professional.

His eyes lit with understanding. 'But you don't want it.'

'It's the only life I know. Why would I leave it?' Except to honor the last thing asked of her by the man who had raised her and educated her. And perhaps to chase her impossible dream of a family of her own. 'Your grandfather wants me safe before…' She had to catch her breath. This, too, was difficult to say out loud. 'Before he can't watch out for me any more.' Wren swallowed, watching Luce's face. Would he hate her for it because his grandfather was giving to her the one thing he would not give to his grandson—freedom from the network?

Luce gave nothing away but stayed silent. His own gaze steady, matching hers, while the fire crackled gently and the mantel clock ticked.

'I am to simply disappear. But after today, I wonder if that is possible or if it is even fair for me to inflict my presence on an unsuspecting quiet village knowing that someday my past might catch up with me. Maybe you're right and it is not really possible to leave the game, even if one leaves their name behind.'

If he was right, it meant her impossible dream remained out of reach.

'Who will you be?' Luce asked with a quiet matter-of-factness.

In their world, aliases and shifting identities were commonplace. But this would be the last time. If she were a cat, it would be her ninth life. There would be no further iterations of her.

She shook her head. 'That's just it. I don't know. I was no one before your grandfather found me. I was just Wren. I had no history. I had nothing. There is nothing for me to go back to, even if that were possible. I am supposed to walk into the mist and remake myself from whole cloth. I don't have a title to help me do it.'

'Even with a title it's not that easy. While I do sometimes wish to lay down the mantle of a Horseman, and while I do want to live a life apart from that, I do not want to walk away from my family, or my brothers any more than you want to walk away from the network.' Luce gave her a half-smile. 'So, I stay. Perhaps it's for the best. Every time I think I can strike out for myself, something brings me back in.'

'Like a girl with a code stabbing men on your doorstep?' She gave a soft laugh. 'I fear I have disrupted your plans for a quiet winter.'

His gaze rested on hers, his own voice gentle. Somewhere in the discussion of her retirement, the anger had left their conversation. They were Luce and Wren once more. 'Maybe that's the universe's way of telling me I should not leave.'

'I wish the universe would tell me the same thing. I would like to stay, too, but your grandfather will not hear of it.' She studied the fire, aware that she was holding back on this issue as well. She'd only given him part of the truth behind the need for her to retire and only part of the reason those men were here looking for her. What a fraud she was, withholding three truths from this man who'd saved her life, with whom she'd been infatuated with for years. If this was how she treated the people she cared for, perhaps she didn't deserve to have better? Perhaps too many years as an agent had stripped her of the ability to truly love.

'I think the scariest thing about retirement is who I will become. Who am I if I am not part of the Sandmore network? What is my value? My worth to anyone?' She felt Luce's eyes on her.

'You define yourself too much by your extrinsic value. You are a very worthy person, Wren Audley, regardless of what name you take next.' He wouldn't believe that much longer, not when all the secrets came out. At least she would be long gone by then. She wouldn't have to face him with the knowledge of what she'd withheld. But heaven help her, here was a good man and she wanted him anyway.

'As are you, Luce Parkhurst, Viscount Waring. Brother, son, grandson,' she said softly, moving her gaze to his face, her breath catching at what she saw there: understanding, empathy, commiseration. *Visibility. He saw her.* Again. It wasn't a one-time occurrence. For someone who was used to being invisible and playing parts, being seen was exciting, intoxicating and yet one more step into a vast unknown territory.

Perhaps he understood her so well because these were concerns for him too; the youngest of four brothers, looking for his place and having found it here at Tillingbourne after years of fighting to establish himself with his family, with his brothers and with his grandfather. How like her luck to discover this man when nothing could come of it here at the end of this particular life, when she must disappear entirely from the world he inhabited.

Time would run out for them. Their time together was already running out thanks to the vicar's inconvenient guests. Last night, there'd been slow kisses and the promise of time aplenty to think it through, to take it slow. But a fateful meeting on the street in the village today had changed that timetable, sped it up and moved everything forward so that now she was down to last things whether she liked it or not. There would be the dinner. The snow would melt. Then she'd have to follow the Stepan lead and vanish into the unknown where no one, not even Luce, could follow. Where she would be entirely alone.

Urgency sparked. Desperation sizzled. 'I don't want to go.' The confession came out in a rush. Those were dangerous words. She was putting herself above the mission. The longer she stayed, the harder it was to keep her word to the earl.

'Then stay. As long as you like. We can have all winter.' Luce's voice was a low, seductive whisper, his words imbued with temptation followed by simple logic. 'We have nowhere to be.'

He believed that because she'd allowed him to believe it, because she'd lied to him and withheld from him. Her secrets were becoming a drumbeat in her head, one that was increasingly harder to quell.

'You have to find a wife,' she whispered the reminder. They both had somewhere to be. The only difference was that he'd been honest about it.

'I'm not asking for for ever, Wren. I am just asking for now,' he made the argument.

For a little while, the fantasy could be theirs. They *could* choose each other for a short time and the rest, secrets and all, be damned. For a little while, the fantasy would be safe enough.

'Yes.' She breathed the word, already out of her chair. Already moving towards him, before the rest of the words left her mouth before logic could change her mind. 'I'll stay. For a little while.' In his house, in his life and in his arms for as long as she could. Before she had to leave. Before he learned the truth about her mission. Before he realised she'd withheld information shortly after promising not to. Before he despised her. Before that dismal ending, there would be a passionate memory to take into the unknown and to hold against the lonely nights to come.

His mouth was on hers, his kiss hard and hungry, sealing their choice, temporarily silencing the traitorous tattoo in her head. She was not the only one spurred on by desperation and urgency. He understood the rules, too. Understood that this spark between them was a rare, precious flame that could burn bright for only a short time like a comet making a once-in-a-lifetime-appearance. Now that they'd decided on this path, there was no reason to defer pleasure and every reason to pursue it. Time was fleeting, passion ephemeral.

She tugged at his jacket, shoving it from his shoulders with deft hands that had suddenly become clumsy with haste. A haste to feed the fire, to be consumed by the heat of its blaze, to give over to it and see where it led. What was about to happen between them would be heady and explosive, powerful and profound in its promise to fulfil and to overwhelm. She cursed as her fingers fumbled with his waistcoat buttons. 'Men wear too many damn clothes.'

Contrary to her less than competent efforts, Luce's hands were making short, enviously ept, work of the buttons on her bodice. Her simple, borrowed gown, could be fastened—and in this case *unfastened*—from the front, designed for a woman who hadn't the luxury of a maid. He gave a low growl and nipped at her neck. 'Consider it quid pro quo for all the layers a woman usually wears.'

'Quid pro quo? Really?' She looked up at him and laughed, the waistcoat forgotten. 'Only you, Luce Parkhurst, would quote Latin during foreplay.'

'Only because *you* would understand it,' he teased sliding the blue dress from her, his eyes moving over her, lighting up as if he'd just unwrapped a gift. She ought to have felt naked, exposed, vulnerable standing there before him in her chemise, but all she felt was power in knowing *she* inspired the look in his eyes.

'You're beautiful.' Two simple words, uttered in male, primal honesty, changed the tenor of the interlude entirely. What Wren had thought would be a ravenous ravaging of mouths and bodies between two people desperate to claim some modicum of completion, to slake their burning curiosity in regard to the other, was now transmuted into something that bordered on reverent. But it was no less potent, no less intense, for its reverence.

Her mouth went dry. She had not anticipated real love-making. This was to have been a rapid joining, a conflagration of heat that was there and gone in an explosion of passion. It had certainly, and agreeably, started that way. She understood those couplings. But this, oh *this*, with Luce's dark eyes hot upon her, telling her she was beautiful with the sincerity of an honest man who had no hidden agenda, she hardly knew what to make of it.

Luce stepped back, his gaze never leaving her, and finished unbuttoning the waistcoat himself before pulling his shirt over his head in a deft movement that drew her attention to the flex and play of muscles in his arms. It was hard to decide where to look first. She wanted to look everywhere all at once; his arms, his shoulders, his upper chest, the lean muscled lines that defined his torso and drew the eye downward. She schooled her gaze to patience, working her way down his body with slow intent, careful not to miss a thing. He was quite a specimen.

'Most men look better *in* their clothes than out,' she commented dryly, her gaze returning to meet his after a long perusal that had left her hot and wanting. All the man had to do was walk into a room without his shirt and he could have any woman he wanted.

'Do you think I am most men?' Luce gave her a sharp look that had her pulse racing with the reminder that he was definitely not most men.

'No. Not at all.' She stepped towards him. 'I want to touch you,' she whispered, her palms pressed against his chest, her fingertips revelling in the hard sculpted structure of him. 'You feel like granite.' A veritable stone wall to protect the woman he loved.

In the fantasy she was weaving, that woman could be her.

'If you think my chest is hard...' He gave her a slow, wicked smile. His hand captured hers and moved it lower until she closed her hand over the length of him. Her breath caught and she gave a delighted shudder. He was long, hard and hot through his trousers. His was no mere bulge but a veritable log.

'Dear lord, we must get you out of these trousers at once.' She was only half playing at the mock seriousness in her tone. Her breath was coming fast now as she undid the fastenings and pushed his trousers past his hips. Then and only then could she feast with her eyes and her touch. And what a feast it was. She took the length of him in hand and gave a slow, experimental stroke, delicately thumbing his tip until moisture beaded.

'You are positively magnificent,' she murmured against his mouth.

'Shall we get rid of your chemise now?' Luce's hand was at the hem of her garment. She hesitated.

'*You* are muscled perfection, Luce. But I am not. I have no such perfection to offer you in return.' Her scar was still fresh, still violently red against the paleness of her skin. For the first time since he'd undressed her, she felt self-conscious.

Luce gave a slow, reassuring smile. 'I've seen your scar. I'm the one who stitched you up.' He'd probably seen more than that, too, although he'd been gentleman enough never to bring it up.

'I'm not ready for it to be on display.' She pressed a kiss against his jaw. 'You can still touch me. Here.' She gently disengaged his hand from the hem of the chemise and placed it on her breast, her body thrilling to his caress. This was not a mere touch. It was an invocation, the beginning of a promise of pleasure. 'And here.' She pressed his hand to her mons and moved against it. Luce groaned behind gritted teeth.

The heat and the hurry was building between them again, matching pace with Luce's reverent adoration. She knelt on the carpet before the fire and tugged him down with her and he came, gathering her to him, surrounding her with the strength of his arms and his body as he covered her.

Oh, how she revelled in that strength and the care he took with it to keep all that power braced above her instead of on her. She could not have borne it. She opened her body to him and invited him in.

How lovely to be able to do that, to be the one who decided. Lovelier still—the word was not enough— was the feel of him, the slide of his body against hers, the glide of his phallus as it met with her wetness. *This* was perfection and she wanted to hold it close. She wanted it to last and last. She wrapped her legs about his hips, prepared to guide, to coach.

'I know what I'm doing.' He gave a low lusty laugh at her ear. 'Trust me, come along with me. We can do it together.' He moved a hand to her hip, training it to his rhythm. He slid deeper and she fell into it with a gasp—part pleasure, part epiphany. *This* was what it meant to have a *lover*. A man who thought of her first. Who thought of *them* and what they could achieve together.

He picked up the pace, the rhythm becoming a staccato tempo and her body answered, her legs tightening as she felt his body gather itself, the muscles of his arms taut with strain, the cords of his neck standing out, the waves of his dark hair falling into his face. She reached out to push his hair back, bracketing his face with her hands. Dear God, she wanted to see him, all of him when the moment came. Those dark eyes, that wicked mouth. She arched her back, pushing her hips up into his, craving closeness to him in the extreme as the critical moment neared. Her pulse beat a rapid tattoo against her skin—*this, this, this*. And then pleasure was upon her, sweeping over her until all she could articulate was a series of desperate disbelieving sounds as he tore himself from her with a groan, his body spending beside her, a gentleman until the last.

While her body was still in the echoes of passion, he reached for the velvety throw and dragged it over them. He gathered her to him, nestling her against his body, and there they stayed for a long while without words. Speech seemed almost plebian after that. A tool that belonged to mortals while she and Luce had soared with the gods. Her body was soaring there still and she never wanted to come down. This was heaven; to lie in his arms beside the library fire. To feel peace seep through her bones like the most pleasant of elixirs. She had not imagined such a feeling was possible. But now that she knew it was…well, that posed a whole other line of questions and problems that she did not want to think about, not yet.

Chapter Ten

For every action there was an equal and opposite reaction. It was an absolute law of science and of sex. Making love to Wren Audley was no exception. Luce closed his eyes, attuning his body to the nuances of hers. He listened to the soft inhalations of her breathing, felt the rise and fall of those inhalations against his chest. She slept as someone who was complete, at peace. Content and sure.

Those were no small things when one lived as they did, knowing that at any time the game could change. That players could switch sides. That people were seldom who they said they were and the only constant was danger. A person learned to sleep on edge in that world, learned to awake at the smallest invasion of space or sound. One did not go too deeply into Morpheus' realm. That she had done so tonight, lying in his arms, filled Luce with a sense of pride. A woman and her pleasure were safe with him, even when it was for business.

This had most definitely not been business tonight. This had all been for personal pleasure. His attraction to her had been instant from the moment she'd literally landed on his doorstep, bleeding, and it had only intensified with the constancy of her presence. The facets of her on daily display tantalised him with her intelligence, tempted him with her boldness. In hindsight, tonight had been inevitable. But what came next?

Curiosity slaked was not the same as curiosity sated, of being satisfied to the fullest degree. The former was a temporary condition, the latter permanent. His body was already rousing again, wanting her again. Wanting what it was they had created between them again. Proof that once with her had slaked a temporary need but it had not sated it.

There was a fear too, that lay beneath that proof—that twice or thrice, a week or a month, might not sate him either. If it could not sate, it would have to suffice. There was no question of permanence here. It simply wasn't possible. Grandfather would forgive him for sleeping with an agent. Grandfather would not forgive him for disrupting that agent's retirement plans—which had, no doubt, been achieved at great effort and expense on Grandfather's part.

It was no small thing to disappear alive and *never* be found. Not even by him. Should he try to find her, he could very well end up endangering her. She would not thank him for that.

Luce gently pushed her hair back, exposing the delicate bones of her face. Ethereal. That was absolutely the right word for her. She slept like an angel. In retirement, she could sleep like this every night, with no worries. Perhaps she would sleep like this beside another man, a man who would know nothing of her. Who would never know how deadly she was with a stiletto. How she'd camped in the hills with guerillas outside of Athens or how she'd pickpocketed great statesmen at his grandfather's dinner table when she was twelve or that she'd survived the streets of London. Everything that man would know about her would be a lie—a false history designed to hide the real one. It seemed unfair that man would get to have her for the rest of their lives. She deserved a man who understood her and with whom she could be herself, stiletto stories and all.

Was that man him? Was that where his thoughts were leading? Did he think *she* deserved *him*? That he deserved her? It was quite narcissistic to think he deserved her enough to disrupt her chance at real retirement. She might say she didn't want it, but she would come to appreciate it and the things that came with it—peace, quiet, the ability to walk down a village street and not worry about who you met coming around a corner. There would be no more upsets like the one today. The stress of constant alertness would fade replaced by the ability to relax.

He had no right to steal that independence, that freedom, from her even if it meant letting happiness slip through his fingers. When he was with her, everything he hungered for was close enough to touch.

Was it really though? His conscience posited the sharp reminder. She'd withheld information from him. He'd been furious with her earlier today. Perhaps he should be alarmed at how quickly he'd ignored that, how easy it had been to shift his focus, to forget that they were a game within a game.

She stirred against him and woke, slowly and drowsily, a content smile lighting her face when her eyes met his, a reminder why he'd so easily forgotten. 'It wasn't a dream, then.' Her hand was warm on his chest, her fingertip tracing circles and lines as if she were painting him.

'Are you all right? We didn't aggravate your injury?' Luce adjusted his arm about her.

'No, it's fine, but perhaps I should be on top next time.' She slanted him a teasing look. How he loved a woman who knew her own mind.

'Should I carry you to bed before that happens?' Luce arched a brow.

'Do you have to? I want to stay right here, by the fire, in your arms. We have everything we need. A blanket, pillows from the sofa, each other and... brandy.' Dear God, had any woman ever made him so hard so fast with a single word? There was a significant amount of wicked promise in the way she said it.

Luce levered himself up on one arm, letting his gaze linger on her mouth as he took the lure. 'Were you thinking of drinking the brandy...or perhaps something else?'

She flicked a tongue across her bottom lip. Mischief lit her quicksilver eyes, her voice seductively low and throaty. 'I was thinking about lapping it up off your cock, or should I say your *membrum virile* since we do love our Latin. What do you think of that?'

'Not phallus?' Luce flipped onto his back, watching her pad across the room to retrieve the decanter. He would have liked her naked but the thin linen didn't hide much, and the firelight was on his side, outlining the trim figure and the rounded derriere beneath the fabric.

'Are you trying to trick me?' She gave a look of mock scolding as she returned, decanter in hand.

'Phallus originated in the Greek, with an os instead of us. Latin co-opted it and changed the spelling. It's not truly Latin.'

She knelt beside him with a coy smile, appreciating that he'd tossed aside the blanket, while he thought he might burst from being so frankly appreciated.

'At any rate, *membrum virile* is far more apt a term when a man has a cock like yours. *Membrum virile* indeed.' Her hand closed around him. His body was ready to enjoy this singular treat but his mind had fixed on something she'd said.

He covered her hand with his and kept his tone light as if this were nothing more than pillow banter. 'Have you seen many cocks, then?' A concern had taken root and he would not put his own pleasure ahead of it.

She laughed and swung her hair to one side. 'Enough to know that yours is magnificent, as is your skill in wielding it. You needn't worry.' It was what every man wanted to hear—that he'd been a lover nonpareil. And that was the concern.

'That's not why I asked.' He disengaged her hand from him. A herculean effort to be sure, but the right effort. 'You're not required to do this.' Did she think it was expected? He did not want to be a routine to her, did not want to be 'every man'.

She met his eyes evenly, unabashed by the question or its potential implications. Her voice was soft and sincere, her hand cradled his jaw, holding his gaze to her. 'Believe me, Luce Parkhurst, when I tell you this: You are a man beyond compare in bed and out. I have taken men to bed in the course of my information gathering and sometimes in the course of loneliness. No doubt you have done so with women for reasons of the same. But before tonight, I had never taken a *lover*, a man *I* chose to be with for entirely personal reasons, simply because of my *feelings* for him. A man *not* for the game, but a man for me alone, where there is no ulterior purpose. I have never done so before and I think it unlikely I will ever do so again.' She leaned close to him, whispering, her hair brushing his chest and her scent in his nostrils, 'I've waited my whole life for you, Luce. Not for a man *like* you—one who is noble and true—but for *you*.'

Her words overwhelmed him. *Waiting for him. Just him.* In her words, he was not one of many, but a unique entity, an individual. The very thing he craved. He'd thought to seek that individuality in a place, at Tillingbourne. He'd not expected to find it with a person.

He opened his mouth to speak but she pressed a slender finger to it. 'I don't need you to say anything. I expect nothing. No promises, no flattering words. You're a Horseman. I am well aware of your reputation and that you're called the Four Horsemen for reasons beyond delivering apocalyptic revenge for England.'

She gave an impish smile.

'You and your brothers are rakes who deliver extraordinary rides of a more intimate nature. I've heard the talk in drawing rooms across Europe. We needn't pretend with each other, Luce.'

Luce levered into a half-upright sitting position. 'Not as many lovers as you think. In that regard, my reputation may be exaggerated.' But not overestimated. He might not be Caine, who'd been a thorough embodiment of the word 'rake' before his marriage to Mary, but he'd done his fair share. He'd had a steady parade of women who served their purpose and moved on at his request. He'd never met a woman whom he had wanted to stay. Not until now.

'You're too modest.' She pressed him back down. 'You needn't act the monk with me. I like a man with some experience under his belt and a little discernment. Now, shall we get back to the brandy?'

'Yes.' He sighed the word as she took the stopper out of the decanter and drizzled careful droplets on his membrum. She bent her head to him and drew her tongue along his ridge until his breath came in shuddered exhalations as wave after wave of pleasure shook him. Had he ever been so worshipped?

She laved him as if she took great pleasure in pleasing him, as if this was pleasure for her as well. She mouthed the tip of him and he wound his hands into the depths of her hair, searching for something to anchor himself in the sea of sensation washing over him.

'Wren—' he called her name in warning. He would not be able to withstand it much longer.

She lifted her head from between his legs and his breath caught at the sight of her wet lips, the smokiness of want in her silver-grey eyes, an absolute passion-fantasy come to life. He wanted to remember this moment always. She gave him a smile, knowledge in her eyes as she crawled up his body and straddled him. She bent to his mouth and kissed him, letting him taste the brandy and sex on her tongue. 'Me on top this time, you promised,' she whispered against his mouth, her hand guiding his membrum to her entrance, her hips rising up and then lowering as she slid onto him.

She began to move and his body ran riot, his eyes feasting on the sight of her. Her hands in her hair, drawing it up, letting it spill through her fingers, and drawing it up again. Her breasts thrust forward against the fabric of her chemise, nipples hard and pink beneath. He filled his hands with them as she sighed her joy and his body gathered for completion. Too late, he realised his mistake. He was not in control. She was. Would she think to come off him in time? His hands slipped to her hips in warning. He struggled for coherency. He was nearly too far gone to care about anything except the sight of her—her eyes shut, her head thrown back, her long lovely neck exposed. She was lost entirely to the pleasure riding them both.

She opened her eyes at the last and leaned over him, her hair a curtain about them both as if this moment existed out of time and sealed his climax with a kiss. He spent in glorious release, his mouth swallowing her cries as she joined him there on pleasure's shores. It had been beautiful, stunning and irrevocable. He hoped she wouldn't pay for it, but the thought echoed in his mind even as the echoes of pleasure lapped his body—*for every action there is an equal and opposite reaction.* Somehow, in some way, they would pay.

Wren never would have guessed such a reaction to love-making existed. That having done it once, she'd want to do it again. Once was usually enough to erase any mystique a man might hold. Men without their clothes were an antidote to many desires.

But not this one. Luce Parkhurst was not an antidote. He was an addiction she wanted to feed.

Sex with Luce Parkhurst had not cured her of infatuation or curiosity. It had instead inflamed both. She'd been reckless with him just now, confident that the calendar was on her side, that she could afford this indulgence just the once.

His hand was at her breast as they lay together, listening to the room—the tick of the mantel clock, the occasional pop of the fire from the warm flicker of flames.

'This is the kind of peace I've only ever dreamed about,' she said softly. 'Warmth, security, comfort.' She did not dare define 'comfort' too much for fear of crossing an unspoken line. They owed each other nothing but the moment. She expected nothing. They had lives that needed to carry on beyond this affair.

'You shall have those things when you retire.' Luce drew a circle through the thin fabric about her areola, his voice offering quiet reassurance in the dark. She wanted to argue with that. Wanted to point out that she had those things now because of him. It was his arms that created the warmth, not the fire. His arms that offered her security and provided the comfort. She could not duplicate those things on her own.

'You have those things without retiring.' She

looked up at him, proffering the small challenge. 'You've had them all your life. I envied your family, you know. Through the earl, I could watch you all from afar. I thrived on your letters and reports like some children thrive on fairy tales.'

'Grandfather read them to you?' Luce gave a laugh. 'They're hardly reading for a child.'

'They were for me. Your grandfather caught me in his office one day, sitting in a corner reading a letter from one of you. He said if I liked them so much, he'd read them to me at night before I went to bed. They were like my version of Arabian Nights, all those adventures. I knew that was what I wanted to do, what I was made to do.' She nestled her head into the corner of his shoulder. 'Your grandfather is a good man. You have a good family, Luce. You're very lucky. I would give anything for a family of my own.'

She'd never voiced that secret out loud to anyone. There'd been no one to tell, no one to entrust that secret to. Not even the earl. If the earl knew, he would probably have pulled her out of the game and tried to find her a husband. He was a problem solver like Luce. He couldn't stand to let a problem remain unresolved. She couldn't let him do that. It wasn't as simple as merely finding a man. She wanted to love that man the way the countess had loved the earl; the way the Parkhurst husbands and wives loved each other.

Luce reached for her hand and laced his fingers through hers. 'Perhaps you will have a family in retirement. Maybe that's the best reason of all to leave the game. You'll have a chance to make your life over completely.'

'Your brothers didn't have to leave the game to have that. You don't have to leave the game. I hear you're an uncle now and about to be an uncle again in the summer.' She held their hands up to the firelight, watching the flames play through them. He did not have to tell lies to have a family. That would not be the case for her. Lies would be the foundation and protection of any family she sought to create. They could never know the real her and that web of deceit still might not be enough.

She caught the grin on his face. 'I am. My sister, Guenevere's, baby was born at the end of December. I stopped to see him on my way home from Kieran's wedding. They named him James Henry. James is one of the former Duke of Creighton's names and Henry is of course for my grandfather. So, young Jamie is named after two great men. And you've heard right. Mary and Caine are expecting. They announced it over Christmas. Grandfather must have told you. That information is still fairly new.' He gave a laugh. 'I think we've officially entered that season of life where everyone will be having babies. I expect to be overrun with nieces and nephews over the next ten years.'

From the sound of it, he wouldn't mind that season of life a bit.

'You like children. You haven't stopped smiling since you started talking about them.' She could easily imagine him with a child on his shoulders, trotting them through the library, stopping to have them take a book down from a high shelf, or playing in the snow outdoors with them, showing them how to make a snowball. It was too easy to see him here at the abbey—the abbey finished, a family of his own surrounding him. She swallowed against the emotion it raised.

He would go on to his dreams while it seemed unlikely she would ever find the right man for hers. Because she'd already found him and she could not have him. Luce Parkhurst was not for her. She had to leave the game and he had to stay. He was an earl's grandson, a viscount in his own right, and she was a street rat. He was honourable and noble. He wrestled with his conscience and measured the greater good against his own happiness while she withheld information from him about his beloved brother. She was not truthful and yet she had her reasons. Surely, her heart argued, Luce would understand that. Neither of them were as white as snow. Moral ambiguity was a part of a Horseman's life as much as it was a part of any Sandmore agent's life. She hoped there would be clemency for her. In that they were alike.

She snuggled against him. 'Sometimes I can't decide if we're alike or different. You love winter and I love summer. You love the cold and I love the warmth. You want to leave the game and I want to stay because I have nothing and no one outside of it and you have everything—a home, a title, financial security. But then I think beneath the surface of all that, we both love England. We've dedicated our lives to its safety. We have lived similar lives edged in danger that have shaped who we are. We've had experiences, travels, and educations that few can understand or appreciate outside of ourselves. What do you think, Luce? Are we more alike or are we different?'

Her answer was a quiet snore. She gave a soft laugh and smoothed back his tangled hair. Well, would wonders never cease? Luce Parkhurst was human after all, and it only made her love him more. That would be yet another secret she'd have to keep to herself. No good could come of telling anyone, especially not Luce.

Chapter Eleven

No good could come of playing out domestic fantasies with a woman who could rouse him with a glance, send him over the edge with a touch or scorch him with a word. A woman who *would* leave him. They'd promised themselves only a short time. Despite those promises, Wren Audley had become a fixture in his life and in his home, to the extent that brandy would never taste the same and he would never look at the chair or the carpet in the library without thinking of her as she'd been last night—neck arched, snowflake-colored tresses cascading, her head thrown back in abject pleasure. He may have to replace the furniture if he was meant to survive this. He'd certainly never step foot into the guest chamber and not think of her bleeding and pale on the bed. But that seemed non-unique. He couldn't stop thinking of her whether she was in a room or not. His attraction to her had transcended proximity. She'd taken up residence in his mind.

Luce looked up from where he stood at the long dining room table polishing silver to watch her with Mrs Hartley, selecting china and glassware for their supper with the vicar and his guests. Today, she wore one of her new ready-made dresses, a garnet wool that she managed to wear without needing any corsetry, the curves beneath the gown undeniably her own. His hands had traced those slight curves, cupped the perfect apples that were her breasts. She caught him staring. She met his gaze and gave a knowing smile that indicated her thoughts were aligned with his.

'Do you prefer the Wedgwood with the Etruscan pattern or the blue?'

The question shot a bolt of domestic premonition through him. One night of loving and here he was imagining her, *seeing her* in his home as his hostess, as his viscountess, *as someone permanent* when he knew he had to give her up for the game, for her own good. He'd fallen for the one woman he couldn't keep.

His conscience mocked him. *My dear boy, it wasn't just one night of loving that brought you here. That was just the sharp relief that brought the depth of your desire into focus. You've been thinking of her nonstop for weeks now—long before she was in your bed.*

Perhaps the old adage was true that when one saved a life one felt responsible for it. He flashed her a smile that betrayed none of his inner turmoil. 'You decide.'

'We'll use the blue, Mrs Hartley. It sets a more traditional tone, I think.' She smiled back, hidden meaning dancing in her eyes. 'Which is the mood we want to set for the evening. It is Lord Waring's first entertainment in residence. We must lead as we mean to go on.'

We. Such a short word but a powerful one. She'd dropped that word into the conversation with ease, as if the two of them hosted dinner parties all the time and all else that was implied in it. That they were together, a single unit acting in harmony. 'Thank you, Mrs Hartley.' Luce dismissed the housekeeper with a polite nod, wanting the dining room to himself.

'You are very welcome.' The housekeeper gave his rolled-up sleeves a disapproving stare. 'We have footmen to polish the silver. Rowley and the others can do it.'

'They certainly can, Mrs Hartley. However, time is short and their efforts are needed elsewhere if we mean to receive the vicar with a modicum of decency.' The abbey was staffed to take care of a single bachelor living quietly, not hosting dinner parties. Luce had not planned to hire more staff until...until he brought his bride home at midsummer, whoever she might be. His gut twisted at the prospect. He could not imagine—did not *want* to imagine—another woman sitting in Wren's chair, touching Wren's velvety throw.

Mrs Hartley pursed her lips in concession. 'It would be best if word of such efforts on your part didn't get out. It wouldn't do.'

'I understand, Mrs Hartley,' Luce replied with the gravity the response deserved. Rank and file was everything to servants who took pride in knowing their place and doing their jobs.

Mrs Hartley exited and Wren came to stand beside him, giving his arm a playful punch. 'You will give that dear woman an apoplexy. The viscount polishing silver!'

'It must be done.' Luce grinned. 'Do you know what else must be done?' he growled wickedly at her ear, his hands at her waist. 'This.' He kissed the tender pulse beneath her ear. 'And this.' His mouth dropped to trail kisses along the line of her jaw, breathing her in. She smelled of summertime—strawberries and roses, the soft sweetness of the berry, the feminine sophistication of the rose. 'You smell good.' Luce nuzzled her neck. 'Is this the soap you got in town?' He'd buy all the shop had.

'Does it meet with your approval Mr Lover-of-all-things-winter?' she teased. 'I would have thought it too summery for you.'

'But not too summery for you. It suits you perfectly.' He gave her a wicked look and hoisted her up to the table. 'Do you smell this good everywhere?'

To his ever-lasting pleasure, Wren spread her legs and drew her skirts back, her mischief matching his wickedness. 'Come find out, *if* you think you can before Mrs Hartley returns.'

He knelt, his hands at her parted thighs. He breathed her in. 'My dear, have you ever climaxed on a fifteenth-century trestle table used by monks?'

'Am I about to?' She leaned back, bracing herself with her hands, her eyes dark with excitement. The scent of feminine arousal mixing with the soft strawberries in the space between them.

'You most certainly are,' Luce whispered wickedly and put his mouth to good use at her strawberry scented core.

Open doors, returning housekeepers and wandering servants all ceased to be a priority at the first lick of his tongue. Wren dug her hands into the walnut surface of the table, a moan escaping her despite her efforts for silence. What servants couldn't see, they could still hear, but she was very close to not caring about that either. This was a delicious payback for last night when she'd mouthed him with the brandy. Yet even in the midst of such ecstasy, the nasty reminder intruded. There would be a price for this pleasure. Every day she withheld her secrets she was betraying him, and he would hate her for it. Her heart pounded a single message in every beat. *Tell him. Tell him.* But how could she betray the earl? To tell would be to fail in her final mission.

Luce flicked his tongue over the secret centre of her pleasure and a primal groan purled up her throat. She thumped the flat of her hand on the table, begging for obliteration that would take her past the doubts in her mind. She was beyond control. Beyond caring who heard her. Dear heavens, he was a master at this—driving her to the edge of completion and then drawing her back until all she wanted was the release that taunting her on the horizon of her desire. Her body was a riot of sensation. A contradiction of wants. She wanted him to hurry yet she wanted him to linger. She wanted him to give her release yet she wanted him to extend this decadent limbo for as long as possible. She *could* endure this pleasure yet she could *not* endure it. She would surely die if she could not claim that pleasure soon…

And then he set her free. His own breathing laboured. His hands gripping her thighs hard as he let her claim release, let her soar among the clouds, her face raised to the timbered ceiling and its blackened Tudor beams. Her eyes closed as her soul roamed another realm. A realm that only pleasure could access and to which Luce was the key.

She moved a languid hand to his head resting at her thigh and tangled her fingers gently in his hair.

'Luce,' she whispered his name as if that one word was enough, as if it contained all meaning necessary to convey the emotions of the moment. This had been both worshipful and wicked, pious and profane.

He looked up from his intimate crouch, an enviable, self-satisfied smile on his decadent mouth. 'I believe the answer is yes, to both questions.'

'Yes,' she sighed softly, 'I do believe you're right.' She would have liked to have remained there on the table until every last echo of pleasure had passed but that would have been too long.

'Mrs Hartley is expecting me to go over the menu for tomorrow night.'

If she didn't go to Mrs Hartley, Mrs Hartley would come looking for her and Wren would rather not be found sitting on the table, her skirts askew and her cheeks flushed.

She drew her skirts down and whet her lips. 'Do I look ravaged?'

'Only I would know.' Luce leaned forward for a kiss, something soft in his eyes.

'It will be our secret,' he whispered at her ear. 'You can think about this when the vicar sits down to supper. Then you'll smile and the vicar will ask you why you're smiling. You will have to make something up, of course.'

'Lie to the vicar? How wicked.' Wren wrapped her arms about his neck and drew him close, intent on a little mischief of her own. 'Maybe I'll tell him the truth,' she murmured, 'that the day before, Lord Waring pleasured me most thoroughly with his mouth at this very table and it was so divine I cannot stop thinking about it.'

Luce gave a primal growl. 'You minx. You'd give him a fit before the first course.'

She tapped him on the nose. 'Will I do it or not? Now *you* have something to think about as well while you polish the silver.'

She'd levelled the pitch with her parting remark, but knowing Luce would also be distracted in his chores did *not* make discussing menus any easier. The domesticity of the chore in fact inspired further distraction.

What would it be like to be part of this home?

To support the running of it for the man who lived within its walls? To raise a family with him? To balance life at Tillingbourne with life within the network? To be part of the Parkhurst clan?

But that was not the promise they'd made each other.

It was supremely difficult to concentrate with the echoes of Luce's touch so fresh on her body. Marking her, tempting her to confess her secrets, luring her with dreams of an impossible future. To no longer be on the outside looking in on all that love and togetherness? To have an anchor in this world when the earl passed? To support Luce, to never leave the game? To be his partner in all levels of his life—his home, his family and his work. Living in a village with Luce would never be boring.

'Miss, did you have a preference on the venison or the roast? Mrs Hartley prompted and Wren had the distinct feeling she'd let her thoughts wander in the midst of a question.

'A roast. You do beef so nicely, Mrs Hartley. Perhaps your gravy to go alongside and one of your syllabubs for dessert?'

Wren recovered only to be distracted once more with the appearance of Luce at the sitting room door, brandishing a note and wearing a smile. 'What is it?'

'The vicar has written to ask if we might postpone our supper for a night so that we could all attend the assembly in town. The town officials thought it would be a good idea to offer some impromptu entertainment for all those stranded here by the weather. There will be dancing and refreshment at the Hound and Fox tomorrow evening in the upstairs assembly rooms.' He flashed her a boyish grin. 'What do you think? Are you up for a bit of dancing, Wren?'

'Most definitely.' Her mind was already reeling with possibilities as she rose, menus forgotten. The vicar's guests would be there. She could dance with them. In a crowd it would be easy to slip a hand into a pocket...

Luce gripped her forearm and pulled her into the hallway. 'What are you thinking, Wren?' his voice was gruff, his gaze stern.

She flashed a feminine smile. 'What does any girl think of when going to a dance? What am I going to wear? If Mrs Hartley can help me find some ribbon, I can dress up the second gown enough to do for tomorrow. If there are slippers in the attic, perhaps I could borrow them for a night. Slippers never really go out of style and they'll be hidden beneath my skirts.' She shot him an impish grin, meaning to tease him and distract him from reading her true thoughts. 'Unless of course, someone were to pull my skirts up again. Are there many fifteenth-century tables at the tavern?'

Luce growled appreciably, pressing her to the wall. 'I love a woman who knows her own mind.' His mouth was at her ear, sending delicious shivers down her spine. There was something undeniably erotic about intimacy in a public space where one might be interrupted at any moment. 'Are you sure you're not thinking about picking certain guests' pockets tomorrow night instead of waiting for our supper party?'

She slipped beneath his arm. 'No, I was thinking about where I could put my stiletto.' It wasn't a lie but she was betting on the remark being too bold to be believable.

Luce's face broke into a grin. 'You're a dreadful tease, Wren Audley.'

'Are you sure I am teasing?' She'd found that the bolder the claim, the less likely people were to take it seriously. Even Luce wasn't sure what to make of it.

'No stabbing tomorrow, Wren. Just dancing. Promise me?'

'You'd better make sure I don't get bored, then. Perhaps they will have an alcove or two we can use between dances, or perhaps we can bring some brandy...' She paused, delighting in the obsidian darkness of his eyes. 'For the punch bowl, of course. What did you think I meant?'

Luce grabbed her by the hips and drew her to him. 'You know very well what *you* meant, Minx.' He kissed her hard. 'You're insatiable.'

'As are you.'

'What a fine pair we are then.' His gaze lingered and banter was no longer enough to protect her from the reality. Tonight she'd lie in his arms. Tomorrow they'd dance. He'd waltz her around the dance floor like she'd always dreamed of. Dreams really did come true. And like all dreams, this one too would end.

Perhaps if she could give his brother back to him, it would be worth it. This would be her compromise just as Tillingbourne would be his. Partial happiness was better than none at all.

'Go on, Wren, go see to your gown and slippers.' He smiled against her mouth, his forehead pressed to hers. 'I have letters to write, but we'll dine at seven in the library. Yes?'

'Yes,' she answered softly, her breath catching. For a moment she was a real wife—*his* wife—he was her husband and there were no secrets that would come between them. This was their home and this was their happy ever after—a dream that didn't end because it had come true.

Chapter Twelve

Wren pressed a hand to her stomach as if a touch could calm the excited butterflies that fluttered within. She was school-girl giddy as Rose laid out the dress for the assembly that night. She'd hardly eaten a bite from the tray Mrs Hartley had sent up after her bath.

She *knew* her reaction was positively silly but knowing didn't seem to be an antidote. Neither did it seem to matter that she'd danced with Russian princes, Austrian nobles, French ambassadors and assorted heads of state during the years she worked for the earl's network. None of them were Luce Parkhurst. None of them were her own choice. None of them had set her pulse pounding and her heart racing the way he did any time he was near.

When he was near, anything was possible, as yesterday had proven—on the ancient table where anyone could walk in and in the hallway where anyone could pass. It had been decadent and delicious to tease and taste and tempt one another. Tonight, there would be more of that. Then she'd go. Off to find Stepan. Off to disappear.

She told herself there would be relief in leaving, in moving beyond the temptation to tell her secrets. The mission weighed on her daily, intruded on her pleasure. She could not look at Luce and not think about it. But there would also be grief at all she was leaving behind and all she could never come back to. After this, she and Luce could never be the same. His trust would be broken.

Wren touched a finger to the ribbon they'd purloined from an unwearable gown in the attic. 'I think we've prettied this dress up enough for the assembly.'

It was certainly not on par with the gowns she'd been sent to Paris and Vienna with, but neither were the assembly rooms on par with Parisienne ballrooms. There wouldn't be a single crystal chandelier insight tonight.

'You will be the added touch. Your beauty will finish out the dress,' Rose assured her.

'You are too kind.' Wren blushed. She was not used to sincere compliments. Men flirted with her, spoke flattery because they wanted something in return, because seduction was one of many games played in continental ballrooms.

There was a knock on her door and Luce poked his head in. 'I see I am just in time.' He was still dressed in his day clothes and he carried a large white box. 'This has arrived for you.' Luce set the box on the bed. 'Go on, open it.'

Wren removed the lid, thinking to find a cloak inside, something warm to wear. She was not prepared for what lay beneath the tissue: A gown in ice-pink silk, trimmed in delicate falls of lace. Simply but elegantly done. One might wear this to a local assembly or a modest London ballroom and not feel out of place. She glanced at Luce. 'Wherever did you find this?'

'I didn't find it. It was made—altered—for you. It had been left behind by a friend of the squire's daughter who had visited last year. The dressmaker couldn't imagine anyone else looking finer in that fabric than you. I do apologise there aren't any ruffles and trimmings. Time was a factor.'

She drew it from the box and held it against herself. 'It's perfect just the way it is. Luce, thank you, it's perfect.' She held his gaze. Would he see in her eyes that the real perfection wasn't the gown but his thought for her? She was deeply touched—that he'd known her desire to look her best tonight, that she'd been happy to make the gown she had work, but that she was concerned it might not be enough.

'I'm glad you like it,' Luce said quietly, taking out his pocket watch. 'We have only a little time. I'll be back in a half hour to collect you.'

The gown fit to perfection. If it had been meant for someone else, left behind and altered for her, Wren didn't care. It was hers now. Chosen for her by the man she...loved. She tried the powerful word out as Rose finished with the fastenings. Love. Four simple letters. One frightening word. Of course, she loved the earl. Her affection for the old man was real. What she felt for Luce was a different type of intensity, one that she'd never felt before, but she *knew* what it was. *She loved him.*

All the more reason to leave him. Love never worked out well, never lasted. It was fragile and too easily tarnished. Yet here she was, dressed up in ice-pink silk, breathless at the thought of being in love anyway.

'How shall we do your hair, Miss?' Rose asked.

'We'll leave it as it is. I want to wear it down tonight.' It was a little unorthodox given her age to wear her hair down, but this was not London and she would eventually leave here. If anyone chose to gossip about it, she wouldn't be around to be bothered by it. 'You've done well, Rose, thank you. I don't think there's anything else I need.' She smiled to reinforce the friendly nature of the dismissal. 'I'd like a moment to myself before Lord Waring returns.' She still had to strap on her stiletto and she couldn't very well do that in front of Rose or Luce, who had expressly forbidden it. But she'd be damned if she went anywhere without it.

She'd just finished buckling her sheath about her thigh when Luce returned.

'You look stunning,' he said complimenting her.

She blushed. She felt stunning.

Luce looked well himself, turned out in black evening wear, his waistcoat a pale pink damask.

'I wanted to make sure everyone knew who I was with.'

He grinned and then proceeded to study her. 'You do look quite fine, Wren, but I think something is missing.'

For a moment she panicked, a hand going to her hair, almost missing the glimmer of mischief in his eyes as he pulled a slim velvet box from his inner coat pocket.

'A neckline like that needs jewellery.'

She swallowed hard, fighting to hide the inordinate and irrational amount of emotion the blue velvet box raised. Whatever was in there would be on loan only. But like the dress, it was the thoughtfulness that mattered.

She put a hand to the decolletage, doing a little teasing of her own to cover her surprise. 'Are you suggesting my neckline is too low? This is in keeping with current fashion, and I must tell you that I had gowns in Paris that were cut far deeper than this.' She slanted him a flirty smile. 'I had one gown that was cut to here.' She drew her finger down her breastbone and his gaze followed. She leaned forward. 'If a man slanted his gaze very carefully, he could see straight down my gown.'

'Minx.' Luce gave a husky chuckle. 'Then, I'm glad this dress is cut no lower than it is. No one needs to be seeing any of your charms tonight. No one except me.' He flipped open the lid of the box, revealing a simple strand of pearls. 'Will this do?' he asked solemnly, all teasing gone as he lifted the necklace from the box.

'Yes.' It would more than do. She turned swiftly and gave him her back, lifting the length of her hair. She blinked hard against the tears that threatened as he put the necklace about her neck and fastened it.

His hands lingered at her shoulders. 'What is it, Wren? Has the necklace upset you?' She had not been discreet enough to hide her tears.

'No, just the opposite.' She faced him, her fingers gently touching the pearls. There was comfort in their smoothness, their symmetry. 'It pleases me greatly. No one has ever given me jewellery before, not voluntarily at least.' She hastily added, 'Not even for a night. I know I have to return them, that they are merely on loan. Of course, the earl made sure I had jewels but they were for work and this is…not for work.'

Luce gave a quiet grin just for her. 'That's right, there's to be no work tonight. Just fun. Just dancing.'

'Just dancing?' She made a coy enquiry and then gave a teasing pout. 'I was given to understand there might be a little more on offer than just dancing. Did I misunderstand?' She pressed the flat of her palm to his trousers. 'Seems like there might quite a bit more than a little on offer.'

'There most certainly is. Later. Don't start something we can't finish in five minutes,' Luce growled against her throat. 'I am sure it took more than five minutes to get you into that dress. And we are expected.'

She gave him a knowing smile and a last caress. 'I will hold you to that.' The promise would definitely add a delicious edge to the evening.

The evening was made to be enjoyed—brisk, cold and clear. They took their time with the short drive enjoying the winter air and the bright stars overhead from beneath the luxury of warm fur robes. Before they reached the village, Luce pulled the horse to a stop. 'Look, the winter hexagon is out tonight.' Luce traced the sky with a hand.

'Show me.' She used it as an excuse to lean close to him, to breath in the spicy winter scent of him, knowing the opportunity to do so was not infinite.

'It starts with the star, Rigel, at Orion's foot.' His mouth was close to her ear and he took her hand, raising it to the sky with his, so that they traced the stars together. 'Then we move clockwise to the tail's end of Canis Major, on to Sirius in the dog's chest. Then, to Castor and Pollux in Gemini. Follow the line to Auriga, then finish at Aldebaran, the star that makes up the eye for Taurus. For a bonus, Betelgeuse can be found at the middle of the hexagon.'

'Amazing.' Not just the stars, but the man beside her. She sighed against his shoulder, content to linger with the stars, the allure of dancing paling against this quiet moment. 'How do you know so much and remember it?' Astronomy had not been among her subjects.

Luce laughed, a soft sound in the night air. 'The four of us liked to be outdoors. We'd camp near the lake at Sandmore during the summers and Grandfather felt it was not an opportunity to be wasted. He sent our tutor with us to teach us the stars at night. I liked it because of the Latin. But it was Stepan who was the best at it. We all had our gifts. Caine was an excellent marksman at an early age. Kieran is an all-around talent from weapons to conversation. He's always mastered anything he's set his mind to. The problem with him is that he doesn't set his mind to everything. He is rather selective.' Luce chuckled. 'I excelled at language and academia—probably more from circumstance at first than choice.'

'Why is that?' She smiled up at him, enjoying this intimate look into the brotherhood, into *him*.

'Well, I was the youngest by six years and we'd have this swimming competition every summer to see who could race out to the island in the lake fastest. The loser had to do the others' homework for a week. I couldn't hope to compete with them although I tried my best. Inevitably, I ended up doing four Latin assignments instead of one quite often. Later, I was glad for it. I enjoy books and history and languages. They weren't hard for me and my father was a great supporter of learning. We've bonded over books throughout the years.' He gave a teasing smile. 'May I tell you a secret? I think my father likes me best because of it.' He laughed. 'I am joking of course. My father loves all of us.'

Wren thought it was wondrous to have a father at

all. To have one who loved you, who shared such a deep abiding interest in something that also interested you, was beyond her scope of imagining but not beyond her scope of wanting.

A little silence stretched between them. Luce sighed, his breath coming out frosty. 'Stepan was the best at astronomy, though. He was the consummate outdoorsman out of all of us. He could swim like a fish, hike like a bear and track like a fox. He'd take off on day treks and come back with a knapsack full of plants and herbs. He'd spend the next day analysing them. Or he'd go out to the home farm. He loved to work with the farmers and talk about crop rotation. Country folk were his folk. He might have struggled with Latin but the language of the countryside was *his* language. Crops, yields, fallow fields—he knew it all.'

'You miss him.' He'd not talked about Stepan in the weeks she'd been here. For a man who spoke six languages, such silence was an indicator of the depth of his pain. The subject of his brother simply hurt too much yet. What he had mentioned in passing had been perfunctory.

She squeezed his hand beneath the robe in quiet gratitude for the story. No words were necessary. Words would only make it worse. It was enough to be the recipient of these beautiful stories tonight, to be given this rare look inside the Parkhurst world and yet her secret kicked at the bars of its cage with a new ferocity. *Tell him! Tell him! Tell him his brother may be alive. Take away his pain.*

'Luce, I...' she began. The words were nearly there, nearly breathed into existence on the wisps of a frosty night, '... I am so sorry.' Truth faltered in the silence, the secret intact and yet Wren felt as if in keeping the secret she'd somehow failed.

After a while, Luce picked up the reins and chirped to the patient horse. He turned to her all smiles and mischief, as if he hadn't been entirely vulnerable just minutes before. 'I believe I've promised you some dancing tonight.'

'More than dancing I believe was promised.' She smiled back, willing to play along. She understood it all better—the flirting, the fun, the projects and the passions. They were all ways to drive the hurt into oblivion, whether it was late nights spent working on his grandfather's memoir, restoring his home, or solving codes. If he was busy, if he was working on something meaningful, it held the pain at bay and perhaps in its own way kept alive hope that Stepan was out there. Somewhere. And someday he'd find his way home, perhaps guided by the very stars he loved so much.

A wave of guilt over her failure earlier swept over

her. She had the power to give him some hope, real hope. But she'd promised the earl to say nothing until they were sure. That promise grated on her tonight. The man she loved was in pain, living daily with an anguish he kept hidden, and she was sworn to do nothing about it. *Yet.* She consoled herself. She was doing something about it, she simply couldn't tell anyone. *Yet.* In many ways yet was a word of hope, a promise of things to come.

Luce parked the cutter in the tavern's stable yard and helped her down with a laughing caution about watching where she stepped. She laughed, too, their laughter restoring some of the mirth of the evening. For her, though, the evening was already tainted. The secret was eating her alive. It wasn't supposed to be this way. Tonight was supposed to be magical, a moment out of reality, her very own fairy tale. She touched the pearls one last time before they stepped inside. She'd played parts before but never one as difficult as the one tonight.

'You look beautiful. No one will be able to take their eyes off you.' Luce held the door.

'I feel beautiful because I'm with you,' she confessed in a whisper, flirting hard as they stepped over the threshold into the boisterous warmth of the tavern. She couldn't let him guess that she'd held out on him. Couldn't let him guess that in the morning she'd be gone. After their moment under the stars, she knew it was the right choice. If she couldn't tell him, she couldn't stay.

His hand was at her back, his voice at her ear with a final caution. 'Remember, you promised to be good, tonight.'

She leaned close to him with a wicked rejoinder and a warm, throaty laugh to hide her distress. 'So did you. I'm holding you to that.'

Chapter Thirteen

Luce held her close for a country-styled quick-step variation of the waltz, revelling in the feel of her, the speed of them, her hand in his, his hand at her back. Together, they were flying. Had he ever danced like this? So free? 'You're wild!' She laughed up at him as he took a sharp turn that brought her hips against his.

Little Albury was not Almack's. He could risk a bit here and in this crush, who was to gainsay him? The assembly room was full to bursting, sturdy wooden chandeliers hanging from the ceiling with its blackened beams, the floor scuffed and hardy beneath their feet, having survived centuries of such evenings.

Downstairs, refreshments had been set up and conversation flowed with the ale. But at the moment he was only interested in dancing with the woman in his arms. She was wild and reckless tonight, a living flame.

She was already drawing looks and as much as he was revelling in the fun, a sixth sense suggested that something was off. As if this wildness of hers was too much and was a mask for something else. She'd been quiet in the sleigh and there'd been a moment when he'd felt she'd been on the brink of a significant disclosure. But it hadn't come. Perhaps he'd pursue it later tonight at home.

He leaned towards her ear and whispered, 'This might be the only dance I get with you all night. We'll be swarmed after this.'

She gave a merry laugh. 'That's your fault for putting on such a show. Perhaps if we'd tripped over each other endlessly and crashed into other couples people would be less keen to dance with us.'

'What's the fun in that?' Luce gave her a reckless spin. 'If I only get one dance, I want to make the most of it.'

Her eyes went soft. 'Me too,' she whispered and there it was again, that sense that something was not quite right. In the next breath it was gone as she flirted. 'It isn't every day a girl gets to dance like a dream. I feel as if I've waited my whole life to dance with you.'

If happiness had a look it would have been Wren's

face in that moment. That look dispelled his worry and Luce captured it, taking a mental picture for later. Still, the dance was over far sooner than he'd have liked.

He was not far wrong in his predictions about partners. He'd no sooner led Wren from the floor then she'd been besieged with admirers, all wanting a dance. He'd had his own admirers to fend off including Clara Benton's mother who insisted he partner her daughter.

'Grandchildren of earls should be together,' Mrs Benton hinted broadly, shoving her pretty, mortified daughter forward.

Luce had dance partners aplenty but none of them could compete with even the merest corner-eyed glimpse of ice-pink skirts and snowflake hair sailing past with a smile, a laugh. Wren was effortlessly enchanting. There wasn't a man here tonight who wouldn't be in love with her by evening's end. Himself included.

She brought out the sentimental in him. She'd had him babbling about stars and Stepan tonight, hunting through the estate's jewellery for a piece to give her and rush-ordering dresses from the modiste. It wasn't that he hadn't given gifts to women before, it was that the giving was more perfunctory with them. A note sent to Rundell's and a delivery made without him ever laying eyes or hand on the item. These gifts to Wren were personal. Personally selected and personally delivered.

He'd been alive these past weeks in a way he'd not been since Stepan's disappearance, or perhaps in a way he'd never been. He could not recall feeling like this. Like flying, like laughing, like simply being himself with another woman.

In London, they expected the handsome rake, charmingly sharp wit and a daring overture that affirmed his reputation. They didn't want the man who was committed to peace in Europe, who was determined to see the Vienna Accords hold, and pledged to independence for Greece. Nor did they see the man who would rather spend his days restoring a medieval abbey, poring over historic texts and languages or riding the countryside. A man who did not care if he ever set foot in London again. But with Wren he was himself and it was more than enough. When he was with her, he *belonged*. The craving to be seen and understood for himself was satisfied.

'I *said*, Lord Waring, how are you enjoying the weather?' Arabella Malmsby's tone was petulant, her eyes scolding, when Luce brought his thoughts and gaze back to the group surrounding him on the sidelines. He'd returned Miss Benton to her mother and had been immediately besieged for dances. For conversation. Frankly, for anything he was willing to give even if it was distraction, silence and thoughts that had wandered too far afield. Wren had wandered afield, too, it seemed. For a long, unnerving moment he couldn't find her in the crowd and when he did, he was not pleased.

'I like the winter and I love the snow, Miss Malmsby.' He counselled himself to patience and favoured her with a disarming smile before spreading it around the group as he made his departure. 'Please do excuse me, ladies, there are so many people to talk with and I am sure you have young men waiting to dance with you.'

Wren was with Vicar Paterson and his 'guests', smiling and charming as if she had no idea they were the enemy explicitly sent to hunt her.

It was hard going navigating the perimeter of the assembly room. He was stopped numerous times to talk and he had to be polite. These people would be his neighbours. First impressions were everything. He could not be rude, but Wren was moving faster than he was. She was on the dance floor now with Mr Wilkes, the one who had stared at her for an inordinate amount of time in town. Luce told himself not to worry. It was inevitable she'd run into the vicar's dubious guests tonight. Everyone was here and, as the vicar liked to point out, she and his guests had disrupted travel plans in common—something the jovial vicar assumed would bind them together on account of shared experience. There was some comfort in knowing the vicar's guests didn't recognise her. Wren had promised to be good and save her pickpocketing for tomorrow night at supper. He was counting on the latter especially.

At last, he reached the vicar's side. Both of the vicar's guests were in absentia. He knew where Wilkes was—out dancing with Wren.

'Is Mr Paterson dancing as well?' Luce asked, scanning the dance floor and not finding him.

'No, he went downstairs for refreshments.' The vicar smiled. 'Mr Wilkes and your lovely guest are out on the floor somewhere. She is delightful, Lord Waring, an exemplary young lady.' There was a knowing twinkle in his eye that warmed and alarmed Luce.

'She is *just* visiting and stranded because of the weather, Vicar.' Luce didn't bother to point out that if not for the snow such a visit would be completely indecent—a young woman alone at the abbey with only a single gentleman in residence and no chaperone in sight. Thanks to the snow, and the presence of maids and Mrs Hartley, the rules could be somewhat relaxed in this instance.

Luce did another scan of the dance floor for pink skirts and came up empty. A moment of panic took him. Where was she? 'Do you see Wilkes and Miss Audley?' he asked casually, trying not to appear too obvious in his searching.

'Hard to see anyone in this crush.' The vicar offered only a cursory glance about the floor, unconcerned. 'Don't worry, Mr Wilkes strikes me as a very upstanding fellow.'

Too bad Luce was inclined to disagree. Still, Wren wasn't likely to gut the fellow on the dance floor, he reminded himself. She'd be good. She'd given her word.

It was so hard to be good when it would be so easy to be bad and in this case, being bad would be good. Mr Wilkes' coat pocket was *right there* daring her to check it out as they navigated a brisk country dance. All she needed to do was feign a stumble, fall against him long enough to feel his inner pockets and retrieve anything of interest.

Of course, his pockets might be empty. A good agent didn't carry identification on themselves. That was always the risk. In this instance, though, she thought it might be different. He wouldn't want to leave anything behind unguarded at the vicar's. Or there might be a weapon, something that would be entirely out of place and unnecessary at an assembly—unless one intended or anticipated trouble.

Now would be the moment as they came up on the turn. She had him laughing and smiling. But she'd promised Luce to wait. And yet, Luce hadn't counted on such a plum opportunity. Wasn't it an agent's job to adapt, to be flexible as circumstances evolved? How many times had she gone into a situation with one plan and accomplished her goals with another because *things* evolved? Surely, Luce would understand. No doubt, he'd done the same many times as well.

Wren deliberately missed a step and fell hard against Wilkes, her hands clutching first at the lapels of his jacket, pressing her hand against the fabric where the inner pocket was located before dropping down to make a quick pass of his waistcoat pocket as well. The pockets gave nothing away but she had caught a glimpse of a shoulder holster beneath his coat, discreet enough to accommodate a gentleman's small gun like the relatively new Philadelphia Derringer.

'Miss Audley, are you well?' Wilkes righted her, all outward solicitation but the laughing and the earlier smiles were gone. The eyes that met hers were hard flints. Somehow he knew what she'd been up to, perhaps he even guessed what she had seen and what it meant to her. But that was only possible if he knew who she was. A familiar ripple ran through her, part excitement, part fear. All of it the thrill of the game.

She would brazen it out in order to be sure. He wasn't likely to shoot her on the dance floor any more than she was likely to knife him.

'I'm fine, I just lost my footing.' She flashed him a dazzling smile. It took no effort at all to sound breathless. 'Thank you for saving me,' she gushed. Most men needed very little help to see the damsel in distress.

His arm was an iron band about her. 'Perhaps you are feeling faint and need some air? It's a crowd in here to be sure.' They were near the door leading downstairs into the tavern and he was ushering her towards it with unrelenting alacrity. Not that anyone would notice. *Luce would notice.* He'd been watching her all night. Surely, he would see. Unless there were too many people blocking his view. Still, Wilkes wouldn't try anything downstairs with so many people around.

That reassurance didn't last long. He marched her straight to the door and out into the dark stable yard where there were very few people present. It was too cold for people to linger out of doors. Grooms and drivers were huddled in the stables around stoves and warm toddies. The loudness of the music and voices inside made it improbable a scream would be heard. Fine. She wasn't the screaming type anyway. She was the silent type. Silent and deadly. She'd have her stiletto in his gut before he knew what was happening if it came to that. She'd been in more difficult situations, just not after being sliced open.

She tried playing the delicate damsel one more time. 'I appreciate your concern but I am fine and I must insist we go back inside. It is not seemly for us to be out here alone and my escort will be looking for me.' It wouldn't hurt to remind him that someone *would* notice her absence.

The man's flinty stare was malevolent now and it alone would have tipped his hand entirely if his words didn't. He pushed her up against the tavern wall. 'Since when is Falcon concerned about propriety?' His face was close to hers—close enough to smell the sourness of his breath. He gave a cold chuckle. 'I know who you are, just as I know who your 'escort' is. None other than Luce Parkhurst.'

That was all she needed to know. Promises to Luce aside, it was time to be bad. This man had come to do harm. To Luce and to her. It could not be tolerated. She slipped a hand covertly to her skirts, holding his gaze in distraction as she drew them up and reached for her stiletto. Reach and stab, lightning quick. She could see the motion in her mind. Her hand closed around the hilt and she drew the blade.

Too slow. She knew it even as she tried to finish the motion. Her injury delayed the action long enough to alert him. His hand gripped her wrist, pinning it to the wall. 'You're getting sloppy, Falcon.' He banged her wrist against the brick but she didn't let go. She kicked at him, hoping to redirect his energies enough to free her hand.

'You killed two of my friends,' he growled, trapping her against the wall with his bulk, making it difficult to kick with any force. 'It's payback time. I saw you in the pub that night. I never forget a face, especially a pretty one. Too pretty to be a boy like you were pretending. The fellows and I wagered on it. I saw a lock of your hair slip out at the back of your cap. I'd never seen hair that color before. Gerlitz told me you had silver hair and when I saw it, I knew it had to be you. I'd know you anywhere.' Which was more than what most of Europe could say, she thought cheekily. But it only took one. Dear God, the man was heavy. She could hardly breathe. She might just suffocate right here. Damn her skirts. She'd like to give him a real fight.

'Maybe we have a little fun before I end you.' He moved against her. 'You're having fun with Parkhurst, you might as well have fun with me too.'

Wren turned her head and bit the wrist of the hand holding her knife, redoubling her efforts, but she'd not realised how weak she still was. He gave a yelp and let go, lifting a hand to strike her. She dodged under his arm and ran for the door. Normally she would stand and fight but she was nowhere near fighting prime and he had a gun. The only reason he hadn't used it yet was because he'd had that payback in mind first.

She ran into a wall of a man. The wrong man. Paterson! And the wrong Paterson at that. Dear God, where was Luce? Paterson had her about the waist but she had the advantage. She stabbed hard with the blade to his gut, deep enough to stop him, not deep enough to kill him. He staggered away. But Wilkes was charging her now. She went down beneath him, her knife skittering away out of reach. Fabric ripped, his weight punishing. She punched at him, wriggled and squirmed, making it impossible for him to grab her hands. If she lost the use of them, she'd be done for. If she could get into his coat, grab his pistol. She nearly had it…

'Get off her!' The roar presaged a massive collision of male muscle meeting male muscle. Luce was on Wilkes—a lion on prey. They rolled away. She scrabbled for her knife.

'Luce, he has a gun!' she cried in warning.

Good lord, if anything happened to Luce she would not forgive herself. This had all been her idea. She should not have approached Wilkes and Paterson. She'd thought she was safe, that they did not know who she was. She'd danced a little too close to the fire despite her promise to Luce. If he should pay for her indiscretion…

Luce was astride Wilkes, pummelling him into submission. A gun would not be necessary. The stable yard was filling with guests now and there was help aplenty for Luce. The men were tied up while the vicar looked on stunned.

'They weren't from Yorkshire, I'm afraid,' Luce said grimly, poor Vicar Paterson nodding in disbelief while his mind tried to sort it all out.

Luce went to Wren, draping his jacket about her. 'Are you all right?' he asked quietly, tenderly, but she heard the anger rumbling beneath. When the crisis had passed, there would be a reckoning. She'd broken her word. Again.

'Luce, I am so sorry.' Was she destined to ruin everything between them? She'd ruined their day in the village and now this.

'I guess there's no need to wait for a dinner party,' he said wryly. 'We might as well interrogate them now.'

Yes and no. Panic flooded her, a very different panic than the panic she'd felt fighting in the yard and realising she was too weak. Wilkes knew who she was. All of it would come out. Her search for Stepan. The other reason she had to retire... She could not stop it. She couldn't reasonably argue against interrogation without looking odd. She gripped his arm, stalling him. 'Luce, first, there is something I have to tell you.'

He covered her hand. 'Let it wait, Wren. Let's see to the men while they're still mulling over their injuries and thinking they might want to save their skins.' But who was going to save hers when it all came out? The clock above the stable block struck midnight, its chimes filling the night sky—a sky she'd looked up into so peacefully just hours before. Betelgeuse winked at her. Time had run out for her fantasy.

Chapter Fourteen

'Time has run out for you, gentlemen.' Luce paced the length of the storeroom, coat off, expression grim, tone far cooler and more controlled than he actually was. He would have his answers and his vengeance. Rage, multifaceted and complex, still coursed through him. The righteous rage of seeing someone he cared for attacked, harmed. He would not soon forget the sight of Wren struggling futilely on the ground. There was impotent rage, too, at having not found her sooner, he could have prevented all of it from happening, and a rage he couldn't name directed at *her*. Rage that she'd tried to handle it by herself when they'd planned to do it together tomorrow night at a carefully orchestrated supper where he could protect her.

Luce stopped in front of the men, impatient as he waited for the doctor to finish treating Paterson's wound. He was aware of Wren in the room, near the door, her own hackles horripilated. Her stiletto clenched in her hand and his coat draped about her. She looked far more like the street scrapper his grandfather had rescued years ago than the demure beauty he'd left Tillingbourne Abbey with earlier this evening. She was angry and bristling. An avenging angel in the flesh, hair flowing about her shoulders, her beautiful ice-pink silk ripped, a red mark on the pale perfection of her skin where Wilkes had landed a blow. She was more than capable of conducting the interrogation herself but Luce would stand between her and her attackers now. It was the least he could do.

The doctor stepped away with a nod and Luce stepped in. 'Let's start with the easy questions. Who are you working for, gentlemen? I will give you this one chance to answer voluntarily. Should you choose not to, we'll forego the magistrate and send you to a place where answers will be retrieved involuntarily.'

They would not leave his grandfather's network alive. But, with cooperation, Luce would settle for turning them over to the local magistrate on charges of drunken conduct. They'd get some time in the local jail and then be free to go—a far better and far lighter sentence than being turned over to his grandfather's minions.

'We aren't telling you anything.' Wilkes' bloody

spittle landed at Luce's feet, courtesy of Luce's fist to his jaw earlier. Some resistance was to be expected, Luce supposed.

'Jail might be the safest place for you,' he reminded them. 'Perhaps you fear your own boss's retribution if you give me a name. Will that be worse than what the network might visit upon you?' He knew it wouldn't be. They'd be safe in jail. And when they were out they'd have a fighting chance, *if* they were clever, to disappear and escape any retribution that might be waiting for them. Wilkes slanted a look at Paterson. Luce could see the reasoning move in their eyes.

'Tell him.' Paterson coughed and spat blood, the effort bringing him pain. Luce wondered if his wound was worse than it had looked.

Wilkes gave him a malevolent look. 'Dieter Gerlitz sent us.' His mouth twisted into a sneer. 'That name means nothing to you, does it? Hah hah.' The laugh cost him. His ribs hurt. Served the bastard right.

Wren stepped forward, fingering her blade, her tangled hair and wrecked ball gown giving her a fierce beauty. Primal desire surged through Luce, savage and sharp. She put the blade to Wilkes' neck. 'Dieter Gerlitz worked for Cabot Roan. He was Roan's right-hand man when it came to munition sales in Europe. He and Roan were selling arms to the Ottomans and hoped to sell to the Greeks via connections in England before the Horsemen foiled their plans that night in Wapping.'

Luce shot her a warning look. 'Put the knife away.' He didn't want Wilkes and Paterson dead. At least not yet and not by her hand. She stepped back and he watched Wilkes breathe a little easier although the man's gaze emanated pure hatred for her.

'Of course *she* knows,' the man growled, wanting to bait him but Luce didn't bite, at least not out loud. Internally, he did wonder what the man meant. What did Wren know? The man's gaze lingered on Wren. 'I bet not even you knows the rest though. You put that blade in me or Paterson here and you'll never know. Not until it's too late.'

Luce shifted his gaze to Wren, gauging her reaction in order to adjust his own guesses as to what Wilkes might be alluding. Clearly, there was information to be had. Wren had gone pale, her eyes two blazing grey lights, her hand subtly flexing around the hilt of her blade as if she knew or guessed what that information might be and would do anything to extract it.

'I don't have to tell you anything.' Wilkes sneered. 'Maybe I'm just playing with you. Sowing doubt. Sowing worry.' Luce hated Wilkes' eyes on her. He should have given the man a black eye instead of a sore jaw. But that was what Wilkes wanted. He wanted this to be about emotions, about forgetting what the goal of the interaction was. Luce needed information. That would be the real revenge, not the short-term, base satisfaction of wrecking violence for violence.

'I don't think so,' Luce replied coolly. He split his gaze between Wren and Paterson. Wren *knew* there was information and Paterson was hurt badly. 'Your friend here is going to need more than bandages.' Already, blood was slowly seeping through the doctor's hasty work. Wren had done more damage than originally suspected. Paterson was paling, struggling against unconsciousness and pain. 'We have laudanum. We can get him stitches if need be. But you have to pay in information.'

'That's extortion,' Wilkes bit out. 'The Hippocratic oath...'

'Holds no sway with me. I am not a physician,' Luce snapped. 'It's not extortion, it's a trade. Or perhaps you'd like to join your comrade in feeling the effects of Miss Audley's blade?'

'Miss Audley. That's sweet. She isn't any Miss, any more than you're really a lord. Look at you two, giving yourselves airs.' There it was again, this indicator that Wilkes knew something about her. But that was not the goal of this interrogation. He would not let Wilkes distract him.

'Tell him. It won't matter in the long run,' Paterson urged hoarsely, starting to slouch in his chair. 'Get me the drugs.'

For a moment, Wilkes looked nervous, concerned about his comrade's condition. It was good to note the man had a modicum of loyalty. Luce would continue to use that as long as he needed to.

'It's about your brother,' Wilkes snarled. He might confess but he wouldn't be nice about it. Luce felt the man's gaze shift to him and carefully schooled his features. Wilkes had been trying to provoke him from the start. Features schooled, but his pulse still raced. Wilkes knew something about Stepan?

'Gerlitz has found him in Essex. He is sending a team to finish the business started in Wapping. The explosives expert your brother killed in the water was Gerlitz's cousin.'

Myriad reactions rocketed through Luce. Joy that Stepan was alive. Fear that Stepan was in danger. A thousand questions jockeyed for his attention but now was not the time for it. Wren was on the move, her blade pressed once more to Wilkes' throat.

'That is not a given.' Luce had the impression her words were for him, not for Wilkes. 'There is a supposition only that Stepan is in Essex. There is no proof.'

Luce stiffened, another flood of realisations sweeping him. 'You knew?' He threw the accusation at her.

Wilkes chuckled. 'Seems like the two of you have a lot to talk about.'

No, he would not let this scoundrel of a man sow his doubt. Wilkes wanted a wedge between them. Luce would not give him the satisfaction. Luce stepped forward, waving Wren away. He gripped the man's lapels and tipped back the chair. 'Where's the team now?' How much time did he have to get to Stepan? To warn him? To save him? The Essex coast was up to four days away from the Surrey Hills by horse. 'Tell me or there's no laudanum, no magistrate, no protection of jail. I'll feed you back to Gerlitz myself and tell him how you betrayed him.'

Paterson moaned. The doctor stepped forward, but Luce waved him off.

'Cap Gris-Nez, that's the last I knew,' Wilkes offered and Luce beckoned the doctor forward.

Cap Gris-Nez was thirteen miles from Dover on the French side of the Channel.

'Storms would have kept them in port. They won't have been able to cross yet,' Wren added.

'She knows all about Cap Gris-Nez,' Wilkes

hissed. 'It's Falcon's favourite port. Discreet and less public than Calais.' He sneered at Wren. 'It took Gerlitz a while to figure out where you'd disappear to, but he finally did it.'

Luce whirled back to face Wilkes. 'What did you say?'

'You didn't know?' Wilkes gave an evil grin. 'She's Falcon.'

Luce felt as if a carpet had been pulled out from under him. His sharp mind reeled. Wren was Falcon? Stepan was alive? Wren had known all along and had not told him?

'Luce, I can explain.'

He grabbed her arm. 'You damn well will, but not here,' he growled in a low voice. He would not give Wilkes the petty satisfaction of having caught him off guard. He got them to the sleigh and he managed the drive home. The silence between them was very different than the peaceful silence in which they'd arrived in town, expecting a night of fun and revelry. A night that was supposed to have involved stolen kisses and playful seduction in an alcove. All of that was gone now. His lover had betrayed him, trust and all, after having promised not to. Long before they got home, something inside him broke, his hope perhaps? Or was that his heart?

He'd been unaware until now how deeply his affections for Wren had run, of how much he'd given to her. He'd used the word love in his thoughts earlier but he'd not understood what that meant until now when it was shattered, part and parcel of what had broken in him. He knew intuitively this was why he'd never done it before—never given his heart, only his body. *This* hurt. Belonging hurt. This was the price.

His despair was equalled only by the initial feelings of losing Stepan. It was as if the stars had faded from the sky and the joy from the world. He was dead inside again. The life he'd felt these last few weeks, put out.

But none of that could matter now. He could sort out his brokenness later, *after* Stepan was found. Time was of the essence. He would do what he always did when faced with an emotional crisis that threatened to overwhelm him. He would work. By the time he entered the library, aware of Wren trailing silently behind him, Luce Parkhurst, Lord Waring, lover of the exquisite Miss Audley, had been firmly replaced by the fourth Horseman.

Chapter Fifteen

The man who faced her in the library was not Luce Parkhurst, her lover. This was the fourth Horseman. Death. Moros. A man who prevented death where he could and took lives when he couldn't in order to protect the greater good. He would have killed for her tonight, of that she was sure, just as he'd been prepared to kill for her the night she'd arrived. Gone was the man who'd laughed with her on the dance floor, traced the stars with her and who'd made wild love to her on his dining room table.

'Luce, please let me explain. I tried to tell you tonight.' It was perhaps not the best response, but Luce had flustered her more than fending off Wilkes, more than stabbing Paterson, more than interrogating a man at knife point. Those were all activities she was quite familiar with. She knew how to handle them, how to respond. She was out of her depth here. She had no idea how to respond to Luce. Lover and Horseman.

Work and pleasure had all been conflated on the drive back to Tillingbourne. He stared at her with eyes that said she was his work now, part of a job and nothing more. And her own heart, which had been so warm before, began to freeze. Perhaps for the best. The chill between them would protect her, give her the strength to argue for herself, but cold things were also brittle things. To freeze meant also to risk fracture. Later. When all this was over, when she was anonymous, then she would allow herself the luxury of that. Until that time, Falcon must remain strong. Falcon never cracked.

'Tonight? That's your excuse? You tried to tell me tonight? Do you think telling me half an hour before the despicable Mr Wilkes announced it, would have made it any better? You should have told me when I asked you directly if there was anything else I needed to know.'

'I did not believe you *needed* to know at that time.' She met his gaze coolly, her own mask in place now. It was not Wren and Luce in the library any longer but Falcon and a Horseman. 'Do not harangue me about unilateral decision making. It is an occupational requirement in our line of work. We make unilateral decisions all the time about when to make a move, who to save, who to trust, who needs to know what. You've done it, too.'

'I didn't need to know about my brother? How dare you make that decision for me.'

'I didn't make it. Your grandfather did.' She took supreme satisfaction in deflecting the accusation. She felt guilty about many things. About hurting him and about withholding information from him, but at the same time she did not feel guilty about keeping her word to the earl and doing her *job*. If she arbitrarily decided which orders to follow she'd have been dead long before this.

'My grandfather?' The revelation had stunned him for the moment. 'Whyever not? If Stepan is out there, we should have gone after right away. I would have summoned Caine. He could have been here by now.'

'Which is precisely why he didn't want you to know. Not yet.' They'd divided the room in half, each pacing their own lengths like caged tigers. She stopped to face him. 'Think for a moment. Gerlitz believes Stepan is there. Your grandfather believes it too. Gerlitz is sending a team to claim his revenge. They would be happy to entrap all the Horsemen in one fell swoop. What better way to do that than to use the rumour of Stepan as bait? Gerlitz wants the Horsemen to muster and ride to their brother's aid.

Why do you think Paterson encouraged Wilkes to tell you? Because Paterson wanted medical help? Highly plausible but not probable. The answers came too easily tonight and deep down you know that.'

She watched Luce's gaze turn stormy. He'd not liked having that truth uttered out loud.

'You have everything you need to go after your brother, just as Gerlitz intended.'

Luce's eyes narrowed. 'So they weren't here for you, after all?'

'No. They were here for me but they were also here to make sure their news was imparted.' Would he guess the rest? The rest truly didn't matter except to her and Falcon's damnable pride.

'Wilkes recognised you.' Luce said as he sat— perhaps a sign that he was moving into a different facet of his offensive as he lay siege to the various levels of her betrayal. 'He'd been looking for you. Wilkes and Gerlitz and whoever they've told know who you are. You've been made.' Luce was quiet for a moment, another hidden reality revealing itself to his agile mind. 'That's why you're retiring, why Grandfather wants—no—*needs* to keep you safe.' His eyes were steely. 'Yet another thing you've cleverly disguised from me. You said Grandfather was retiring you for sentimental reasons but in truth, he needs to protect the network.' His gaze bored through her. 'If you're caught, you could expose a great many things. Capturing you would be quite the prize.'

'It *is* out of sentiment. That is not a lie!' she snapped. How dare he insinuate that the earl did not hold her in affection, that this was merely a business decision; that she was being kicked out, exiled from the network she'd been trained to serve and given her life to. How dare he hit her where it would hurt the most.

But oh, she *did* know how he dared. He was hurting her because she'd hurt him. She'd withheld information from him not once but twice. The second time after she'd given her word and led him to believe that she could be trusted, that they were a team, that the rules of the game had been suspended for them for a short while.

'How did it happen? You being made as Falcon? If you're going to use my house as a hide-out, I think I need to know.'

'I was followed to Cap Gris-Nez this past summer on my way home from Belgium.' She gave Luce a few moments to place that journey on the timeline in his mind. It had been the trip on which she'd shadowed Celeste Sharpton, Cabot Roan's ward and now Kieran Parkhurst's wife.

'I travelled a few days on Celeste's tail. She never

knew I was there but others did. It was a dangerous move. I travel alone for good reason. It's easier to hide. I am a professional and she was most definitely a novice. Roan's people knew her trajectory, knew she was headed to London to find the Horsemen. I kept her safe but at risk to myself it turned out. When Caine killed Roan in the autumn, I thought I was safe, that perhaps no one beyond Roan would have guessed. Then Gerlitz surfaced and began making noise in Roan's wake. It became naïve to assume no one knew. That was when the earl made his plans for me. He decided winter would be the best time to disappear. Travel is difficult for many and the world is quiet. It wouldn't be until spring before anyone thought to remark on my absence.'

She sighed and sank into the chair opposite him. 'Are you happy now? I've marched my shame out for you. I slipped up once in an act of unasked for kindness and it has cost me everything. Even my identity, such as it is.'

Luce was silent for a long while. 'For a moment, when you first told me Grandfather was *allowing* you to retire I was admittedly jealous. He would not countenance me leaving the game.' Luce's stare was dark and piercing. 'I thought he must love you fiercely to arrange it all for you.' Luce shook his head. 'But I see now that it was a business decision and I understand it better. Just as I understand you better.'

'You are being hateful.' Wren scowled. 'You want to hurt me by demeaning the one relationship I treasure.'

'I am being truthful.' Luce's reply was sharp. 'Which is *not* the thing you treasure most.'

Family, belonging, being loved. Those were her treasures. He was stripping them from her with his words and she could not stop him. 'No, it is not. I find the truth can be overrated. The truth is subjective. It is easily twisted and misunderstood. But at least I don't hide from my feelings. I know exactly what I want and what I feel, even when it is risky to do so.' How about that for a little truth telling, she thought. Two could play this game. If he insisted on deconstructing her psyche, she could do the same and he could see how he liked it.

'I do not hide my feelings,' Luce countered.

She smirked. 'You do it all the time, especially when you're hurting or scared. If you don't believe me, answer me this. What did you do this summer after Stepan disappeared?' When Luce said nothing, she supplied the answer. 'You came to Tillingbourne and threw yourself into plans to restore the library. Except for earlier this evening, you've not talked about Stepan at all even though I know his loss is killing you. Instead of addressing those feelings, you've buried yourself in work here at Tillingbourne writing your grandfather's memoir. Trying to prove yourself even though you've already done so a thousand times over. You're doing it again tonight with me.' He was focusing on the work, the interrogation and the facts instead of what his heart was feeling.

She bit her lip, her own hurt showing through as she laid the truths out. All she wanted to do was go to him, to take him in her arms and soothe away the hurt. To put joy back in his eyes when he looked at her. He'd been her hero tonight. He'd saved her when she couldn't save herself, just as he had that first night. She wanted to tell him that her feelings for him hadn't changed because of tonight. But he would not have her, not now. For him, everything had changed tonight. Whatever had existed between them was finished and done. All that remained was to tell the last truth.

'We had something brilliant and bright between us, something wondrous I've not experienced anywhere ever, with anyone. Not just passion but a connection. Tonight offered some revelations that have been difficult to process and you are unwilling to process them. We haven't discussed one thing even remotely interpersonal about what happened this evening, only the business of the evening, because that is what Luce Parkhurst does when his emotions get too difficult for him to handle.'

The conversation was getting out of control. He was not going to be told 'truth' about who he was from a woman who'd deceived him twice. Luce rose. 'I don't have to listen to this. My brother is out there. I need to pack and make preparations for leaving in the morning. Trap or not, I have to get to him.'

She rose with him, grabbing his arm. '*I* have to get to him. Have you not heard a word I've said? It could be a trap. It is better that I go, I am not a Horseman. If the worst happens, I am expendable. I am already lost to the network anyway. This is exactly why your grandfather didn't want you to know. He knew you'd go charging in.'

'It *is* a rather natural response to discovering your brother is in danger,' Luce groused.

'We don't even know if it *is* Stepan. It could just be bait to draw you out. *I* am being sent to do the preliminary scouting. Not you.'

To keep him safe. Because his grandfather loved him. Luce was starting to regret his earlier words, challenging her claim to his grandfather's affections out of his own insecurities. She'd hurt him badly tonight and he'd struck out in equal measure.

'That was before you were wounded.' Luce took a steadying breath against his emotions, against her touch. 'You saw for yourself tonight you are not fully recovered. If you were attacked again you wouldn't be able to fend anyone off.' And yet she'd almost managed to elude two men while dressed in a . Still, 'almost' didn't count when weapons were involved. 'You can't possibly think to manage on your own.'

'Neither can you.' Her eyes flashed quicksilver. 'You don't know where you're going. Last I checked, Essex was a pretty big area.' But she knew, of course. It was one more thing she'd not told him. She was going to hold that piece of information as leverage until she had what she wanted from him.

'If I say we'll go together, will you tell me?' Luce sighed.

She shook her head. 'No. You will simply leave without me. I'll wake up tomorrow morning and you'll be gone. Or the next morning at an inn.'

'What does it matter? You'll just follow me anyway,' Luce argued.

'This could be a dangerous journey. We should stay together. We don't know who or what will be waiting for us at the end of it. Your grandfather will be furious I've broken my word to him and told you. The least I can do is keep you safe.'

'Grandfather will be furious his best agent has been wounded and attacked twice. The least *I* can do is keep *you* safe,' Luce replied dryly.

Wren stuck out her hand. 'Travel truce then? We'll find Stepan and then we will be free of each other.'

Luce shook her hand, his emotions a mixture of sadness and regret—regret that things could not be different and had not been different. 'Truce. Get some sleep. We'll ride as soon as the sun is up.'

He poured himself a brandy after she left. He could live with sadness and regret if it meant Stepan might lie at the end of the journey. He ought to be filled with elation. The puzzle of his missing brother could be on the brink of being solved. Surely, that was worth losing Wren—Falcon.

Another compromise on top of the compromises he'd already made. It should not surprise him. His life was littered with them. It was how many men's lives were lived, not just his. It was the way of the world. The way men like him advanced. He ought not find it so chafing. He was a Horseman because loyalty to his brothers and family demanded it. In return, there was fulfilment in the travel and in using his elite skills in service to his country.

To be fair, he did not come away from it empty-handed. He would be the married Viscount Waring in a few months because the loyalty of responsibility to the village of Little Albury and Tillingbourne estate demanded it. The crown demanded it. His grandfather's efforts for his future demanded it. And again he did not come away without benefit. In exchange he had a title and the social privilege that went with it. He had a home of his own to shape to his tastes, a community to look after and a legacy to leave to a son.

He sat down behind his desk. Truly, he ought to be more grateful. It was just that every time he found a way to break free, to stand apart, something happened to drag him back in and tie the bonds more tightly. All of it came with a personal cost and every time he paid the price. This time, the price would be Wren. He'd let the fantasy of what might have been get the better of him. He'd forgotten one of the cardinal rules of the game—that no one was ever all they seemed. He'd not known her as well as he thought. She was indeed capable of hiding things from him. Not just once, but twice. And he'd proven capable of believing her when she'd said otherwise.

That was a deadly combination. It could get someone killed, probably him. Such a mistake had nearly gotten Kieran killed. The damnable thing was, Luce had successfully remembered that rule for twelve years and followed it to perfection, keeping his relationships physical, smoothly pleasant, void of any deep ties and disclosures. Why the hell hadn't he followed his own rules with her? Why had he allowed his heart to be engaged? *When* had he allowed it?

Perhaps he hadn't allowed anything. Perhaps his heart had gone on its own volition. Perhaps he'd never really had any say in it. Wren was charming. Her successful track record as an intelligence agent for his grandfather suggested he was not the first man who'd been swept up in her charms or lost his heart. But damn it all if he didn't want to be the last. And that seemed intolerable. He could *not* fall in love with a woman who betrayed him.

He ought to write to his grandfather, to tell him what transpired in the stable yard tonight and what had resulted. He dipped his pen but for the first time, the words wouldn't come. He'd been hammered with emotional blows tonight. Stepan was alive—possibly. Wren was Falcon. Both of those revelations were earth shattering to him, but tonight it was the revelation of her identity as Falcon that his mind focused on—yet another secret she'd kept from him.

Should he hate her for the secret? Or celebrate her for all that he owed her over the years? He may have saved her life on his doorstep but how many times had Falcon's information allowed the Horsemen to succeed? Kept the Horsemen safe? Kept soldiers safe and countless others? Falcon was everywhere and nowhere. Of course, no one expected Falcon to be a woman. Even when she'd stood beside him the night they'd cracked the Ottoman code, discussing Greece and practically exposing her hand, Luce had not thought twice about who Falcon might be. He'd said, instead, 'I thought only Falcon had gone that far south…' Had she laughed about that afterwards? He wouldn't blame her if she had.

She'd been responsible for getting Celeste to England, to a Horseman safely, and it had been her own downfall. Kieran had a wife because of her. Roan, whose unscrupulous arms sales were a threat to peace in Europe, was dead because of her. Caine had fired the pistol, but her information had put it all in motion.

His conscience pricked. Now, she was being punished for that act of kindness to Celeste. Grandfather was forcing her out. He was sorry for that, although he'd not been empathetic tonight. To Luce's shame, he was punishing her too. He'd been mean. Overwhelmed with his own feelings of betrayal because he cared for her and because he wanted more from her than perhaps she was capable of giving under the circumstances. There was truth in her argument that she was just doing her job. His ego had not liked the realisation that when the moment of decision had come she'd chosen the job over him.

She'd chosen loyalty to his grandfather over him and she'd done it not once but twice. There couldn't be much future in a relationship that was trust deficient but how could it be otherwise between two agents who dealt in secrets? The revelation hurt and Luce did not like to hurt.

Was she right about that? That he exchanged examining his feelings for work? When Stepan had first gone missing, he'd been the one who'd spent that night on the docks running from party to party gathering information because he couldn't stand still and wait, didn't want his mind to have even a moment to think about what Stepan's disappearance in the water meant. Was he doing the same thing now? Using the very vital and urgent work of the Horsemen to prevent reconciling the complex feelings the evening raised in him—betrayal, loss, want.

He pushed a hand through his hair. How was it possible he wanted her when he knew she'd betrayed him? He should not want a woman who'd not been truthful with him. He should not crave her, should not want to run down the hall and beg her forgiveness for harsh words.

He needed to leash this vulnerability of his—another reason to keep his heart under wraps. Vulnerability made people reckless and clouded their thoughts, his among them. The same woman who'd deceived him had protected Celeste and had brought vital information that might lead to Stepan. How did one reconcile the good and the bad? Or perhaps she was right: truth was subjective. The truth was whatever he made it. Heroes didn't exist in black and white but in grey. Quicksilver grey.

Chapter Sixteen

In the grey light of a winter's dawn, Falcon and the Horseman set off for Essex. The Horseman on Vercingetorix and Falcon, swathed in a warm cloak with a deep hood covering her hair, mounted on a competent white mare from the Tillingbourne stables. If the Horseman noticed that Falcon hazarded one last backward glance at the abbey and raised a gloved hand in farewell, he said nothing but filed away the meaning behind it. She would not be back.

They travelled in silence, making what speed they could in the snow. The horses were shod for winter weather and that helped, as did the lower elevation as they left the hills. By mid-morning, the snow was behind them and the road was clear. They stopped every couple of hours to rest the horses, check the horses' feet and eat a small snack. At villages, they chose to stay to the side roads and cut across country where possible to avoid being seen. It didn't seem likely they'd be noticed or tracked out here in the vast, empty countryside but such practice was standard protocol for those in the Sandmore network and they followed the practice, riding hard, talking little.

Luce didn't mind either condition. After weeks of being cooped up at home, the hard riding felt good. Vercingetorix was enjoying it as well, his hooves eating up the ground with ease. Wren had given her mare her head, too. At present, the road was dry and clear of traffic. With luck—if the road and the horses' stamina held—they might make thirty miles today. That would put them halfway to Essex. As for the silence, the difficulty of carrying on conversation while riding at more than a trot was a convenient excuse not to do it.

What more was there to say anyway? Two days ago he would have thought they could talk for ever and still not discover everything there was to know about each other. The prospect of peeling one another back layer by layer had seemed delightful, sensual even. But not now. They were together no longer. Bed mates and soulmates no more. They were work partners only.

In the rare chance of working with a partner, one did not tell a workmate anything personal so as not to burden them with knowledge that might be dangerous to them later on. His mind whispered he could apologise for his behaviour last night. He could offer her absolution. He could tell her that he understood why she'd done it. He could tell her he'd stayed awake in his empty bed wishing the evening had gone differently. That he wanted her still. But that would only set him up for more hurt later. It didn't change the fact that she couldn't stay, that he had to wed, or that when the critical moment had come, she'd chosen loyalty to his grandfather over him. It only deferred the hurt a few months.

They slowed and pulled their horses over to the verge in order to let a carriage coming towards them by. Evening shadows were starting to stretch. 'There should be a village around the next bend,' he observed. The presence of a little traffic on the road, too, signalled that would be the case. The carriage was the third one in the last two miles after a veritable dearth of traffic.

'We should stop there for the night.' Something in Wren's voice made him look at her. She was pale and was leaning forward in the saddle, hands fisted in reins and mane.

'You're hurting,' Luce said gruffly. 'You should have said something.'

'You wanted to make thirty miles while we had a chance. We don't know what tomorrow brings,' she countered. He felt as if he was a complete cad.

It was a testament to her resilience that she was on horseback at all after her injury.

'You rode so well today I forgot to consider that may be uncomfortable for you just yet,' Luce apologised. 'I do wish you'd spoken up.' But he knew why she hadn't. Her effort had been her attempt to mend the breach between them, her own apology of sorts.

'Come sit on Vere with me. He can carry two for a short distance and I can pony your mare.'

'Her name is Beatrice and I can finish the day under my own power,' Wren said stubbornly.

'I know you can, but you don't have to.' Luce hoped that softened the offer or perhaps she didn't want to be that close to him. 'Don't be obstinate if the price of it is you not being of any use at journey's end.'

'I'll be fine. A hot bath will solve me.' She shifted in the saddle with a wince and Luce had to hold his tongue not to force the issue. 'Will you tell me a tale the rest of the way?' she asked. 'It will take my mind off the ache. I want to know the story of your horse's name.'

If there was one thing Luce loved to talk about, it was his horse. 'He's named for a Gallic military commander who succeeded in uniting the Gauls against Caesar and nearly put an end to Rome's presence in France. Vere is fifteen years old. He was a gift to me when I officially became a Horseman. He was three then. I trained him and we've been together ever since. My brothers' horses are from the same sire. They received theirs when they became Horsemen, too. Kieran's horse is Tambor, Stepan's horse is Caravel and Caine's horse is Argonaut. He's the oldest. He's over twenty now.'

That gave Luce pause and he continued more solemnly. 'Caine would be lost without him.' As would he without Vere. 'Our horses are like an extension of ourselves. I can't imagine life without them and yet I think must.' Even if Argonaut lived another twelve years—horses did live into their thirties with good health and proper care—Argonaut would not be mission worthy. Today would have been difficult for him. And yet, there was reassurance in knowing Argonaut had made the trip to Wales with no problem. The horse still had a couple good years left, perhaps. Luce reached down and patted Vere's shoulder.

'What sort of horses are they?' Her prompt sounded terse. She must be suffering badly. Guilt stabbed at him hard. Quarrel or not, mission or not, he'd not meant for her to hurt like this.

'Friesian-thoroughbred crosses. Their sire is a Friesian and their dam a thoroughbred.' The village came into view and Luce strained for the sight of an inn that was clean and respectable. By his calculations they were in the north-western part of Kent, perhaps right outside of Sevenoaks. He spied a neatly kept sign and hoped it was a portent of what it looked like on the inside. 'The Horse and Bull seems promising. Shall we try?'

In the stable yard, he dismounted and gave instructions to the ostler. The stalls looked clean and they were mostly full—also a good sign. People stayed here, although he did wonder what their choices would be if they didn't.

'Luce.' Wren's voice held a desperate tone. He turned, her face pale in the lanternlight of the yard. 'I don't think I can dismount on my own.'

He was by her side instantly, arms reaching up. 'Just fall into me, I'll catch you.' He carried her, too, despite her protestations. She could walk, she argued. 'Why walk, my dear, when I can carry you just as easily.'

Inside, he gave orders for a hot bath to be brought up and dinner to be served in the room. 'You will need my assistance tonight. Two rooms is pointless.' He gave her a sharp look when she questioned his choice. 'Besides, I have helped you before. It's no problem.'

The room was large with an antechamber furnished like a small sitting room before giving way to the bedchamber. Luce set her down on the settee and saw to it that the tub was placed before the fire and a dressing screen brought to ensure she had privacy.

'You can go downstairs and get a drink. You needn't stay with me,' Wren called from the tub.

In answer, Luce took up residence in the antechamber's wing-backed chair. 'You can't get out of the tub without me, but I know you'll try if I am not here. So, no, I will not be going downstairs. It's my fault you hurt. I shouldn't have pushed you today.' Damn, he'd wished she'd said something about it. It was proof that a truce wasn't enough. They'd barely talked all day. All the talking they'd done had happened in the last half hour on the road. And yet, there was no going back to how things had been before. But there might be going back to how things had been when she'd first arrived at Tillingbourne, when she'd spent the days in the library with him, wrapped in his robe. Back to before he'd kissed her. Before he'd let his heart go to her.

He helped her out of the tub, reminding her he'd do this for anyone he was on a mission with as she quickly wrapped herself in a towel. He'd like to have reminded her that he'd been the one to stitch her up, that her body held no secrets from him. Instead, he rummaged in his saddlebags for the salve he always travelled with. 'Here, put some of this on the scar and the sore area. It's comfrey. It will help.' They'd both packed light. No valises, just saddlebags, and he had cash to buy whatever they needed along the way. Cash travelled much better than supplies. It had been one of the many lessons Grandfather had drilled into them.

'Thank you,' she said, coming around the screen, dressed once more in his borrowed nightshirt. She lifted the tin to her nose and took a delicate sniff. The sight of her had him swallowing hard against a surge of emotion. She looked so innocent, so fragile, standing there in his nightshirt with her hair loose about her shoulders.

'I want you to be well, Wren.' Whatever had happened between them, he wanted that.

She reached a hand out to touch his arm. 'Luce, it doesn't have to be this way.'

He allowed himself the luxury of covering her warm hand with his. 'It's best this way, I think. It was a mistake to mix business with pleasure.'

'I'm sorry you think that, Luce. I must respectfully disagree with your assessment.'

She might have said more but dinner chose that moment to arrive. There was the bustle of removing the tub, laying the table and removing the covers on the dishes before they were alone again. After the servants had gone, Luce busied himself ladling the hardy meat stew into bowls, slicing the bread and pouring wine. He wanted to be busy. He did not want to return to the conversation that had been interrupted. He was not to get his wish. He'd no sooner taken his chair than Wren picked up the conversation where it had been left.

'Do you loathe me, Luce?' she asked quietly. She sat close enough at the little table that he could breathe in the scent of her soap, all strawberries and memories. It was heady and arousing—two reactions he did not want to have.

'I do not think it is possible to loathe you, Wren. I also think a man must be on his guard around you. You steal hearts, even those hearts that believe they are immune. It is rather surprising to wake up and discover that one is not as immune as one thought. Wine?'

He was doing it again. Burying the need to feel with little tasks—slicing bread, pouring wine. And yet he did *feel*. It was in his acts of kindness. He'd insisted on carrying her upstairs, on overseeing the bath, the fire, the privacy screen. It was in the gifts he gave. The comfrey salve, the ice-pink ball gown, the pearls she'd left behind at Tillingbourne. *Doing* for others was how he let his feelings be shown.

Because, ironically, words failed him when it came to expressing those feelings out loud. But he would not thank her for sharing those thoughts.

'*I* don't loathe *you*, Luce. You said some awful things to me. You were angry and hurt. No one is at their best under those circumstances.' She took a sip of her wine, a delicious full-bodied red perfect for a winter's night, and watched his face for any sign of relenting. Today had been miserable. Up until the last, he'd treated her as if she'd been invisible. 'Last night was difficult. But it is only insurmountable if we want it to be.' Perhaps she had to be the one to make the first overture of peace, to help them move beyond the silent truce that had marked today.

'The difficulty was our own doing. We'd taken things too far. It would not have been a problem if we had let business be business.' Luce was putting up his walls, reasoning away the hurt. She wanted to stop that before the bricks got too high.

'And pleasure go hang? Are you truly telling me that you'd have preferred not to have tested the spark between us? To not know how it felt to be together?' She would not trade those nights for the world. They would be her remembrance of another time once she stepped into retirement.

'We tested the spark and we found our limits,' Luce replied with preternatural calm.

'And what were those limits?' She would make him say them out loud.

'Trust and truthfulness. Now, before you get your hackles up, let me say this. You are an agent for my grandfather. I am an agent for my grandfather. Our lives are about dealing in secrets. The rational part of my mind understands the choice you made. It understands the need to play a part, to dissemble, to decide what people get to know and to see. The Horseman in me understands and forgives Falcon. Although the Horseman in me also knows there's nothing to forgive. It is simply the nature of the game. Complete trust and truthfulness are not part of it. If you want absolution, there it is.' His dark eyes were intent on her.

'I hear a "but" dangling there somewhere, Luce.'

He nodded solemnly. 'But the man in me, Wren, must have those things—truth and trust—from the woman he…cares…for. Our circumstances do not permit those things to be given. Those are the limits we discovered when our fantasy got out of hand.'

'You cannot forgive me or you cannot forgive yourself for that?' She already knew the answer. He could not forgive himself for letting his role slip. For letting the Horseman and the man combine. It had made him vulnerable and that was intolerable for Luce Parkhurst. Without vulnerability he would find it very hard to make his vaunted love match. 'Do you like being immune, Luce?'

Luce levelled her with a stare that said he didn't care for the conversation. 'I like being in control of myself. I like the clarity that comes with a sharp mind. I do not like deceits or surprises. They undermine control and clarity.'

She answered his stare over the rim of her wine glass, a suspicion rising. 'So you've never been in love despite saying that you want a love match? What of the wife you will take this summer? Do you plan to love her?' Wren did not like thinking of the other woman, whomever she might be. But she pitied that woman, too. That woman would never know Luce the way she did. Never see him come undone at climax. Never see him look up at her from between her legs, his eyes full of dark fire, his heart vulnerable.

'I believe we've already discussed the compromise. For Tillingbourne and my obligations to be met, love must be sacrificed, at least in the immediate future. I will have my mother draw up a list of suitable candidates and I will choose one of them with the hope that love may grow after marriage. I think in this case that is the most realistic expectation.'

Another compromise for him, so that he would

be in control of his future and of his feelings. Wren saw that very clearly.

'A certain kind of love *can* grow over time if two people respect one another,' Wren said thoughtfully. 'But one does not cultivate passion like it is a plant in your herbal garden. Your brothers have that love. The Parkhursts are known for falling hard and fast. Your grandfather married your grandmother after a short courtship. Caine knew Lady Mary for barely two months. Kieran married Celeste after an adventure on the road. Do you think you can really have the same finding a bride that way?'

'You're quite the student on our family.' Luce growled. If she did not know him better, she'd understand his remark as an insult, a scold. But she did know better. He was protecting himself, like a wounded animal backed into a corner.

She did not relent. 'I think the Parkhursts are marvellous. I will miss them. I will miss *you*. You are no less extraordinary to me because we've had a falling out. Although, I must say I much prefer falling in.' When he said nothing but stared at her in silence, she reached for his hand and threaded her fingers through it. 'Luce, I want you to know I never meant to hurt you but I also had—and still have—a job to do. I will do it by whatever means necessary. If you can't give me absolution, one network agent to another, then at least give me understanding.'

'Why does it matter?' Luce sounded tired, defeated, as if he'd waged a battle with himself while she'd talked.

She smiled. 'Because I can't go another day with you not talking to me.' He did chuckle at that and she'd consider it a breakthrough. She stifled a yawn. There were things she'd like to discuss. But Luce rose.

'You need sleep.'

'So do you. We'll share the bed.' She would sleep better knowing he was beside her. She took his hand again. 'Lay beside me tonight. We need to stop punishing ourselves because something didn't work out.'

He gave a curt nod in concession to the practicality of the suggestion. They needed a good night's sleep if they were to function well in the face of what lay ahead. She did not pretend that nod meant all was resolved between them, but perhaps it was a start. They needed to be unified by the time they reached Stepan. She didn't know what they might find there or who they might meet. And more selfishly, she didn't wish to leave with the memory of him hating her, when she disappeared into retirement in a few days.

Chapter Seventeen

Wren wondered if she'd ever learn her lesson about wishes. She'd wished to meet Luce in person and she had. She'd wished to work with him on a project and she'd gotten to do that too, and so much more. For a short while, she'd lived the fairy tale with him and seen him at his most personal—at least the most personal he'd allow. Those wishes had come at the cost of his trust, though, and it had been a high price to pay indeed. And she'd still not learned. That first night on the road she'd wished for a better memory to leave with than one of cold silence. She'd gotten that wish too.

Tonight would be their last night on the journey to Essex. It had taken them three days, and they'd made good time considering they had to nearly go all the way through Essex to reach their destination. They'd been blessed by passable roads in winter, a lack of traffic and decent inns along the way in which they could recover from long days in the saddle. And she'd been blessed by his presence beside her in bed every night and his conversation during the day.

But it wasn't the same as it had been before. These conversations were the conversations one might have with an acquaintance. The type of small talk he might make with the baker in Little Albury. There were no more forays into family stories or tales of growing up beneath the stars at Sandmore with his brothers. It was polite and technically what she'd asked for—to not be invisible to him.

He was certainly not invisible to her. Whether she rode beside him on wide tracks of road, or rode behind him on narrower ones, she was fully conscious of him, every waking moment. She did not tire of watching him in the saddle, his head bare, his waves tousled. The cold did not affect him at all. He was revelling in the journey, in being outdoors. She craved their evening meals, always taken privately in their room, when she had him to herself even if the conversation remained general.

She had tried to draw him out a few times, even provoke him, but to no avail. He was on guard and his armour was firmly in place. She understood. He was protecting himself. What he might comprehend from a business standpoint, he was struggling to come to grips with from a personal perspective. In that regard, the Parkhurst pattern where husbands and wives seemingly told one another everything, trusted each other with all things, had set him up for disappointment. Twice.

This evening, though, as they settled into the inn at Southend-on-Sea, their final destination, Luce was in high spirits. Perhaps it was the excitement of potentially being reunited with his brother tomorrow. She hoped it wasn't the prospect of getting rid of her. 'Will you be able to sleep tonight?' she asked as they sat down to supper. Was this their *last* supper? It could be. She'd been doing that all day, counting things off in terms of lasts.

'I do not want to get my hopes up. It might not be him and we will have come a long way for nothing.' But she could hear the hope in his voice. He thought it would be Stepan. She hoped for his sake it was.

Wren tried to bolster Luce's hopes. 'There's a good chance it will be. Our information is excellent. One of the agents Caine sent out this fall reported that there was a stranger meeting Stepan's description living in a Quaker settlement near Southend-on-Sea. He'd not been able to see the stranger but the man's story is particularly compelling.'

'The story is hearsay from third parties. It is not the stranger's own telling.' Luce's caution tore at her. Had she done this to him? Created a caution that prevented him from embracing the possibility of joy openly? The higher one flew, the further and the harder the fall. 'Caine's man did not set eyes on him.'

'But the odds, Luce,' she said in protest. 'A tall, dark-haired, dark-eyed man washing up on shore at *that time*?'

'I will admit it is more than the other enquiries have revealed, but that doesn't make it true. What of the knife wound? What does the man have to say for himself?'

'We will find out tomorrow. Now, come to bed.' She held out her hand to him, wishing he was coming to bed for more than the practicalities of rest and sleep. But he'd made his choices and she had made hers.

The next day found Luce restless and up at dawn. He'd been unable to sleep with the knowledge that Stepan might be alive and that he would see him in the morning. There was the knowledge, too, that once Stepan was—hopefully—found, Wren would leave him. He took himself out to watch the winter sun rise, to take a brisk walk in the quiet village lanes, anything to keep himself busy, to keep the questions at bay that had plagued him through the long night.

He stopped to check on the horses, positing some answers in his mind as he fed apple pieces to Vercingetorix. If it *was* Stepan why hadn't he contacted them? Why hadn't he found his way home? There'd been enough time.

Luce stroked Vere's long face. If Stepan had been seriously injured, a long convalescence would have kept him from home. As would an illness, perhaps he had caught something from spending so much time in the water—a fever or chill that had proven near deadly. Especially if there was a lack of medical care. These were isolated parts here where the Thames emptied into the sea.

How long *had* Stepan been in the water? Had he really drifted this far down the river? By Luce's calculations, it was approximately forty miles from the Thames in London to its outlet in Southend-on-Sea—not all of it fast-running water either. A man would have opportunity to paddle ashore at myriad points. Caine had posted men to the various hamlets along the waterway in the hope that Stepan would drag himself ashore.

Luce reached for another slice of apple. Injury and illness would explain the delay in returning, but they did not explain why he hadn't sent a note.

'Why would he not send word?' Luce asked Vere quietly. No money for franking? But surely, some good soul in the village would have helped him send word. Family would have come for him and stayed with him until he could travel.

These questions shaded his joy at the prospect of today's findings and beneath those questions was worry. His gut told him something awful had happened to Stepan, something terrible enough to prevent him from sending word. They might find him but in what shape? The worst thought of all nudged at his conscience. Would it have been better if he'd not washed ashore? Better for whom? Him or his family? Luce would rather live with the not knowing if it spared Stepan from incurable suffering.

The stable was rousing and getting busier as inn guests woke and prepared to travel. It was a reminder to him that Wren would be waiting. They would eat breakfast and then head to the settlement. After six months of not knowing, resolution was just hours away. Maybe. He'd spent so much time thinking about what if the man was Stepan, he'd not considered the consequences if the man wasn't. It would mean Stepan was still missing. Still lost. Still dead. It was a testament to just how much his thoughts had subtly slipped towards the hopeful, the accepting, despite his questioning. Not unlike how his heart had slipped towards Wren, falling for her without his permission.

She would be out of his life soon. Once the situation with Stepan was resolved, she could get on with her retirement, sliding into nothingness and erasing the very presence of herself within the network. His hand halted its stroking. It would be as if she'd never been. His traitorous heart rebelled at the thought. His heart had stopped caring about her betrayals. His heart argued all too easily on her behalf that she'd found herself in an untenable situation. His heart had craved the nights beside her on their journey, recapturing a little of the closeness that had existed between them.

He had to make his heart understand that it was better this way. Even if he had taken her olive branches and re-engaged, it would only have been for a handful of nights. He would have prolonged further heartbreak by a matter of days. It changed nothing. She was not returning to Tillingbourne with him when this was over. She was disappearing. It was necessary so that Gerlitz and others could not find her. He could not tempt her with a reason to stay. Nor could he tempt himself. He'd have to let her go in the spring when he went to London anyway. He would not ask her to risk her freedom for such temporary terms as the ones he could offer. They had found their limits.

His conscience whispered: *Then learn to live with the limits and ask for longer terms. Ask for permanent terms.* The solution was simple enough. This little piece of logic regarding terms had been working its way to the surface since he'd seen her in the pink gown and put the pearls about her neck. He'd not wanted anyone or anything as fiercely as he'd wanted her in that moment. Not just carnally, but for ever. To make her his viscountess. She'd looked like one, standing there in that gown, her hair down. So regal, so elegant, so *his*. Looking at her, he'd felt so *hers* as well. The things he'd told her, the stories he'd shared. He'd never unburdened himself like he had with her. No one in London would measure up. He would for ever be comparing those girls to her and they would all come up lacking. But having her would mean accepting limits. Could he do that?

There were footsteps behind him and a soft voice. 'I thought I'd find you out here when you didn't come in for breakfast.' Wren's hand was gentle on his arm. 'Couldn't sleep? The bed was cold. You've been up for a while.'

'I meant to come in and eat with you.' He'd spent all morning waiting for time to speed up and now it was running away from him.

'I saved you some bread and cheese, and I packed our saddlebags in case we decide to stay in the settlement tonight. We can leave when you're ready.' She was taking care of him, thinking of things for him the way he had for her. When had someone taken care of him? As a Horseman, he was always looking out for others. He'd been beastly to her when they'd quarrelled. He didn't deserve her kindnesses.

He smiled. 'I'm ready. Let's saddle up the horses and go. The morning promises to be crisp and cold. Perfect for a ride.'

The settlement was five miles from Southend-on-Sea and their horses covered the distance easily. Luce brought his horse to a walk and took in the little hamlet with its thatched roofs and half-timbered buildings. It was old, dating back to the Quaker settlements that had thrived in the area in the seventeenth century. To the best of Luce's knowledge, settlements still existed at Epping and Chelmsford as well.

Old it might be, but it was also well kept. Roofs were in good repair and the dirt street was devoid of animal droppings. There was an inn, a dry good store of sorts that probably carried a little bit of everything from fabric to hardware. No tavern, of course, not for Quakers. Alcohol wasn't forbidden but they'd hardly build an edifice dedicated to its consumption just for themselves. At the end of the street, stood the meeting house. 'Nice place.' He glanced at Wren.

'Quiet place. We are attracting attention,' Wren replied, drawing her horse close to his. 'Our moment of escaping notice is gone. We'd best get to work.'

Luce nodded and circled Vere back to the inn to start asking his questions while Wren waited outside with the horses, watching his back. They were blind here. Had Gerlitz's men already arrived?

Inside, the tidy inn was nearly empty except for a man in his late middle years eating a mid-morning breakfast in the dining room.

The innkeeper was skeptical. 'There was someone asking the same questions in the autumn right before the harvest.' He looked Luce up and down. Luce hoped he noted the plain but superior tailoring of his greatcoat and the quality of his boots, suggesting he was a man of some wealth and standing. He was no adventurer.

'I am the man's brother,' Luce offered when the innkeeper proved to be tight-lipped. 'I've come to take him home. He should be with his family.' That much was true if it was Stepan. Luce would worry about that when the time came.

The man eating breakfast looked up from his

food. 'I know the man thee speaks of. He's boarding out at the Kingsley farm. My property abuts it. I will take thee out there.'

'That would be most kind,' Luce accepted the offer, but he didn't miss the calculation in the man's eyes. He was doing this because it served a purpose for him. Luce didn't like being used as another's pawn.

The man lumbered to his feet. 'It would be good for him to be home with his family, his people. My gig is parked outside. It's not far, just a little ways outside of the town here. We're close to the beaches. I'm Francis Hartlett, by the way.'

'Thank you again for your assistance.' Luce didn't offer his own name. He mounted Vere and threw a cautioning look at Wren to say nothing. He needed this man for a short while and that was all. He felt no obligation to make conversation or to discuss his brother with him.

At the Kingsley farmhouse, which looked more like a cottage than a true farmhouse, the man insisted on coming in to make introductions. 'Friend Anne, is thee sister home?' He stepped inside without knocking and Luce liked him even less.

A young woman looked up from a worktable where she was rolling out dough. Luce noted the dislike in her gaze, shown but quickly disguised. 'Friend Hartlett, my sister is in the field with Peter.'

'This is Peter's brother.' Hartlett paused, no doubt hoping Luce would supply a name for himself and for Wren. Luce gave away no surprise over the name. Peter might be an alias Stepan had adopted and there might be a reason for it. He needed to be patient.

'In the field? Very good,' Hartlett said cheerily in the awkward silence Luce had let grow. 'I'll walk our guests out.'

'No need.' Anne hurriedly wiped her hands on her apron. 'I wouldn't want to keep thee. I need to walk down to the field anyway.'

Luce helped her by issuing his own curt farewell. 'Thank you indeed, Friend Hartlett. Perhaps we will see you another time.' He ushered Anne and Wren ahead of him, effectively dismissing the nosy Hartlett by leaving.

They reached the field and Anne pointed to where two people were slowly walking the empty rows, heads close, deep in conversation. 'There they are.'

Luce shielded his eyes against the bright winter sun and stared. Relief and elation coursed through him. Stepan was alive! Stepan was found. There was no mistaking the broad shoulders and unruly dark hair so like his own. 'Wren, it's him,' he breathed the glad words as he felt Wren squeeze his arm in shared joy.

'Ellen, we have company!' Anne waved and beckoned the pair over.

Luce strode forward, unable to wait. He halted. Stepan was walking towards him patiently as if he wasn't surprised at all. Something was wrong. Why didn't Stepan run to him? This was not the reaction of a missing brother found.

'Welcome,' the pretty woman named Ellen greeted them with a smile. 'How can we help thee?'

'I'm Luce Parkhurst and I'm here for my brother.' He rested his gaze on Stepan. What was wrong with him? 'Brother, do you not recognise me?' The euphoria of finding Stepan was quickly being undermined by something else.

'Peter doesn't know his real name. It is unlikely he'd recognise any family,' Ellen Kingsley offered quietly. 'We called him Peter because we pulled him from the water.'

It wasn't an alias then.

'Is it true? Do you not know who I am?' Luce's gaze never left his brother's. He held his breath, waiting for an answer.

Then, in a voice he'd thought never to hear again, Peter said, 'I have no recollection of who you are. I am sorry, Sir.'

In a flash, the puzzle came together. Stepan had not contacted them because he had no memory of who he was, or who they were. Dear God. He'd gotten what he wished for all these long months. His brother was alive but Stepan might as well still be lost.

Beside him, Wren slid her hand quietly into his and he held onto it. Her presence, her touch, anchors against the reality crashing around him. They gave him the strength he needed to get through what came next.

Chapter Eighteen

She would be strong for him, Wren vowed as the little company made their way back to the farmhouse. This could not be how Luce thought today would play out: a brother found, but memories lost. Was it really his brother then if those memories weren't intact? She slid a covert look in his direction. Outwardly, Luce seemed very much in control, but inside he must be reeling. His grip on her hand was tight, almost painful, but she wouldn't let go. Whatever else lay between them, she owed him her life, not once but twice. She would give him a life for a life if she could. He looked in her direction and she let her eyes say what there was no time for words to convey: *be patient, don't rush your brother, this is a lot for him, just as it is a lot for you.*

Inside, they all took seats around the long table that served as worktable and dining table. Wren left Luce's side long enough to help Ellen gather tea things—a mish mash of unmatched mugs and two prettily painted teacups that were clearly considered the family's valuables. Anne had gone to call the boys—whom Wren assumed were the girls' brothers.

Wren did the quick math. Four people plus Stepan lived in this space but, despite the overpopulation, the cottage was clean and warm. A ladder led up to a loft where the brothers probably slept. There was a bed frame with a stuffed mattress in the corner of the main room for the girls. Perhaps it had once belonged to their parents. Clothes hung on pegs. Cooking was done over the fire in the stone fireplace.

This was a long way from the lifestyle of the Horsemen, Wren mused as she and Ellen set out tea and a loaf of bread. Yet, Stepan seemed at home. He was comfortable in the unbleached linen shirt and work trousers. He was comfortable with Ellen, too. Wren did not miss the quick brush of their hands as Ellen passed by him, nor the synchronicity between them as Ellen set out a crock of butter and a jar of jam while Stepan cut slices of bread. Well, that was an interesting wrinkle. She glanced at Luce. Did he see it, too?

'People were asking questions in the settlement, earlier this fall.' Ellen's tone carried a hint of defensiveness, a warning. She was eager to protect Stepan. Another item to note. 'But they didn't come out here.' Probably because they didn't have an eager guide to show them the way, Wren thought. Why would Hartlett be so eager to befriend a stranger? Especially when Hartlett didn't seem the friendly sort in general. He had the face of someone who lived in an attitude of perpetual sourness, although it had lit up when he'd asked where Ellen was and it had dimmed when Anne had told him Ellen was with Peter.

Stepan touched Ellen's hand gently. 'It's all right. Let's hear what these people have to say. Nothing needs to be decided today.' There was definitely something burgeoning here. This was the Kingsley cottage but Stepan carried weight and position here. Typical Parkhurst male, Wren thought. Charming everyone in sight. Caring for them, too. Stepan was a hard worker, a provider given what she'd seen in the fields.

The cottage door opened, admitting two rambunctious boys in early adolescence and Anne. Stepan motioned them over to take seats at the table and they immediately settled down. 'Mr Parkhurst, Miss Audley, this is Phillip and Andrew. Boys, Mr Parkhurst believes I am his brother,' Stepan said calmly, slicing them bread.

'I *know* you are my brother,' Luce said smoothly,

directing the conversation to where it needed to go, no matter how difficult. 'I would like to hear your story, how you've come to be here, and then I would like to share mine.' It was a good strategy, focusing everything on Stepan instead of Luce making himself centre stage with demands.

Stepan exchanged a warm look with Ellen. 'This good woman found me on the beach not far from here. I was half dead and half drowned, but somehow there was enough life left in me worth saving. Her brothers—' he stopped here to nod towards Andrew and Phillip '—fetched me home in a quilt and laid me on that bed over there, where I stayed for far too long recovering from wounds and a fever. I've been here ever since. I was able to see the harvest brought in, but it is meagre payment for what this family has given me—a home, care and a place in the community.'

'An injury?' Luce pursued the point. 'A knife wound on your arm by chance?'

'Yes.' Stepan rolled up his sleeve revealing a tanned forearm and a healed scar higher up near his bicep. His brow knit; an expression so reminiscent of Luce. Even Wren, who'd never met either of the brothers in person until a few weeks ago, could see the resemblance. Wren glanced at Ellen. The woman had gone pale. She'd seen the resemblance, too. Her thoughts were clear: anyone could guess or hear about a knife wound, but one could not fake a resemblance. She was concerned and fearful. If the stranger at the table was Stepan's brother, she would lose him. She did not want to give him up.

Stepan rolled down his sleeve, his gaze steady on Luce. 'Perhaps you should tell me your story now.'

'I am Lucien Parkhurst and you are my brother, Stepan Parkhurst. We are the grandsons of the Earl of Sandmore.' Luce spoke slowly, giving the man time to digest the news. 'We have two older brothers, Kieran and Caine, and a younger sister, Guenevere. She had her baby last month, a boy.' He made no mention of the network or of the Four Horsemen. He paused and Wren knew what Luce was waiting for, hoping for: a switch to flip in the man's mind, one that would bring all the memories flooding back.

There was a little rustle around the table. Andrew and Phillip had exchanged excited glances at the mention of the earl, but a look from Stepan quieted them. The boys adored him, obeyed him.

'An earl's grandson?' Peter queried in disbelief. 'If you'd said I was a sailor who had fallen overboard I might have believed that. How would an earl's grandson come to be washed up on shore where the Thames meets the North Sea?'

'You were lost during an altercation on the docks

in Wapping in July.' Luce's announcement was met with shock. Ellen gasped and quickly covered her mouth, her distress evident. Stepan took her hand, steadying her with his gaze.

'I assume that's what the other enquirers mentioned as well. This is not the first time you've heard of the incident in Wapping,' Luce continued.

Stepan nodded. 'It is not. It just seems a little extreme. It's a long way from here in lifestyle and in distance.'

'May I tell you about our family?'

Luce was doing an admirable job of keeping his emotions under control. How frustrating it must be for him to have Stepan right there in front of him but unable to remember who he was.

'Yes, please. Perhaps it will jog something loose. I've been unable to remember a thing.'

Stepan was lying about that last part. Wren noted the way his hand had discreetly tightened on Ellen's hand. He *had* remembered some things. Perhaps he just didn't know what they meant.

Luce did his best. As the afternoon gave way to shadows he told stories of the four boys growing up at Willow Park, at Sandmore. Stories of camp outs, swimming races and horses. Of how Stepan had delayed his entry to school by a year so that Luce could go with him. But Stepan recalled nothing. It wasn't going to happen today.

Wren shot Luce a signalling look. 'It's getting late. We should be going. We thank you for your hospitality today and your patience.'

Luce rose, admitting to temporary defeat. 'I will call tomorrow and discuss a few other matters.' It was not a question or a request.

They said their goodbyes and Wren noticed that while the farewells were cordial, there was no begging them to stay for supper or a desire to put them up for the night. Ellen Kingsley and Stepan wanted them gone. It was understandable. They had a lot to discuss, as did she and Luce. There would have been no space or privacy in which to do that work in the cramped cottage and unexpected company would drain the family's food resources in the heart of midwinter. She knew a little about that.

'He didn't know me.' The knowledge settled with leaden intensity in Luce's heart as they made their slow way back to the inn at the settlement, taking care in the dark to keep the horses safe. 'I was stunned when he didn't recall who I was, but it made sense. It explained his absence, his lack of contact. I told myself I could fix that. I thought I could make him remember me.'

In retrospect he felt rather naïve as he confessed to Wren. 'I was certain if I told enough stories, gave him enough details, his mind would crack open like a safe and all the memories would come spilling out. I don't know why that didn't work.'

'We don't know how trauma functions. Perhaps there is something he unconsciously doesn't want to remember,' Wren offered. She was trying to help and her efforts touched him. She'd been beside him all day not only because this was her mission. She'd let her concern for him be palpable and it had sustained him through the long, disappointing afternoon. 'His brain might be trying very hard to block something out. We can consult doctors in London. I am sure your grandfather knows someone who is an amnesia specialist.'

'We can if there's time and if he's willing.'

'Do you think he's not willing? I think people who discover they're the grandson of an earl would be quite willing to pursue their true identity.'

'My brother seemed very happy in that cottage today.' Luce had been envious of how happy he'd seemed for a man with no memory. Content even, as if he'd found his place in this world. It was akin to how Luce almost felt at Tillingbourne. Perhaps he too would feel entirely content there once the restoration was complete.

They reached the inn and swung down from the horses, the conversation temporarily stalled. Inside, supper was laid out for them in the dining room where they were the only two diners.

'I think his contentment had something to do with Ellen Kingsley.' Wren dropped the remark into the meal between sips of wine.

How observant of her. 'I noticed it too. The brushing of hands when Ellen set out the tea.'

'How he'd touch her hand to assure her,' Wren added. 'She doesn't want to lose him. She's afraid.'

Luce nodded. 'He's protecting her.'

You could take away the name but you couldn't take away a Parkhurst's honor. His brother might not know who he was, but he was a Parkhurst through and through. A Horseman to his bones, protecting the vulnerable. The lead in his heart eased. He reached for Wren's hand, thinking too late how alike it was to his brother's gesture with Ellen.

'Thank you for being there today. It was difficult and disappointing, but you made it bearable. You gave me the strength to get through it.' His gaze lingered on hers, letting her see in his eyes how important it was to him that he say those words. She would know how hard it was to say them, too, for he who was so self-reliant, who valued his privacy even when it came to his feelings as she'd so accurately accused the night it all fell apart for them.

The innkeeper came to clear their plates and bring dessert, a dried apple pie with fresh cream. The exchange gave Luce time to regroup and gather himself.

'A specialist may help; it's a good idea. But Stepan still has to be warned. He has to accept that there is danger coming for him and by extension, those he cares for.' That was a predominant worry. If Stepan didn't want to believe who he was, then he'd not believe there was any danger to him, that Gerlitz's men were coming. 'I want time alone with him tomorrow to discuss the Horsemen and the danger. I must make him accept that at least.'

'I will go with you and with your permission, chat that through with Ellen. She wants to protect him, perhaps she'll see reason and maybe I can learn what she needs protecting from as well.'

Sweet heavens, they made a good partnership. Luce took a bite of the dried apple pie but he couldn't have told anyone what it tasted like. All of his attentions were for Wren. 'We're a good team. Talking through the day like this, is not only useful but cathartic.' It was also a subtle slap on his wrists. He'd stubbornly thrown away something beautiful and priceless when he'd ended things with her for the sake of principles. Not that it mattered any more. Their time was over. The thought turned the pie flavourless in his mouth. Losing her was becoming too real.

'Luce, what is it? Is the pie not good? You've only had a bite. Mine was delicious. If you're not going to eat it, may I have it?' She smiled, oblivious to his turmoil.

Luce forked a bite of pie and fed it to her. 'I want to ask you something, Wren. Feel free to say no,' he said solemnly. 'Would you come to bed with me?'

Her quicksilver eyes stilled. She swallowed slowly and for a moment he thought she was going to refuse. 'Is this the Horseman asking Falcon, or Luce asking Wren?' It mattered, he realised. One of them had forgiven her, the other hadn't.

'Both. I can't change our circumstances, but neither can I stop wanting you.'

Her voice was low. 'Are you sure it's what you want, Luce? You had a difficult day. You're craving connection. Something to fill the disappointment over Stepan.'

'I've never stopped wanting you, Wren. Even when I felt you'd betrayed me, I still wanted you. I shall want you until my last breath. I crave *you*, difficult day or not. It is killing me to lose you,' he confessed. She wanted to see his emotions, well there they were.

She raised his hand to her lips in reward and he felt the cares of the last hours melt away. Of all he'd lost, he'd not lost her. Not yet. There was enormous comfort in that.

'It will kill me to lose you, too, Luce.' Then she smiled. 'What are you waiting for then? Take me to bed, Luce Parkhurst.'

Chapter Nineteen

If this was a penitent, deliberately vulnerable Luce Parkhurst, she'd take some more. They wasted no time upstairs, loosening clothes as they went, tearing them off themselves and each other once they reached their room. They fell to the bed together. Mouths, arms, legs entangled. He was on her, in her. She revelled in it. In him and in the wanting. Tonight she wanted to burn. Wanted to be obliterated, consumed and he did, too. In the fire there could be forgetfulness, the past could be suppressed, the future was non-existent. To burn with him was to be free with him and to soar with him one more time.

She felt the glorious gathering of his body as she clung to him, legs wrapped tight around his hips, arms twined about his neck, hips pressed into his, bodies joined. So connected that it was impossible to say where one started and the other ended. Was she wrapped about him or was he wrapped about her? It would be too difficult to decide. She only knew this; what it felt like, what it meant to be one.

Her own release swept her fast and strong like a rainstorm breaking over a land that had been dry for too long. She gave loud, throaty voice to that deluge, the sound of her pleasure like the roll of thunder across the sky.

Afterwards came the calm. That time of peace when they lay together in a place between who they were and what had happened. Happy. Content for the moment because moments were all they could have. 'I think we may have shocked the innkeeper,' Luce said drowsily. 'I am not sure these walls are used to such sounds.'

Wren nestled closer. 'It's not even the most shocking thing about us. What would the innkeeper think if he really knew us? If he knew how we met?'

The idea made Luce chuckle. 'I'd never thought of it that way before. How *would* we tell people how we met? How would we tell our children?' He cleared his throat and affected the polite drawl of a self-important gentleman. 'Well, son, how I met your mother was like this: she was stabbing people on my doorstep at midnight in the midst of the first snowfall the Surrey Hills had seen for years.'

'It's a good thing we won't have to tell anyone then.' She gave a soft laugh in the darkness, glad for its shield. He'd only been joking but there'd been a bittersweet quality behind it, a reminder that they and whatever they'd been together would vanish when she did. There'd be no bond linking them. No remnant to remind the world that they'd been here, *together*.

'Is it a good thing, though? For us not to be together? After moments like these, days like these, I wonder if it truly is?' His hand began to move slowly up and down her arm in a thoughtful caress and she had the sense he was thinking out loud, talking to himself, arguing against his original position that they'd reached their limits. 'We are good together, as partners, as lovers. We broke the Ottoman code. We found Stepan. We thwarted two of Gerlitz's men. All in the span of a few weeks. And as lovers—' he gave a low laugh in the dark '—we match each other in appetite and passion to say the least.'

'Such things cannot last, do not last. We've already proven that, too. We've reached our limits, as you say,' she reminded gently. For all their strengths, the possibility between them had been fragile. It had been like crystal—bright and beautiful—and it had shattered at the slightest provocation.

'We ruined ourselves, Luce. It wasn't a threat from outside that broke us. It was us. It came from the inside. We did this. There are things you cannot tolerate and they are things we cannot change unless we change ourselves instead.' She did not want to do this. Did not want to lie here in the dark dissecting what could have been. Absolutely nothing could come of it. But Luce was a puzzle solver and that translated rather easily to problem solver. *He* wasn't performing a post-mortem. He was re-working the puzzle. Where she saw broken endings, he saw pieces to be refitted in new beginnings.

'Perhaps I can change. Perhaps I can accept those limits if it means having this wondrous thing between us.' His hand on her arm stilled, its grip tightening. She braced although she doubted it would offer any protection. Luce was good at overwhelming people with his charm, his reasoning. She was no more immune to him than he was to her. 'I want you to stay.' Five words said quietly in the dark but which carried with them the power to alter lives. Not just hers, but his.

She sighed, breathing in the possibility those words offered and breathed out the improbability of them actually happening. Her hand played on his chest, drawing the slow circles he liked.

'Luce, I am flattered to be asked but it can't change anything, only prolong it, which might be quite dangerous for us both. I do not want Gerlitz's men to come to Tillingbourne or the village. I do not want to watch you ride away in the spring to London knowing that you will return with a wife. I'd rather be the one who rides away first.' She mounted her protest gently.

'Come spring,' Luce broke in fiercely, his hand trapping hers on his chest. 'Nothing will change. I am not asking you to stay temporarily, Wren. I am asking you to stay for ever. As my wife, as my partner in my home and with the Horsemen.'

Luce Parkhurst had just proposed. In bed, nonetheless, and the one thought running through her head was that when something sounded too good to be true it probably was. This proposal was not the exception. She levered up on one elbow to face him, finding the strength from somewhere deep inside to let logic do the reasoning for them both. 'You need to go to London and find a wife there for the sake of your title and your estate.'

Luce rolled to his side, matching her in posture. 'Why would I do that when I have a perfectly good wifely candidate right here? One that I *can* see myself with for the rest of my life.'

'You are compromising your principles for me. I don't want to be another trade you make in life.'

'When a rule doesn't make sense it should be changed. Perhaps it was wrong to cast truth and trust in absolute molds to begin with. Why should those things be absolutes when nothing else in the world we inhabit is? Perhaps it was never right to think they should be. Maybe the Horseman in me was right all along and the man was simply too stubborn to see it.'

The words shook her. To be wanted by this man who knew exactly what she was—a street rat, an informant, a woman who'd lived a less than pristine life albeit an adventurous one—was overwhelming. 'Women like me are not viscountess material.'

'Men like me—fourth sons of third sons—are not precisely viscount material either. But here we both are.' Luce gave a shrug of his shoulder. 'I had no title until six months ago and it was most unorthodox in how it came about, as were the reasons for it. Perhaps it makes sense that such an unorthodox viscount should have a viscountess who is the same?'

'I can almost hear you smiling,' she replied wryly. 'Stop right there. You know you have a silver tongue. You can make it sound plausible in the moment. Long enough for me to say yes.'

His hand was at her hip. 'Then say yes and we can celebrate right now in bed.' There was a flirting lilt to his voice and she wanted with all of her heart to say yes. To be loved, to be cared for by this man, to be part of his family, his world, meant everything. It was beyond all expectation and for good reason.

She stroked his cheek with a soft hand. 'What happens when the moment is over? Persuasion only alters perception, Luce. It does not alter reality. Reality is solid. Immoveable. Empirical.'

He captured her hand and kissed her palm. 'Reality is what we make it. I thought we were agreed that people see what we show them.'

Heavens, he never gave up. 'I am to vanish. How can I stay? We can change my name. We can make up a history and that will fool people in society. But someone, somewhere, knows better and they will come one day. They will put you, our family, the network, all the things I care for, in danger.'

'I will protect you, our family, all of it. This is the promise Kieran made Celeste and that Caine made Mary. Now, I make it to you. A Horseman's life is inherently dangerous and the game does not stop. What you say for yourself is also true for me. In that, we are together.' He insisted on spiking her guns. 'Why should we let the potential of risk keep us from the reality of happiness?' He paused. 'Unless you *want* to vanish? I was under the impression you did not prefer it, that it was something you were compelled towards.'

'It is because it makes sense. I can be responsible for my own fate without entangling others.'

The sacrifice of one for the benefit of many. That

was how the earl had put it to her when she'd protested. Wasn't that what the whole purpose of the network was? What the purpose of the work of the Horsemen was? A few might sacrifice in order to prevent war, to stop the slaughter of thousands. Stepan's sacrifice had secured safe delivery of arms to Greece so that the cause of independence might continue.

'If I am found, Luce, no one will suffer. No one depends on me.' Perhaps she didn't have enough courage to be part of a family. How brave the Parkhursts were to love so openly, to care so deeply for one another. The risk of one was a risk to all and yet they embraced it.

Luce let go of her hand and rolled onto his back, a hand behind his head, but he did not let go of the issue. 'It is natural to choose what seems safest to you when faced with a difficult decision. Easy decisions have clear alternatives and clear consequences. This does not. One might say there is danger either way. It is just which risk you're willing to take. I'd like you to take that chance on me. On us. Aristotle says...'

'Do *not* quote Aristotle to me while my heart is breaking. I *must* refuse, Luce, and you damn well know it. What would your grandfather say?' They hadn't even discussed the earl. That was just one more ripple on a pond already flooded with ripples, with consequences, if they were to wed. 'He'd be furious. His grandson married to Falcon. To a street rat.'

'I think we should ask him instead of deciding for him. He had no problem with Kieran marrying Cabot Roan's ward—his enemy's ward—this would be a far more amicable arrangement.'

His tenacity was wearying. He would wear her down at this rate. 'May I think on it, Luce?' She moved back into his arms, hoping to put an end to the conversation. She *would* think on it, she just wasn't sure she'd come to a different conclusion. But Luce would keep them both up all night with his arguments if he thought there was a chance.

'You may think on it, but not indefinitely. I will demand an answer.'

She knew he was only half joking despite his playful tone. Damn it all, she'd hurt him. Again. He wanted her and she'd made him fight for her only to be rebuffed. But she couldn't say yes until she truly believed it was possible. She thought for a moment of Stepan and Ellen. Perhaps she wasn't the only one who was holding back.

'Luce, do you think Stepan doesn't want to be found?' she asked quietly.

'Why would you think that? Why wouldn't he

want to be found, to have the missing memories restored at least factually even if he can't restore them for himself?'

'Because he's content. Remembering means he'll have to choose. He cannot have both lives: the peaceful Quaker farmer and the gallivanting, rakish, sometimes-*violent* Horseman. He cannot have both families. You saw how he was today with those boys. They worshipped him, responded to the slightest glance from him. He has made that family his own in the short time he's been there. Our presence here threatens that.'

'*We* threaten nothing.' Luce's admonishment came softly in the dark. 'His choice has already been made. He *can't* choose them. It doesn't change what he is, what he'll always be.'

My point exactly, she thought silently. Did Luce realise he'd turned his own argument from earlier? Reality was unalterable. Stepan could forget who he was, put on a farmer's boots and tramp fields, but he would still be a Horseman. She could call herself a viscountess and be the lady of the manor, but somewhere out there someone would know she'd been a spy. The past would always be there in the background. No one walked away from anything. Except perhaps happiness.

Chapter Twenty

'You are happy here.' Luce stood in the bare fields with Stepan, both of them bareheaded in the cold. He'd thought several times about Wren's comment. That Stepan may not want to give this up, may not welcome his intrusion with the truth especially if that truth cost him the lovely Ellen Kingsley.

Stepan did not shirk from the comment. 'I am, I feel that I belong here, that I can do good here. People need me. The Kingsleys need me.'

'You have another family that needs you as well. Brothers that need you. You belong there, too.' Luce looked about the wide-open space, the spread of the land. Whoever—Dickens and Vivaldi, among others—said winter was the season of death didn't know better. Winter was a time of rebirth. Even now, the land was fortifying itself for spring. Was his brother doing the same? Was he fortifying himself, preparing to be reborn? But as who? Peter the farmer or Stepan the Horseman? He saw the appeal. Stepan had always loved the land.

Stepan was thoughtful for a while. 'You tell me that I am a hero because I jumped into the water and killed a man attempting to blow up a ship. You tell me that was a fairly normal occurrence in my life, that I worked in diplomacy and such things were *de rigueur*. I don't want to be that person any more. I want to stay here. Ellen and I discussed it last night.'

That was not an acceptable answer. Luce kicked at the hard earth with the toe of his boot. 'You would stay and live a lie? Would you be comfortable with the ethics of that? Of dragging Andrew and Phillip and Ellen into that? It's one thing to live a life because you don't know any better, but you do. You *know* you're not Peter. You know you weren't born to *this* life. Even if you don't believe me, you know you were washed up on shore. That you came from somewhere else and that you *are* someone else. Peter the farmer is a pretence.'

'A man has a right to make his life over. I have been given a second chance.'

'Some men, not you,' Luce ground out, his anger rising. It was an impossible situation to stand here and *see* his brother talking to him but denying his identity altogether. This man was and yet was not Stepan.

'There is more to it than what I shared yesterday at the table. There are things I did not want to say in front of them.' He held Stepan's gaze, forcing his brother to look at him, willing him to see the undeniable resemblance between them. 'There are others looking for you. A man named Gerlitz is seeking revenge. The man you killed in Wapping was his cousin. Gerlitz has discovered someone who could be Stepan Parkhurst is living here. His men are coming. They know who you really are. You can't pretend them away. They will not listen when you tell them you want to leave that life. There is no leaving the game, only surviving it, as we used to say.'

Luce did not think he'd ever done something so frustrating. This gave new meaning to the expression banging one's head against a brick wall. Was he even making a dent? It was heart wrenching, too. He and Stepan had once been so close. That was gone now as long as Stepan didn't remember.

'I will surrender myself to them if I must in order to protect Ellen and the boys,' Stepan said nobly. It was exactly what Stepan would say. Emotion rose.

'That will not deter them.' Luce laid out another hard truth. 'You killed the man's cousin. He is not beyond destroying something or someone you hold dear in front of you before he destroys you. There are things worse than death. Death is easy, dying for a cause, for a loved one is simple.' Stepan seemed to blanch at that. Progress at last, perhaps. Luce pushed his small advantage.

'We can get you help. There are specialists who deal in memory loss. Come with us, we can be in London the day after tomorrow. We can go to Sandmore. You can see Grandfather. Or we can go to Willow Park and see our parents. The familiar might do you a world of good in remembering.'

'And leave Ellen unprotected?' Stepan countered.

'She's of no interest to Gerlitz without you. Leaving will protect her. The farther away you are from her, the safer she is. We can protect you in London or at Sandmore.' Luce made the arguments patiently, methodically. A flicker of hope sparked. If he could lead Stepan towards the logic of this choice, he might be able save him, reach him.

'That's not the only protection she needs. Who will protect her from Hartlett if I am gone?' He slanted a scolding glance at Luce. 'It's not fancy living here. It's not all daggers in the dark, but we do have a life here. Our own dramas are not so insignificant. Ellen has been running the family farm since her parents' deaths but the community would like to see her wed. Her brothers are young, too young to be the men of the house. She needs a man about the place. Hartlett's a widower. His land abuts Ellen's. The community feels it would be a good match, or at least they did before I came along.'

Ah, that explained Hartlett's sour face yesterday and his willingness to bring Luce out. Hartlett would befriend anyone who helped rid the place of his competition for the comely Ellen and the wealth that would come in joining the properties.

'Ellen needs me, and I need her. I feel complete when I am with her.' There was a flash of sharpness in Stepan's gaze. 'I do not have a wife or an arrangement with anyone do I?' It was the first point of interest he'd taken in his identity.

'No, there's no one like that waiting for you. Do you have an understanding with Ellen?' It was time to ask that question now that his brother had brought it up.

'No, nothing formal, but she is dear to me. I had hoped to discuss intentions with her come spring. I can't live here indefinitely without declaring myself. It isn't fair to her reputation. But your arrival has complicated that.'

Luce refused to say he was sorry. 'My arrival will be the least of your complications if Gerlitz finds you here.'

'What of the woman you're travelling with? Miss Audley? Are you betrothed?'

'I have proposed, but she's not accepted. Yet,' Luce added hastily. 'I have laid the world at her feet and still she resists even though our feelings are mutual.'

'Have you said the words?' Stepan asked. 'Have you said, "I love you"? Women set a great store by those three words.'

Had he told her? He'd thought the words, he'd admitted them to himself. He'd certainly shown her time and again the esteem in which he held her. There'd been gifts and he'd worshipped her quite completely with his body.

'I don't know if three words would change Wren's mind. She, um…' How to explain why she resisted? 'Well, it's complicated is all.'

'Love is always complicated.' Stepan gave him a man-to-man smile and for a moment Luce had his brother back. This was like the conversations they used to have.

Luce cleared his throat. What would Grandfather say if he had to tell the old man he'd failed to bring Stepan back? 'Why don't you bring Ellen, Anne and the boys to London?' Luce lobbied. 'The farm won't need minding for a few months yet.'

'You are relentless.' Stepan laughed. 'I have no worries that Miss Audley will be yours with all that tenacity on your side.' Luce hoped he was right.

Stepan had put it perfectly when he said Ellen completed him. Wren completed *him*, something that had not been driven home to him in its entirety until yesterday, watching her with the Kingsleys, subtly supporting him with her observations, lending him her strength with her touch, her eyes, knowing what he needed before he had to ask. Because she knew that he would not ask, asking was not *his* strength. Perhaps she knew that so well because she was fiercely independent, too, not wanting anyone to be inconvenienced for her sake. The real inconvenience though would be losing her. No, not inconvenience but tragedy. The real *tragedy* would be losing her. In her, he found the wholeness he'd been chasing all his life.

'We've been out here for a while.' Stepan clapped him on the shoulder. 'Shall we go in? The ladies will be wondering what we've gotten up to.'

Luce fell into stride with his brother, matching him step for step, another reminder of their similarity, their innate synchronicity. There was urgency in their steps. Perhaps his brother was as eager to get back to Ellen as he was to get back to Wren? He had told her so much, made so many arguments but perhaps Stepan was right. For all he'd told her, he hadn't told her enough. For all of his words, he hadn't given her the right ones. I love you. He did love her.

He felt Stepan's hand on his arm. 'Are you expecting anyone?' Stepan asked. 'There's horses outside that aren't yours.'

'No, no one.' Luce felt cold fear steal over him. Gerlitz was here. He knew it. 'Where are the boys and Anne?'

'Helping at a neighbour's.' They exchanged knowing looks. There was only Wren and Ellen in the house.

Luce's mind was already sorting through his options. 'There are four horses, so four men. Perhaps two are stationed as lookouts. We have to take them out quietly before they can raise the alarm. The other two are in the house.' Wren would have her stiletto. Would she be able to use it without endangering Ellen? 'Do you have a weapon on you?' Stepan shook his head.

'Then our first stop is the barn. Grab a pitchfork, lumber, a scythe, whatever is handy,' Luce instructed. 'Lead us in, you'll know the best way to reach the barn without detection.'

His brother nodded grimly. 'We can't be seen from the house if we come up on the west side.'

It was slow going, slower than Luce would have liked. The distance suddenly seemed infinite. But there was no margin for error. They ran where they could, they crouched when they had to and they made the barn without detection. Stepan armed himself with a butchering knife. They approached the cottage cautiously, careful to avoid detection from the horses. There was no one stationed outside. Perhaps Gerlitz's men counted on the horses to raise the alarm.

'All four must be inside.' Luce didn't feel comfortable with that assessment. It seemed off to him. These were professionals. They would not set themselves up to be taken by surprise purposely. There ought to be a sentry, someone outside. But where?

'Do we go in hard and fast, take them by surprise? Capitalise on disruption?' Stepan asked.

Luce shook his head. 'Something in between. We go in fast, grab the man closest to the door, make him a hostage, survey the room and start negotiating. Show no mercy. Every word you speak will matter. If you say it, you must mean it. Be prepared to carry it out.'

Stepan nodded. 'I'll go in first and do the grab. You negotiate.'

A pistol cocked ominously behind them and a rough voice spoke. 'A good plan but I know a better one. Why don't you gentlemen step inside and join us for tea? I think you'll know some of our guests. Lovely ladies.'

That would not do. They'd have no surprise, no negotiating power. They'd all be trapped inside in a very small space. No room to manoeuvre. Out here, Luce had a chance. From the sound of the man's voice, he was close. Too close and too confident in the advantage his gun gave him. Luce wagered he could reach him before he recovered from his shock.

Luce whirled and charge, lowering his head like a battering ram and catching the man in the stomach. The gun fired into the air. The man went down dropping the weapon as he fell. Luce grabbed the weapon, wielding it like a club and delivering a blow that rendered the man unconscious. 'One down,' he said grimly but Stepan had melted away, looking for another way in, another way to Ellen.

'That's all you'll get, Horseman.' The cottage door opened and a roughly dressed man emerged, holding Wren against him, a pistol to her head. Wren was pale, her quicksilver eyes wide, her jaw set with determination. 'Unless of course, you don't value her. Then you might get past me.' He gave a shrug as if his life and Wren's life were of no consequence. 'Of course, we have the other woman, too. Get past me, and her throat will be slit before you can reach her.

So, rushing me doesn't seem to accomplish anything for you.' He offered his analysis with a toothless grin.

'What do you want?' Luce asked in even tones. 'She is nothing to you. Let her go and negotiate with me.'

The man spat. 'She *is* something. She is Falcon. Not the same as a Horseman of course, but still. Falcon has betrayed us before. She's the one that got word to you about the sabotage on the Greek arms. She got our boss's cousin killed. She killed our comrades a few weeks ago.'

'Got two more of them just a few days back,' Wren managed through gritted teeth. 'You're running out of friends.'

Luce stifled a chuckle. He didn't want her bravado to get her killed right in front of him.

'Shut your mouth, missy. You're in no position to talk.' The man wrenched her arm and Luce saw her wince. 'You save her, you lose the other one. You'll never get to both in time.'

Wren held his gaze and Luce feared she was saying goodbye, that she had concluded as he had that he couldn't rush this man, couldn't draw his knife before the man could fire. He might get the man afterwards, but it wouldn't matter. It wouldn't save her. 'Take me instead,' Luce offered the trade, his arms held out wide in surrender. 'You've got two Horsemen here. Surely that equals the score.'

'Or maybe, while you two gents are talking, a girl can save herself.' Wren's eyes flashed and she moved with lightning speed. A foot to his instep, an arm coming up to smash into her captor's arm at short range and full force, jarring the gun loose but not before it fired. Luce half expected to feel the bullet hit him as he ran forward, his knife out. But there was nothing, not even the wind of passage. Stepan was behind him, then pushing past him into the cottage with a guttural yell to dispatch the man inside.

A blade glinted in Wren's hand and her captor fell, clutching himself. But Wren fell, too, stumbling away and grabbing at the side of the cottage for purchase, her hands red, blood everywhere.

'No! Wren!' Luce lurched towards her but the fourth man spilled from the cottage, blocking him. Luce dispatched him with a ferocious stab and shoved him aside. He wanted only to get to Wren. Wren who was down. Wren who was bleeding. Wren whom he loved but hadn't told.

He knelt beside her. There was so much blood. Dear God, the bullet. His first thought had been she had not been fast enough to divert it's trajectory. 'Are you hit?' He gathered her to him, his hands running over her looking for the injury. 'Are you hurt?'

'It's not my blood,' she managed shakily. 'It's his. At least it's mostly his. I think.' She sagged against him and real terror took Luce.

'Luce!' Stepan was beside him. Ellen with him, frightened but unharmed. 'Is she…?'

'Fainted,' Luce said with a conviction he forced himself to believe. He lifted Wren in his arms. 'She might have been shot. I can't find an injury, though.'

'Bring her inside.' Ellen led the way, stepping over the carnage and clearing the table. 'Lay her down here. I'll bring a lamp.'

For Luce it was too reminiscent of first meeting her—Wren, bleeding and lifeless in his arms. He'd been drawn to her even then and that attraction had only grown.

'Wren,' he whispered her name in desperation as he laid her down. 'Don't you dare die on me.'

'Look.' Stepan nudged him. 'It's just a graze here at her hairline. She'll be fine.'

Luce wasn't sure *he'd* be fine. The bullet had come *that* close to her. Her manoeuvre had nearly gotten her killed. If she'd been a bit slower, her aim less sure…it didn't bear thinking on. What did bear thinking on was everything he wanted to say to her when she awoke, starting with how dare she pull such a foolish stunt and ending with I love you.

Chapter Twenty-One

She loved him. She was *not* going to lose him, not this way—in the heat of battle to a foe dedicated to cutting down the most noble of men she'd ever encountered. A man noble enough to love her, to want to marry her. Wren stirred, fighting with herself to wake up. Luce was likely to have a few things to say about this afternoon. But so did she. Best to get it over with so they could move on to more important things, things this afternoon had thrown into sharp relief for her. Besides, there were worse things than opening one's eyes and finding Luce Parkhurst hovering over them, every emotion he felt unleashed at last and reflected in his dark eyes.

'Wren!' She felt the weight of the bed take him as she looked into those dark eyes, a new sense of relief swamping her. The man had tried to die for her today. If she'd hesitated a second longer he might have been successful. 'How do you feel?' He held a mug of tea for her. 'Ellen put willow bark in it.' Wren shook her head. She was not interested in sipping.

'I am fine. A little sore, my head hurts a bit.' The gun had gone off close to her ear and the sound had been literally quite deafening. 'Are you well?' She looked him over, seeking any sign of injury and finding none.

'Yes.' Luce gripped her hand. 'You had me so worried—'

She interrupted before he could get a full head of steam worked on. '*You* had *me* worried. What fool notion was going through your head? You are never to do such a thing again, not for me.' She harangued. 'You could have been killed and where would that have left me? I wouldn't have anyone to marry.' The quickest way to end an argument was to take away the conflict. There was nothing to fight against and it had completely disarmed Luce for the moment.

'Marry me? Do you mean that?' A ghost of a smile took his mouth but she did not believe for a moment that he would not extract his own scold for her actions today. 'Love may be unconditional, but I am not. There are conditions I need to impose for my own personal sanity. You are never to try such a stunt again. Second, you are never to risk your life for mine. If you can abide by those conditions then

I can abide by yours. This is not a jest, Wren. Today, when I saw that pistol at your temple…' His voice broke and she levered herself up, instinct compelling her to reach for him.

'Luce, it worked, I am fine. You are fine. Nothing bad happened,' she soothed. He should not be in agony when she was near.

'But it could have.' He had her face between his hands, his eyes two dark pools of intention and emotion.

'But it didn't. You have to trust me, Luce, or this is never going to work. We live in a dangerous world and that isn't going to change. Marriage means there will be no retirement for either of us. We will have to find a way to balance life and the game. To balance Luce and Wren with the Falcon and the Horseman. Minute by minute, moment by moment. Those are my conditions. Can you meet them?' she asked softly. This too was not said in jest nor as a mere romantic gesture. There must be this between them. Her breath caught and held. This was the point of no return for them. A real test of their ability to commit to each other beyond words. If he could not do this, she would have no choice but to leave.

Luce gave a low laugh. 'I knew early on when you arrived that life with you would be a series of compromises and I was not wrong.'

'Did you really think that?' She smiled. 'And what do you think now? Is it worth it?' She hoped it would be.

Luce nodded, touching his forehead to hers. 'If a man says he'll do anything for love—and I *do* love you, Wren Audley—he'd best demonstrate that when the need arises.' He whispered wickedly, 'I am sure you are aware that my need arises quite often when you're around.'

'As does mine.' She kissed him then, this wondrous man who would be her husband, but more importantly would be her partner.

That partnership would begin the balancing of work and pleasure immediately. There was the issue of Stepan to resolve and there was the earl to inform about their impending marriage. Both were considerations of the heart and considerations of the practical as well.

Wren watched Luce walk outside into the yard with his brother to clean up the carnage; three dead men to bury and one unconscious man who would need to be transported to the local jail. Amid the work, the brothers would have a chance to talk one last time. Luce would not waste the opportunity to press his case. Surely, today's events proved the need to return with them along with the necessity of Stepan actively acknowledging who he was and doing all he could to retrieve his memories. But when Luce returned two hours later, she knew from a single glance his arguments had been unsuccessful. Her heart went out to him. This would be a difficult blow for Luce who both loved his brother and was not used to failure.

He'd failed. Luce returned to the cottage with his brother, the long shadows presaging evening starting to fall. His time was up. He needed to get Wren back to the inn and travelling in the dark was less than ideal. They'd done it yesterday but she'd not been hurt yesterday. Inside the cottage, Luce looked at Ellen and then at his brother. Those two were in accord on this and he could not penetrate either of their obstinance. Still, he had to try one last time.

'Ellen, are you certain you will not come? After today, you can see the danger is real.' Luce offered his plea. 'The violence is real.' Quakers did not hold with violence and yet Ellen held with his brother. 'There is no guarantee Gerlitz's men won't come again.' And he wouldn't be here to protect them, to warn them.

Stepan stepped up beside him. 'Then you'll send the earl's men as we discussed,' he said firmly. 'You will not sway Ellen. We are together on this.' Luce felt his hand on his shoulder, offering a brotherly squeeze. 'I know this is not the resolution you wanted, but I am not prepared to give it. Not at this time.'

'Gerlitz, all of it, is a hydra,' Luce argued with his brother. 'Caine brought down Cabot Roan, systematically dismantled his arms empire. It has positively impacted the sale of arms to British enemies, but it still isn't enough to stop them from coming for revenge. Roan's business partners lost money and lost family members, and they will have their own private vendettas to wage long into the future. We chop off one head only to have two more grow.'

'I know,' Stepan said patiently. 'I can do very little about that, but I can do a lot here and this is where I want to be. For now.' Ellen moved to stand beside him and took his hand in a gesture of undivided loyalty and unity. Luce glanced at Wren. He understood a little something about those things.

'Very well. Wren and I will leave for Sandmore in the morning. Our grandfather will post a discreet company of men to patrol the area so that you are as safe as we can make you until this particular threat has passed.' He reached into his coat pocket, withdrawing several pound notes and placed them on the table. 'Use this for whatever you need and when you are ready, use some of it for passage to London. Parkhurst House is your home and it's always open to you. Or come to Sandmore if you prefer the country. Grandfather would love to see you.' He let his gaze offer the imperative behind that. *Grandfather would love to see you once more before he passes. Don't wait too long.*

Business completed. Luce drew a steadying breath. There was nothing left to say now except goodbye. 'I don't want to leave you here,' he confessed to Stepan as he drew his brother into an embrace. 'I lost you once already.'

Stepan hugged him in return although Luce knew it didn't mean the same to him, this man who was his brother in fact but who felt no emotional connection to him, hardly knew him beyond the acquaintance of a few days. This man would be glad to see him gone. He'd disrupted this man's life. For him, order could now be restored. But for Luce the upheaval would continue.

Outside, Luce helped Wren mount before swinging up on Vercingetorix. Overhead early evening stars made their faint appearance. Wren leaned between their horses and took his hand. 'Think of the good, Luce. All is not lost,' she said quietly.

And he did. All the way back to the inn and in the days of travel that lay ahead two thoughts sustained him. Wren Audley was going to marry him and his brother was alive, which ought to be miracles enough for any man in a single lifetime.

It was difficult to tell if Grandfather agreed with him on the impact of those miracles. His grandfather sat for a long while in silence, letting those three words *Stepan is alive* hang in the air, while the fire flickered and popped in the study at Sandmore on a cold February afternoon.

This room had been a part of the most important events of his life. He and his brothers had taken lessons in here on occasion growing up. It was where Grandfather had solemnly invited each of them into his network as Horsemen when they'd come of age. He and his brothers had joked between themselves that some grandfathers gave their grandsons watches when they entered adulthood but their grandfather had given them a calling. Despite the joking, Luce remembered being feverishly jealous of the three brothers who'd gone before him. How he'd coveted the day he'd been taken in and given his place alongside those brothers. After years of trying to catch up, he was finally one of them. This had also been the room in which Grandfather had shared the news of their titles—the latest milestone to be passed here.

'I felt such news should be delivered in person,' Luce gently broke in when the silence showed no sign of ending. 'We came straight from Southend-on-Sea.'

His grandfather turned his dark gaze in Luce's direction, his eyes bright with unshed tears. 'It should, my boy. You were right to bring it in person. Forgive me my silence. So profound is my relief, so overwhelmed am I at your news. I had hoped, of course, but hope can be dangerous and disappointing. Especially at my age.' He reached for a handkerchief with a hand that trembled just the slightest.

His age was showing. Some would say at last. One did not attain almost eighty-nine years of life without acquiring some wear. Wren had been right about that. He looked tired. There were bags at his eyes that no amount of sleep would cure and he was thin. A tea tray had been brought but he'd only eaten a small sandwich.

'Are you upset that I could not bring him back?' That one failure had burdened his heart the entire trip.

Grandfather shook his head. Despite his weakness a moment ago, his voice was strong now, his mind clear. 'No. For the network, it is unfortunate. The Horsemen need him. We can help him recall his memories, get him fully healed. All of it would be easier if he were here. His family needs him but this news will definitely suffice. It will mean everything to your parents, your brothers and sister. You were right to leave him money and to tell him we'll send men. We have to trust now that Stepan will come when he's ready.' Grandfather reached for his hand. 'My boy, you did it. You brought him back to us as best you could. We know he is alive and for now that is enough, more than enough.'

It was. Luce had come to accept that on the journey. Wren had helped, though, reminding him of what truly mattered. Happiness, contentment, were not to be taken lightly but enjoyed. Stepan deserved that as well. 'I didn't do it alone,' Luce cautiously broached the next miracle he wanted to share. 'Wren was an enormous part of this.'

'As she should have been.' Grandfather was stern. 'She was not to have told you at all. I shall have to have words with her. You were not to be worried in case it was a goose chase.'

'No, you will not have words with her over it,' Luce said protectively, although he doubted Wren would appreciate the defence if she was in the room. After greeting Grandfather, Wren had insisted this interview be conducted between just the two of them and had taken herself off to refresh herself. 'As you know, I can be quite persuasive.'

Grandfather gave him a sharp eye. 'Exactly how

persuasive, my boy? You know she is to retire, leave the game. I have it all arranged.'

Luce gathered his courage. Even at thirty-two, it was hard to stare down his grandfather. 'Those plans have changed. We plan to marry.'

Again, the long silence. He'd managed to overwhelm his grandfather twice in the span of an hour. Luce waited. His grandfather gave a slow smile, his eye twinkling. 'You aren't going to *ask* for her hand? You're just going to take it?' His tone suggested he wasn't entirely displeased and it suggested something else Luce wasn't quite sure he understood yet.

'I am not taking anything.' Luce chuckled. 'You know Wren. No one takes a thing from her. This was our decision. Together. We have decided to wed.'

Grandfather seemed to think it over. 'She understands what this means? No retirement, likely ever.'

Luce nodded. 'She never wanted that. She said you wanted to see her protected. She couldn't bear to disagree with you after all you've done for her. If protection was your goal, you have succeeded in that. I will be there.'

'So you will.' Grandfather's gaze was steady. 'That pleases me greatly. More than you know. She told you how we met on Audley Street? I was in town for the first time since your grandmother had passed. I had my work as always and the war kept me busy, but my heart was empty. You boys were grown, off to school in your case and Stepan's, off to the Continent with the other two. My heart needed to be filled and there she was, the prettiest, most fragile-looking child I'd ever seen. Most unique, too, after being surrounded with all the dark-haired, dark-eyed Parkhursts. I'd never seen hair like that. She was an angel with her hand in my pocket. The universe moved at that moment and I knew I should care for her, take her from the streets. It was easy to see what would become of her if she stayed.'

His grandfather leaned forward. 'I've never told anyone this, not even Wren. I felt as if your grandmother was with me, her voice in my ear saying, *Henry, save the child. Let her fill your heart.* And so I did. The only time I've ever done anything so rash.'

Luce thought that was debatable but at least now he knew Wren was the only orphan he'd taken in. He needn't worry on that account.

'Now, she will truly be a part of our family. You are both dear to me. This fills me with wordless joy, Lucien. The circle is complete.' Grandfather smiled contentedly.

The circle *was* complete. That elusive something Luce had not been able to put his finger on immediately became clear. Why, the old schemer...

'You planned this,' Luce posited his burgeoning hypothesis.

Grandfather gave him a sly look. 'One cannot plan anything, really. One can only put events in motion and let nature take its course. I did not plan for her to be chased and stabbed. That note sent fear through me, to think she'd been harmed. But I knew she was in good hands with you. Nor did I plan for Gerlitz's men to come after you so soon, but her injury worked against me there. Gerlitz had time to regroup.'

'But you did plan on her telling me about Stepan, despite your words to the contrary to her and again just now to me.' Luce caught his grandfather out.

'I counted on you persuading her,' Grandfather admitted.

'Just as you counted on us falling in love? How could you have been so sure so little time would have been enough to make the connection?' But he knew how. Wren's words came back to him: Parkhursts fell fast and hard.

'Count on nothing, my boy. You know that.' Grandfather admonished. 'Assumptions are dangerous, but I did want to give you a chance to meet when the time was right.' It had been right. Luce could see that now in hindsight. He was facing a matrimonial deadline and Wren had been facing the danger of being recognised. She needed protection, more than Grandfather could offer her. But Luce could provide it. In lieu of that, disappearance would have to do.

'Wren suspects nothing,' Luce said.

'Neither did you.'

'We worried about your approval,' Luce scolded. That had been another burden he'd carried on the journey.

'I always approve of love, my boy. Kieran's wedding should have proven that.' Grandfather rubbed his hands on his thighs. 'Now, when's the wedding to be and where? I'd like it to be here at the bride's home, at Sandmore, as soon as possible—which means as soon as the family can gather.'

At the bride's home. Wren would like to hear that. But Luce had not liked that last part about 'as soon as possible'.

'Why the haste? Are you ill?'

Grandfather gave him a warm smile. 'I am not ill, my boy. I am old. All time is precious now. But don't you worry. I only thought to suggest haste because I'll be busy this spring planning my eighty-ninth birthday,' he added cheekily and Luce laughed.

'Then yes, if earlier is better for your very busy calendar, we'll do it "as soon as possible". Thank you.' Luce rose. 'If you will excuse me, I would like to go and tell Wren the news.'

'Shall I write to the family with your news?' Grandfather said, waving him off. 'My afternoon is clear and I am guessing that very shortly yours won't be.' There was a roguish gleam in his eye. 'I will see the two of you at dinner and we'll celebrate.'

'He said that? Really? We're to be married in the bride's home?' Wren was teary eyed as she lay in his arms, as Luce knew she would be.

'He did say that.' And much more. Maybe someday, he'd tell her about Grandfather's shenanigans. 'He also said we should wed as soon as possible. I'll see to it that we have a special license, but you'll need to see to the rest. Plan whatever kind of ceremony you want, whatever decorations you want.'

She sighed against him. 'I wish we could have snow so we could drive off in your sleigh.'

'We're too close to the sea, I'm afraid. No snow for you, not this late in the season.' He held her close with a laugh. 'But I am glad to hear you're readjusting your perspective on winter.'

'I've adjusted my perspective on many things since I met you: marriage, love, home, family. These are all things I never thought I could have. But you've made that possible. You're quite the most extraordinary man I've ever met and now you are mine for ever.' She looked up at him, her eyes silvery, her hair tangled from love-making. She'd never looked more glorious to him than she did right now—a picture of love, of happiness, of for ever.

Luce would have to amend those words just ten days later as the wood doors opened at the back of the Sandmore chapel and Wren stood there for a moment framed in late winter sunlight. She made the most spectacular winter bride in a gown of pale blue velvet that had belonged to his grandmother, her hair loose, hanging in wavy tresses down her back. His grandfather stepped forward beside Wren and presented his arm for a slow, stately walk down the aisle, offering everyone ample time to appreciate the glory of the bride, especially Luce.

He mentally added this picture of her to his ever-growing collection of his wife. His wife! The thought, the words, would not cease to fill him with satisfaction, with contentment. It would be official shortly although he'd thought of her as his wife since the day she'd accepted his proposal.

The last days leading up to the wedding had been filled with unexpected joy, watching her with his family as they'd arrived, piece by piece. The first to arrive had been his parents. His mother had taken one look at Wren and swept her into her arms, declaring, 'Another daughter to love! One can never have too many, not with these boys around.'

Caine and Mary had arrived next from Newmarket, Mary starting to show the signs of their blessed event expected this summer. Mary had been the one who'd helped Wren decide on a wedding dress. Guenevere, Devlin and the new baby had braved the journey, surprising Grandfather with a request to do the baby's christening at Sandmore before they returned home. Kieran and Celeste had the furthest to come, all the way from Wales. They'd only arrived last night to complete the reunion although they'd all been together at Christmas not so long ago. Celeste had hugged Wren, eyes glistening with gratitude. 'The boys told me what you did for me. Thank you, Sister.'

Luce knew how much that one word would mean to Wren, who'd craved a family, who yearned for siblings. She had those aplenty now in her three sisters and three brothers by marriage. She had new cousins and aunts and uncles by marriage as well. Luce had made her a family tree to keep it all straight as a wedding gift. He'd left blank spaces on the tree, too, for a future that was rapidly approaching. Looking around at the faces of his family it was hard to believe it had only been two months since they'd all been together. So much had changed. And for the better. He'd found Wren, and love and new hope. Stepan was alive and there was hope in that, too, that someday they'd all be together again. But for now, for this moment, when he took Wren's hand from Grandfather, he had more than enough in the present to be thankful for, more than any one man had a right to. He'd not thought to find a wife let alone love in unprepossessing Little Albury.

'What are you thinking?' Wren whispered, eyes shining, as the vicar started the service.

Luce grinned. 'That love found me when I least expected it and where I least expected it.'

'On your doorstep?' she murmured with a laugh that earned a censorious look from the vicar. Luce exchanged a conspiratorial grin with Wren. This was the beginning of a life that would be unconventional in all ways. How could it be otherwise when the fourth Horseman married Falcon? Together they were destined to fly. And if they fell, and they probably would on occasion as both of them were too stubborn to prevent it, well they'd do that together too. They'd waited their whole lives for this. This was their time and there wasn't a moment to lose in claiming it.

Epilogue I

April

No expense had been spared for the Earl of Sandmore's eighty-ninth birthday fete held at his estate amid the glory of spring time in England. Wood anemone, cowslips, the dog violets and the roundhead rampion were all in full bloom. The sky was blue overhead and all was right in Luce Parkhurst's world because he strolled the garden paths of Sandmore with his wife beside him. Somewhere ahead of them, his brothers strolled with their wives, their laughter occasionally reaching them on the breeze, but Luce had lagged behind on purpose, wanting a moment alone with Wren.

'Does it feel good to be back?' he asked, stopping to pluck a bluebell and tuck it behind her ear. It still was a marvel to him that she was his, or as she would say, he was hers. It was a marvel, too, to be able to share Sandmore with her as a place they'd both grown up. Coming to Sandmore for Grandfather's birthday had been a chance to retrace those youthful steps together—the lake, the garden paths and the school room on the third floor.

'Yes, it is good to visit but it's not home, Luce,' she offered quietly. 'Tillingbourne is home. It is where I belong because you are there, because our family is there.'

He lifted her hand to his lips and kissed it. Tillingbourne was still under restoration but renovations aside, the place had undergone a transformation over the past few months. Sharing space did that to a place. There were more cut flowers in vases and fewer Holland covers on the furniture. There was more noise, too. Wren had turned the abbey into a gathering place for the women in the village, a place where they were as likely to meet to knit blankets as they were to learn to how to defend themselves should the need ever arise. Luce had caught her on several occasions giving tips in self-defence in the ballroom.

There were children, too. Wren had insisted that no woman be left out of her gatherings because she needed child care. Luce didn't mind. If he needed solitude he could always escape to his library and Wren would know where to find him.

'You miss Tillingbourne and it's only been a week,' he commented.

'A very busy week,' she countered. 'We travelled. We had the family party, then the public party.' Luce had presented the memoir to his grandfather at the family gathering. He'd read the introduction out loud after supper and managed to bring a few tears to his grandfather's eyes.

'Is being a Parkhurst all you hoped?' Luce teased gently. In between the parties, there'd been long afternoons with lawn games and late nights as he and his brothers and their wives talked over endless card games. It was grand to be together, but Luce understood. He, too, would be eager to leave tomorrow and return to Tillingbourne, to their life.

'More than I hoped.' She smiled and took his hand. 'You've given me so many gifts over the past months, Luce. Being part of your family is one of the greatest.' Her eyes glistened and he raised a thumb to wipe them away. She'd been emotional this week, crying at Grandfather's party, tearing up as she'd hugged her new sisters in-law upon arrival. His stiletto-wielding wife had sentimental depths. It was sweet.

'But yes, it is a lot. I am amazed Grandfather is still on his feet. I'm exhausted.' She slid him a shy look. 'Perhaps I'll need to get used to that.'

Luce knit his brow. 'It won't always be exhausting being a Parkhurst.' He hoped that wasn't a lie. It might be. The Horsemen would be called forth again at some point in the future—a week from now, a month from now, no one ever really knew. But they had come to terms with that.

Wren gave a soft smile. 'No, not always, but it will be for a few months. I have it on good authority from Mary that the first trimester can be tiring.'

Mary was due in the summer with her and Caine's first child. She was in blooming good looks and had spent most of the week toting Guenevere's baby about on her hip. Practicing, she called it... Wait. Luce's mind came to a full stop.

'You have it on good authority? What exactly does that mean?' Luce began to put other pieces together. The crying from a woman who was not given to tears, the exhaustion from a woman who was never tired. There'd been other little giveaways, too, in bed.

'You're the problem solver. Put it together.' She smiled impishly.

'Are *we* expecting a child?' he asked, unable to keep amazed disbelief from his voice.

Her smile disappeared. 'Is it too soon?'

'No, not at all,' Luce rushed to reassure her. 'It is an embarrassment of riches. A wife, a child, a home, love, happiness. I've been gifted these things all at once.' His own eyes stung. He wrapped her in his arms and held on tight while they both shed tears of joy. 'When do we think our child might make its arrival?' He was already doing the math, already guessing, already impatient to meet him or her.

'November.'

A wedding night baby. Or before, Luce thought, remembering the night she'd taken him astride. *For everything there is an equal and opposite reaction.* Indeed there was. Perhaps by November, Stepan might be here. He hoped every day that Stepan would choose to return, but for now it had been an immense relief to the family just to know he was alive.

'Do you want to tell our family before we leave?' she asked. He could hear them up ahead. Little Jamie was squealing with delight as his father tossed him high.

He nodded. 'Yes, if it's all right with you.'

'Then let's catch up to them.' She tugged at his hand and drew him down the path towards the laughter and voices. He went willingly. He wanted his brothers to know, he wanted to celebrate with them, with his parents, with his grandfather. That's what families were for and he had one of the best. It was high time he embraced that fully.

Epilogue II

Late October, 1827

'I think it's time.' Stepan had waited until the boys and Anne had gone up to the loft. Dinner was done, the dishes put away. He could have Ellen to himself for this discussion without any interruption.

Ellen untied her apron and sat down slowly across from him at the table, her eyes meeting his. 'You've been restless this past week. Have you remembered anything more?' She did not pester him about remembering. He was always thankful for that kindness especially after the visit last winter, which had answered their questions even if it hadn't jarred his memories loose.

'No, nothing new.' Since Lucien Parkhurst had left, there'd been dreams, though. Still, dreams weren't memories, not exactly.

She reached for his hand and kept silent. She had

a good instinct for that—for knowing when to talk and when to wait for him to do it.

'The crops are in. There is nothing more we can do for the farm. I think we should go to the family for the holidays. Perhaps see a specialist in London.'

'You feel guilty,' Ellen said softly.

'Yes. It is not right to make my family suffer, even if I don't remember them. I have parents, Ellen. A grandfather. They believed I was dead, lost to them. I cannot imagine the grief of losing a child, even a grown child. By not going to them, I feel I am perpetuating that grief, that suffering, for them.'

He reached for her hands, gripping them in his need for reassurance. This decision had not been lightly made. 'It does not need to change anything, Ellen.' This was the argument he'd convinced himself of in the long nights. 'We will go and then we will come back and all will be as it was. We can bring Anne and the boys. Lucien left plenty of money.'

Ellen gave a solemn nod. 'I know you think nothing will change but it will. You have another family whether you remember them or not. Lucien said you were a hero. If you go to them, everything will change. You are not normally naïve. Be honest about that with yourself.'

'I do not *will* for this to change,' Stepan assured her.

'It may not be up to your will.'

'If we face it together, we will survive it. I don't mean to lose you, Ellen. You needn't fear on that account.' Maybe he could not control reactions to his reappearance, or the things others did, but he could control his own heart and his heart belonged with her.

Ellen drew a deep breath and he knew what it cost her. She'd never been beyond Southend-on-Sea in all her years. 'I knew this moment would come. If you think we should go now, then we will go. We'll make preparations in the morning.'

'Thank you, Ellen.' She'd given him the strength to take the next step. He was going home for the holidays to a place he didn't remember, stepping into a life he no longer knew, but he was doing it with the woman he loved and doing it *for* her. He could offer her nothing until his past was resolved.

THE END.... FOR NOW.

* * * * *

MILLS & BOON®

Coming next month

CINDERELLA'S CHARADE WITH THE DUKE
Jeanine Englert

'I would like to extend your offer of employment not only as Millie's governess, but also as my fake betrothed. I think a Lady Penelope Denning would do nicely,' he said, his words rushing out. 'But if you prefer another name, I am open to such possibilities. Do you think you could do that?'

She could have sworn he said something about pretending to be his betrothed, but surely she had misheard every word. 'I am sorry, Your Grace. I do not think I understood you properly. I would love to remain on as Lady Millie's governess, but that last part... Did you say you wish for me, an orphan from Stow, to also pretend to be your betrothed as some other person entirely?'

A beat of silence passed and then His Grace sat back in his chair, his hands sliding down the curved wooden armrests before covering the painted gold flowers at the ends. He met her gaze. 'Yes, Miss Potts, that is *exactly* what I wish for you to do.'

Not even Ophelia would have anticipated this request. Hattie was torn between the shock of silence and the wild laughter of disbelief and confusion. He stared at her and waited.

She asked the only thing she could think of. 'Why?'

'A fair question,' he replied.

This whole scene was ridiculous. Why would *this* man need a woman like her to be his pretend betrothed? He was a duke, he was handsome and had all the time and wealth in the world at his disposal. He could find an eager wife in the time it would take him to blink.

He paused in front of the portrait of the late Marchioness and faced Hattie. 'In the simplest terms, Miss Potts, I cannot take a new bride, but the *ton* will give me and my daughter no peace until I am adequately…unavailable to help quash the rumours they create to sell their gossip sheets. I cannot ask a woman of high Society to fill such a role as they all know one another and will talk about such a ruse and embarrass me.

'So, my hope was that you being from Stow and far removed from here and someone who cares for my daughter and whom my daughter adores would help me with this…endeavour.'

'You mean lie to everyone?'

'Yes.'

Continue reading

CINDERELLA'S CHARADE WITH THE DUKE
Jeanine Englert

Available next month
millsandboon.co.uk

Copyright © 2025 Jeanine Englert

COMING SOON!

We really hope you enjoyed reading this book. If you're looking for more romance be sure to head to the shops when new books are available on

Thursday 23rd October

To see which titles are coming soon, please visit
millsandboon.co.uk/nextmonth

MILLS & BOON

MILLS & BOON TRUE LOVE IS HAVING A MAKEOVER!

Introducing

Love Always

Swoon-worthy romances, where love takes centre stage. Same heartwarming stories, stylish new look!

Look out for our brand new look

OUT NOW

MILLS & BOON

FOUR BRAND NEW BOOKS FROM
MILLS & BOON MODERN

Indulge in desire, drama, and breathtaking romance – where passion knows no bounds!

OUT NOW

Eight Modern stories published every month, find them all at:

millsandboon.co.uk

OUT NOW!

BUSINESS WITH PLEASURE

THE TYCOON'S AFFAIR COLLECTION

MAYA BLAKE

Available at
millsandboon.co.uk

MILLS & BOON

LET'S TALK
Romance

For exclusive extracts, competitions and special offers, find us online:

- MillsandBoon
- @MillsandBoon
- @MillsandBoonUK
- @MillsandBoonUK

Get in touch on 01413 063 232

For all the latest titles coming soon, visit
millsandboon.co.uk/nextmonth